DEMON LOVER

Below the Widow's Walk, the ocean was alive. The rushing surf carried on it whispering voices, taunting me. Frothy arms reached up into the night sky and beckoned me downward. My hair was wild, having blown free of its coiffure, and it undulated upward on the wind like silver waves in the moonlight. Spindrift floated about and settled on the rocks at my feet.

I felt myself a wild and reckless creature, here among the elements. I was curious; I craved new sensations. Beneath heavy brows, his steel blue eyes glittered fiercely. He was a dangerous man, a devil of a man by all accounts, but a fever had overtaken me. He threaded a hand through my hair, and when his mouth captured mine, I did not fight him. . . .

LAUREL COLLINS

DARK SURRENDER

For Michael,
my husband,
for his love and understanding,
and his tolerance of my midnight trysts with the
typewriter.

And for my dearest friend,
Marie,
who listened when no one else would.

Book Margins, Inc.

A BMI Edition

Published by special arrangement with Dorchester
Publishing Co., Inc.

Printed in the United States of America.

DARK SURRENDER

1

Boston Harbor
slipped over the horizon. I faced windward, my cloak
flagging out behind me as the hood slipped back and
the breezes played over my bare head. Above, the
crewmen perched in the rigging were securing yards
of sail. With only a sigh to mourn what had been left
behind, I walked to the taffrail and, in the eddying
green water that was the wake of the packet ship, I
saw my father's face. There were so many things yet
to ask him, but it was too late for questions. I would
never believe that he had gambled away my inheritance. Papa was far too sensible a man to have tossed
away his money at the gaming tables. Had he not
come from amidst the idle Boston aristocracy and
used his own inheritance to build a textile mill to rival
any in the country?

Removing my gloves, I tucked them into my waist-
band and held my head up to the breeze. For a
moment I was distracted by a gentleman on the
fo'c'sle, indolently leaning on the rail. He seemed to
be watching me as well, but when our eyes met, he
turned and headed for the companionway. I went on
studying the coastline off the port side which we

would follow northward. All at once, I heard a voice
behind me.

"Mademoiselle?"

I turned to take stock of the man who drew up
beside me. It was the same man who had been
watching me a few minutes before. I noted his spread-
legged stance, the arrogant carriage of his dark head,
the corners of his mouth turning up now to form an
impudent smile. All told me to be wary. He was so tall
that I found that I had to tilt my head back at an
uncomfortable angle to enable my gray eyes to look
into his blue ones. As I met the half-lidded stare, I
could sense undercurrents of such intensity that I
unconsciously took a step backward. My voice was
surprisingly steady.

"*Oui, monsieur? Qu'est-ce que vous voulez?*"

"I—I am not French."

He seemed to be caught off stride by my speaking
French, and I managed a smile as he grew less
formidable. "Nor am I," I explained, "I merely
responded in kind when you addressed me."

His laugh rang out across the deck. "Of course. May
I explain? I have only just come from New Orleans,
where the proper form of address for a young lady
is—"

"I quite understand."

"It will take some time for me to reaccustom myself
to the staid pace of New England," he commented.

"You sound disappointed. Perhaps then you should
not have left?"

"Perhaps. However, eventually we must all turn
homeward and confront our demons."

I thought that his voice was like that of my own
conscience. I was running from demons: from the
vicious gossip about my father's downfall, and from
an engagement that had been intended, more than
anything, to join two fortunes. I wondered what
Phillip would do when he received my letter. Might

he try to discover where I'd gone and come after me? No, I was sure I knew him better than that. I had made it too easy for him. Phillip was a politician, first and foremost, and if he let me go out of his life, my father's scandal could not taint his campaign.

"I must compliment you on your accent," the man beside me said, trying to draw me out of my silence. "Surely you could convince the Emperor himself that you were a kinswoman."

"My mother was French," I told him, "and I was sent to school in Paris at an early age."

While I spoke, his eyes traveled to my hands, examining the long, tapered nails and the amethyst ring. His gaze lingered over the fitted bodice of my lavender-striped foulard, and I almost wished that I was dressed in the less stylish mourning garb that I should have been wearing.

He lifted his hand then and fluttered my scarf before my eyes. "This is yours, I believe."

"Why, yes."

My hand crept up to my throat as if I were still unsure that it was gone. He rolled his hand in a fluid gesture. "It floated across the deck to me. An omen, you might say. Fate has destined that we should meet."

I deflected his romantic nonsense with a toss of my head. "More likely a stern sou'wester and a carelessly tied knot."

My fingers reached out to the soft fabric but he promptly drew it back. "Please, allow me."

With a firm grip on either end of the scarf, he slipped it over my head. I tensed.

"Unless you would prefer that I send down for your maid," he mocked.

"I am traveling alone," I said, without thinking.

I was certain that he relished the look of discomfort in my eyes. They darted from side to side, for I was not sure what he intended.

"Surely you don't expect me to believe that you got into this fine gown all on your own?"

The innuendo was clear. I pushed my shoulders back defiantly and glared up at this insolent man. "I manage quite well by myself, sir."

He looked down at me with a twisted smile. "I'm sure you do."

He could not have known what a sore point this was with me. The truth was that without my maid I was lost. This morning I had fumbled with the back fastenings of my dress until my fingers were numb. I was unaccustomed to dressing my own hair, and rather than an elegant cascade of curls, I had to settle for a simple chignon.

I wanted to escape this man but the scarf around my neck held me fast. Regarding him coldly, I waited for release. He was not a foot from me now and drew a long breath. "Somewhere," he began, "there is a man responsible for you—"

With this, he pulled the ends of the scarf closer to him and bent his head down until our faces nearly touched. Having captured my gaze thus, he stared into the depths of my eyes as if to read my thoughts. "Father or lover, I don't know which."

His demeanor was cool, and only the congestion in his voice gave a hint that my proximity affected him in the least. "He'll come to regret that he ever let you out of his sight."

He covered my mouth with his own, as if it were a most natural reaction. I was startled to find that I did not protest, though neither did I yield at first. He tasted of whiskey, which seemed to intoxicate me more than it had him. This was an assault on all my senses, and he coaxed me until I responded. When at last he drew away, it was a painful separation, and we regarded one another, faces masked in confusion.

Drawing a ragged breath, I stepped backward, con-sternated by the effervescent sensation which had

spread over me. There was an instant of hesitation
while I regained my wits, and then my eyes widened
in shock as if only now did I realize what had
transpired between us. My arm shot out, and I
slapped him hard across the face. The resounding
crack of my hand on his jaw brought him back to life.
I whirled around and stalked off toward the
companionway, his derisive laughter building to a
fever pitch as I disappeared below deck.

Fleeing to the safety of my cabin, I shut the door
with a shuddering slam. I dropped onto the bunk,
pressing both palms up to my flushed cheeks. How
dare he? How dare he! I was not some tavern doxy to
be taken at his leisure. Clenching my fists so hard that
my nails dug into the flesh of my palms, I shrieked.
To vent my anger, I began throwing whatever was in
reach at the closed door—a cushion, hairbrush, shoe.

"Diable! Il est un mauvais drôle!"

I ranted on in French, a habit which, along with my
volatile temper, I had inherited from my mother.
Before too long, a disembodied male voice called out
from the other side of the door. "Miss? Miss, are you
all right in there?"

The unfamiliar voice startled me back to reality. I
was not at home in my own room where my behavior
went unquestioned. There was a long silence and
then with one final burst of anger, I hurled a book in
the direction of the voice. Its spine hit the door
squarely, pages aflutter, and fell to the floor with a
heavy thud. "Leave me alone!" I wailed and threw
myself face down on the bunk.

I lay there for a long time, ashamed of the outburst.
Though I told myself that such behavior was childish,
it always seemed that my emotions would build until
release was inevitable. I was not so angry with the
brash man who had accosted me on deck as with
myself. How many times this past week had I told
myself that I would manage on my own? A hundred?

A thousand? Perhaps more. Yet with the first episode of difficulty I had only stood there, stupid as a schoolgirl. This was a fine start. Perhaps I was not so adventurous as I imagined myself. I decided not to venture on deck again.

To pass the time, I reread the letter that had offered me an escape from Boston. It was from Matthew Wyndham, who had been a good friend of my father. Having heard of my financial straits, he was offering me a position as governess to his seven-year-old daughter, Susannah. I did not delude myself into believing that the position had been offered on the merit of my credentials. It seemed that Mr. Wyndham felt somehow responsible that my father had died in his house. It was no more than circumstance, of course, as Papa had had a heart condition for some time. There was no doubt, though, that I was deeply indebted to Matthew Wyndham.

No sooner had the bowfast of the packet *Nora Jean* been secured than a swirling mass of storm clouds rolled in, muddying the morning sky. A grizzled old man named McKeon met me on the dock. He told me that he was from the Wyndham estate and ushered me into a waiting carriage. The old man maneuvered handily through the glut of traffic: a tangle of wagons, stevedores loading and unloading cargo, and scores of sailors impatient for their ale, which was to be had in plenty at the grogshops up the street.

Much of the scene was lost on me, though, as I contemplated my upcoming meeting with Mr. Matthew Wyndham. We left the cobblestoned streets of the village for a wide dirt road. It inclined so gradually that I was surprised when, through a break in the trees, I was treated to a picture-postcard view of the village of Wyndham Harbor. It was a patchwork of rooftops from this height, and the deep natural harbor seemed a pond afloat with tiny boats. It was a tidy little village, apart from the rougher elements near the wharves. The main street was cobblestoned and bordered by plank walks serving rows of shops with painted wooden signboards hanging over their doors.

Ahead, the wood was verdant and the undergrowth dense. Ash trees formed an archway overhead, their delicate leaves tracing patterns on the overcast sky. I was anxious for a glimpse of the place that was to be my new home, and what was no more than a quarter-of-an-hour drive seemed to drag on endlessly. I was pleased and more than a little excited when at last we reached a clearing with elaborate wrought-iron gates barring the way. Mr. McKeon pulled up sharply on the reins and let go a high-pitched whistle. A small boy appeared from behind a thicket. He was barefoot, his clothes faded and worn, and his black hair an unkempt thatch.

"That's me grandson, Tim," the old man said.

Without a word, the boy strained on tiptoe to reach the gate latch. I was aware that he was staring at me. He intercepted my gaze with his own hypnotic one, and instinctively I brought a hand to my throat and lightly touched the small brass ring that hung there suspended on a chain as if it were a charm to break a spell. The ring was my only legacy from my father. He'd sent it to me only a week before he died, without explanation. It was not expensive like so many of the other presents he'd given me through the years, and it left a green ring on my finger when I tried to wear it, but it was his last gift to me and especially dear so I wore it on a chain round my neck.

I was uncomfortable under the scrutiny of the boy's luminous blue eyes, and it struck me that I had experienced this same type of appraisal before, though I could not quite recall the circumstance. It was as if he regarded me with a man's eyes, I decided, and then chastised myself for the thought. Why, he couldn't be more than seven years old! As the gates

opened, he lost interest in me. The horses stepped up
again, pulling the carriage up the drive, and after
latching the gates behind us, little Tim darted across
the lawns and disappeared.

When Wyndcliffe finally came into view, I drew in
a sharp breath. My father had been bewitched by this
place; his friend Matthew Wyndham bade him visit
whenever he liked, and in the last few years when the
troubles of the mill weighed heavy on his mind, Papa
had been able to find some peace within these walls.
His letters had described the house in vivid detail. I
quite expected to be disappointed when I saw it for
myself, but instead felt much of the same fascination.

It was an imposing structure, not at all what one
might expect to find in the midst of the Maine wilder-
ness. The architecture was a mixture of styles:
Georgian symmetry with a modicum of the Gothic
ornamentation that was so overdone nowadays. What
it reminded me of most was a European manor house
that had been magically transported across the ocean,
stone by stone. In fact, though, the walls of Wyndcliffe were of gray granite quarried from the nearby
cliffs, or so Papa had explained in one of his letters.
Those walls were enshrouded now by a swirling fog
which lent to the house an eerie appearance. Spires
and chimneys were silhouetted against the angry sky,
and at the eastern end of the structure, a tall stone
tower rose to be swallowed up by the heavy clouds.
Beyond that tower lay the cliff's edge, already
experiencing the onset of the storm. Frothy waves
were dashed without mercy onto the rocks, sending
geysers of foam hundreds of feet into the air. I found
myself invigorated by the whole of it.

The carriage rounded the broad, circular drive and
Mr. McKeon set me out under the porte cochere. I
thanked him and went boldly up the flagstone steps to
the double doors. The house loomed, huge and silent,

before me, and I hesitated. Wyndcliffe was grander than our Beacon Hill townhouse, but then I had been in grand homes before. The difference on this occasion, I thought, was that I had not come to Wyndcliffe as a guest. I stood there for a long while, gathering up the threads of my dissipated confidence. Finally, with a determined set to my jaw, I rapped the brass knocker against the door. A friendly-looking woman appeared in the doorway. She was short and round and about her ample waist hung a chatelaine with an extraordinary number of keys.

"You must be Miss Dalton," she said. "Do come in, dear. I'm Mrs. Garen."

She motioned for me to follow her and was promptly startled by a sharp crack of thunder as she shut the door behind us. She laid one hand over her full bosom and crossed herself with the other. "I never get used to it . . . the storms, you know."

She reached for my bonnet, gloves and mantle as I removed them. "I'll take you to Mrs. Wyndham right off. The mister had important business in the village and said to leave you in her hands."

My brows knit together. "I understood that Mr. Wyndham is a widower."

She smiled indulgently. "Yes, dear. Mrs. Wyndham is his stepmother."

Mrs. Garen gave me a thorough looking over and took a step closer. Extending a pink hand, she laid it on my arm. "Mrs. Wyndham is a hard woman, but you've naught to fear. She's most all bark and no bite. It's the mister runs this ship, and it will be him you must please."

With a reassuring pat on my arm, she crossed the foyer and started down the hall. I followed close at her heels. As we walked, I wondered about the woman I was to meet. Despite Mrs. Garen's warning, I wanted to picture a silver-haired matron, diligently plying her needle. I hadn't anticipated a female member of the Wyndham family other than the child. Papa had never mentioned her. Perhaps I could make myself useful to her: help with her correspondence or read to her from the ladies' periodicals; then I mightn't be as lonely.

Mrs. Garen had paused beside a door and was tapping her foot impatiently and I realized that I had been daydreaming.

"Go on in, miss. Mrs. Wyndham is waiting on you."

The door before me was open and as I stepped over the threshold without the housekeeper's protection, I held my breath. It was a small sitting room, its furnishings decidedly feminine. The draperies were a pale green damask to match the upholstery, and beneath them were crisscrossed panels of sheer fabric. On some other day, this might have been a sunny room.

"Sit down, Miss Dalton."

It was a deep voice, devoid of emotion, and when I saw the woman to whom it belonged, all hopes of friendship were dashed. Mrs. Garen had not exaggerated in the least. Felicia Wyndham was not a tall woman, but her bearing made her appear so. Her hair, black as a raven's wing and without a thread of gray, was drawn back into a plaited chignon that emphasized the hard lines of her face. She wore an expensive tea gown of crimson faille, simple in design and decorated with only a minimum of black lace.

I did as I was told and seated myself in one of a pair of side chairs facing the divan, folding my hands neatly in my lap. Mrs. Wyndham kept her distance and did not move to seat herself. She slowly assessed me with a cool gaze. Her eyes resembled beads of black jet. Throughout the examination I could not help but feel like a piece of horseflesh. What next?

Would she ask to have a look at my teeth? In spite of my nervous disposition, anger rose in me and I bit down on my tongue to quell it. Mrs. Wyndham made a slow approach and circled around me, coming to a halt behind the divan and resting her hands upon it.

"You're not quite the orphaned waif my stepson would have us believe."

I felt as though I'd bitten clean through my tongue. I would not be intimidated by this woman. Choosing my words carefully, I affected a light voice. "I cannot imagine where he would have gotten such an impression. He indicated in our correspondence that my father had spoken of me to him many times."

"Nonetheless, we were not expecting someone as 'accomplished' as yourself."

"Thank you," I said, though quite aware that she had not meant to compliment me.

She ignored me and began her oration. "I am Felicia Wyndham," she said. "Matthew is my stepson. He is often occupied with the family business, and so I handle the running of the household as I did when my husband was alive. If there are any problems, you may address them to me.

"Your duties will be to see to Susannah's lessons and be sure that for the remainder of the day she is suitably occupied. We do have a classroom here, and you will take all of your meals there, except on those occasions when we feel that the child needs supervision at table. You shall have one day per week on which you may conduct your personal business. Now, is all of this clear to you?"

I was beginning to feel the uncomfortable weight of responsibility. 'Yes, ma'am."

"Good. Now there is one final point I wish to make. I am aware of your straitened circumstances, and while you may find my stepson an eligible widower and this house and the Wyndham holdings a great temptation, I do assure you that Mr. Wyndham has neither the time nor the inclination for a liaison with a subordinate. The business receives his wholehearted attention. So if you have come here with thoughts of bettering your station, I would advise that you look elsewhere.''

I was astounded. Never would I have expected such indelicacy. I seethed, though my gray eyes were deceptively placid. I had no taste for this Wyndham welcoming committee and nearly turned on my heel and stomped off to God knows where. But I was my father's daughter, and with his catlike instincts I withdrew into myself to size up this adversary. She shuddered then as though a cold gust of air had blown between us, and it struck me that she was more frightened of me than she let on.

''I am distressed, madam, that you should harbor such imaginings concerning me,'' I said, emotions well reined in, ''and might I remind you that I did not seek out this position; it was offered to me by Mr. Wyndham himself. Furthermore, the gentleman in question is certainly old enough to be my father. Rest assured, Mrs. Wyndham, that I have no aspirations other than to live a quiet life here, concerning myself solely with my duties as Susannah's governess.''

Reaching for the bell pull, Felicia Wyndham sent me a sidelong glance. ''We shall see, Miss Dalton, we shall see.''

Mrs. Garen returned then and advanced cautiously into the room.

''Yes, ma'am?''

''Mrs. Garen, you may take Miss Dalton up to meet her charge now. Oh, and do see that she is shown the classroom.''

She turned to me with a spurious smile. ''You may begin with the child's lessons tomorrow morning. That should allow you ample time to prepare, unless we have overestimated your capabilities.''

She raised an eyebrow, making a question out of the statement.

Rising with as much grace as possible, I hid my trembling hands behind my skirts and forced a pleasant expression onto my face, which by now had lost much of its color. I was unaccustomed to such treatment, and while instinct would have me strike back, I had not the stamina for such sparring. Worst of all, I had to admit that it was not my place to argue.

"My father invested heavily in my education, and my teachers have called me a quick study. I shall not disappoint you, madam."

Mrs. Garen fanned herself with her hand as she escorted me from the sitting room. "The mister picked a fine time to go down to the village," she said to herself.

She took me then on a tour of the house. The interior was less forbidding but at least as impressive in style as its exterior. There was an interesting maze of doors and passageways, and I was glad to have Mrs. Garen ahead to show me the way lest I become hopelessly lost. When we came to the second-floor hall, I observed that while the corridor continued on to my right, on my left the hallway was blocked by a heavy door of carved wood. This aroused my curiosity and Mrs. Garen offered a prompt explanation. "The mister had us shut up the whole east wing on the upper floors. He said it would make less work for us as there wasn't a soul living in those rooms. The family's all here in the west wing."

"There must be quite a few rooms closed off," I guessed.

"Seven on this floor, if you count the tower room, and as many above."

"There must be a magnificent view from the tower room."

"Yes, indeed, miss. From that tower you could look eye-to-eye with old King Neptune himself. I'd take you in for a look, but 'tis a drafty, dusty place. I'd not want you to spoil your fine clothes.''

With that, she went to the first room off the west wing corridor and pointed at the door. ''This is the classroom. A mite more space than you'll be needing, but the first Wyndhams had five young ones to be schooled, you know. You can find your way back here later to see it for yourself, but now I'd guess you'll want to meet the young miss.''

With the prospect of meeting a mere seven-year-old child, apprehension came over me. I had never had to prove myself before. Learning one's lessons was one thing, but teaching them to a young child was something else altogether. And if I faltered, I knew with a certainty that Felicia Wyndham would be there to point out my error.

Mrs. Garen went to the next door and laid her hand on the knob. ''This room is the child's, and yours is the next over. You'll find a door joining them inside.''

Susannah was curled on the windowseat at the far end of her room, knees tucked up under her, her chin resting on her folded arms as she leaned against the sill. She must have heard the door open, yet stared out at the rain as if unaware of any intrusion. ''Miss Susannah? Come and meet your new governess, child.''

''Can't now,'' came the reply, ''I'm waiting . . . watching and waiting.''

''And what, might I ask, are you watching for out there in the rain, missy?'' Mrs. Garen inquired.

''Mama, of course. She never stays long in the garden.''

The housekeeper groaned and shifted her gaze nervously from the child to me and back again. She drew her mouth into a taut line, and a long silence ensued. I felt the color drain from my face and wondered at the game the child was playing. I looked to Mrs. Garen who was awaiting my reaction. "I thought that the child's mother was dead," I whispered.

She threw me an anxious look and went to Susannah, turning her around and drawing the child's small hands into her own. "Come away from the window, child. Miss Dalton has come all the way from Boston. Won't you please say hello to her?"

Susannah rolled her dark eyes upward to consider, sighed heavily and then rose as if it had been her own idea. She was a delicate child, with freckles sprinkled over the bridge of her retroussé nose and auburn ringlets framing a heart-shaped face. She addressed me with a stiff curtsey.

"I'm pleased to make your acquaintance, Miss Dalton."

The child said the words as though they had been rehearsed, and it unsettled me to notice that even while Susannah spoke, she looked through me as if I were invisible.

"I am pleased to meet you, Susannah," I said.

She drew nearer and looked up at me, her eyes wide. "I don't need a governess, truly," she said under her breath. "Mama gives me my lessons and Mrs. Garen looks after me."

I wanted to shake my muddled head to make things right again. This was no game, the child was . . . disturbed, and I feared that I hadn't the abilities to help her.

"We shall begin our lessons tomorrow morning," I informed her, my mind already racing ahead to contemplate what approach I could take with her on the morrow.

She shrugged her slight shoulders. "As you say, miss."

Mrs. Garen swept between us. "That's a good girl. Now off with you. Run down to the kitchen and see

Mrs. Black. She's baked a batch of those ginger cookies you're so partial to."

Before she could finish her sentence, Susannah squealed and dashed out. I stared hard at the toes of my shoes as Mrs. Garen regarded me earnestly. "Please, miss, she's just a baby and her poor mama not yet dead a year. She is wild, but it's only for lack of a stern hand. I've duties of my own and not the time to supervise her properly. Pretending her mama is still alive, that's just a harmless game. Things will change now that you're here. You're just what she needs, a fine lady to pattern herself after."

"It would be quite unfair of me to pass judgment on the child after only one meeting," I admitted.

"Thank you, miss. I'll leave you now, but there's one last thing. I thought you might want to go through your papa's things. We closed up his room and left it all just as it was on that day when—"

There was an awkward pause before she went on. "You're welcome to go up there, if you've a mind to. I'll point out the way if you like."

My father's death was not yet an event of the past to me, and emotion clouded my sensibilities. Of course I should go through his things, but it was the very room in which his life had ended. Words caught in my throat, and when finally a voice came to me, it was decidedly tenuous. "Yes, Mrs. Garen, thank you."

She nodded, which set her white cap to bobbing, and pushing past me, she stepped into the hall. She extended a plump arm and waited until I stood beside her before she pointed her finger to indicate the direction.

"Up those stairs to the third floor. It's the second door on your left."

The house was less appealing when one was alone, I soon discovered. Noises which would have gone unnoticed in the midst of polite conversation were

amplified by solitude. I was acutely aware of the
creak beneath my feet as I climbed the stairs, until the
frenzied tapping of a sudden downpour on the roof
took prominence and enveloped me, only to be
surmounted by the deep rumble of thunder
resounding through the halls. Reaching the upper-
most floor of the house, I decided that it must be
wholly unoccupied as Mrs. Garen had not included it
in her tour. It was exactly what Papa would have
wanted. He disliked noise and commotion.

There were tall mullioned windows at either end of
the long hall but the storm clouds eclipsed the daylight and cast shadows along the deserted corridor.
My heart pounded in my ears as I twisted the knob
and went into the room that had belonged to my
father. The velvet hangings that covered the windows
were drawn, obscuring whatever daylight might have
been available. As my eyes adjusted to the dark, I
literally felt my way across the room with my hands,
the pieces of furniture gradually coming into focus. I
drew aside the draperies, churning up the stale air
and sending a flurry of dust afloat. Choking, I cleared
the air with my hand and turned back to the room.

Yes, this would be Papa's room. It was positively
spartan. He had never had any use for bric-a-brac
cluttering up his life. Absently, I traced a design in the
layer of dust on the writing table. There was barely a
hint that the room had been occupied at all, save a
few sheets of foolscap on the table. I crossed the
room, opened the doors of the armoire, and was
immediately assailed by the scent of my father's pipe
tobacco. I lightly ran my hand over the arm of one
jacket, lifting it up and then slowly letting it slip from
my grasp. The coats were hung in a neat row and
beneath them were arranged several pairs of leather
boots, polished as if their owner might still have use
for them. There were no signs of death here. I felt

then that if I were to settle myself in the chair and wait, he might walk through the door at any moment, but it couldn't be so. I slammed the armoire doors shut. Moving on, I began to pull out drawer after drawer, methodically riffling through the contents. My eyes were bright with unshed tears.

Perhaps I'd thought there'd be more of him in this room, that by going through his belongings I'd somehow be able to understand why he'd let his business matters get into such a state. I'd never believe he gambled it away, but in this room I realized that I'd never have an answer from him.

The last drawer I opened was empty but for a box wrapped in coarse brown paper and tied with twine. I reached for it, feeling its weight and shaking it as a child might a Christmas package. I was conscious of my heartbeat then, and its intense hammering filled the otherwise silent room. The package was addressed, in my father's hand, to me at our Boston home. My hands were unsteady as I slid the twine off the box and removed the paper. My father must have died before this package could be posted. Was this, like the brass ring, yet another unexplained gift? I opened the box and removed the crumpled sheets of tissue from inside. Nestled within was my music box. Papa had given it to me when I was a child. It was an enchanting toy, fashioned after a carousel with a dozen tiny horses, standing in pairs, all sculpted of wood and painted in bright colors. I wound the mechanism, and holding it up I watched as the horses were set into motion. The familiar melody chimed clear in the stillness and transported me to a time long past when I could run into Papa's arms and be safe from the world. I was surprised to find that he had kept it with him all these years. I had given this most precious possession to him on the day that I went to school in France so he might remember me whenever

he played the music. I was not yet ten years old, and
he must have carried it with him for more than twelve
years. Why then, I wondered, had he decided to send
it back to me?

I could feel a presence nearby, even before I heard
the footfall in the doorway. I whirled around, half-
expecting to see no one, but there was, indeed, a
shadowy form on the threshold. I gave out a little cry
and the music box slipped from my grasp. It struck
the wood floor on its side, making an awful clatter,
and dislodging a tiny black stallion from its post. It
rolled lazily across the floor and halted at his feet.

2

The stranger picked up my music box and handed it out to me.

"I'm sorry to have startled you. I should have realized that going through your father's things would be unsettling."

"I should have been more careful," I said and went to retrieve the errant stallion. Without bothering to hide my distress, I tried to put it back in place. My hands were clumsy when confronting the delicate workmanship. It had been a clean separation, though, and to my relief, the broken piece snapped back into place. A little glue and it should be as good as new.

"Did the carousel belong to your father?" the man asked. "It's such an unusual piece of work, and I can't remember having seen it before."

"It was mine, but I gave it to him years ago when I went off to school so that he'd not forget me while I was away."

The stranger stepped into the room. He moved in a slow manner as if contemplating each step before it was taken. His auburn hair was brushed with silver at the temples, and there were reddish highlights in his well-shaped moustache. He regarded me closely.

"I think it highly unlikely that any father would forget so lovely a daughter."

"Thank you," I replied, "I was only a child, and a silly child, perhaps."

"Never that," he said, and smiled at me. "Mrs. Garen told me that you'd come up here. I must apologize for not having been at home to receive you, but my business in the village detained me longer than I had anticipated."

My first thoughts of him had been that here was yet another member of the Wyndham clan, perhaps the younger brother of Matthew that my father had mentioned in his letters. I pieced together the information at hand, though, and when the realization of exactly to whom I was speaking came to me, the corners of my mouth turned up and dimpled. "You are Matthew Wyndham?"

"Why, yes. I'd forgotten that we've not been introduced. I would have recognized you in any case from your father's descriptions. Are you surprised then to find that the shipping magnate and master of the estate is not a more imposing figure?"

"No, it is only that I expected someone, well, someone closer to my father's age. Forgive me if I have offended you."

He laughed then. It was a brittle laugh. "One always thinks of one's parents as ancient. In all honesty, Miss Dalton, I am but a few years younger than your father."

He was more at ease now, I thought, or perhaps it was only that now that I knew his identity, I was not so wary of him.

"May I say then, Mr. Wyndham, that the building of empires must agree with you."

"Well said, Miss Dalton, you flatter me. I see that you have your father's quick mind. Now I think that it would be a good idea for us to talk downstairs in the classroom where the atmosphere is less oppressive. It cannot be comfortable for you here.''

As he ushered me downstairs, there was a short respite in the conversation and I had time to become accustomed to his appearance. Up to this point he had only been a shadowy, somewhat paternal figure in my imagination and not at all the man I was facing now. He was a sturdy man with a strong, intelligent brow and perceptive eyes. I could better understand now why Felicia Wyndham imagined that I might be husband-hunting.

''I trust your journey was pleasant,'' he said.

''Yes, I much preferred to breath clean salt air than the dust and soot one invariably encounters when traveling by rail. Your *Nora Jean* is a grand vessel. The accommodations on board rival any steamship.''

''Ah, but she hasn't a chance in our fast-paced times. The *Nora Jean* is making her last crossing for the Wyndham Lines, I'm afraid. I've sold her to a gentleman in Bristol.''

''What a shame!''

''Such is progress,'' he sighed, but was not lost long in reverie before he pressed on in another direction. ''I must apologize as well, Miss Dalton, for not coming down for your father's funeral. There was an urgent business matter that required my attention.''

''I understand,'' I said.

''It was such a shock for us here, and in all honesty, I must tell you that I feel responsible. If I'd not been so involved in my own work, I might have noticed that Ben was feeling out of sorts. I could have had my own doctor take a look at him and perhaps—''

''You mustn't feel that way,'' I assured him. ''Papa had had a heart condition for some time. The attacks would come on suddenly. They were mild at first. The doctor told him that it was his worrying about the mill. I suppose that when the pressures built up, his heart just couldn't stand the strain.''

Mr. Wyndham seemed to study the brass doorknob

intently before twisting it open. I found the classroom
a cheerful place. There were high ceilings and a pair
of long windows that offered a breathtaking view of
the gardens. On the far wall were bookshelves and
before me a pair of tables and chairs. There was room
for a dozen children here, I thought. Mr. Wyndham
motioned for me to be seated and clasped his hands
behind his back.

"Can you tell me what happened in Boston?" he
asked.

I looked up at him. I needed so much to trust him,
this man who had been my father's friend.

"I'm not sure if you are aware how all of Papa's
troubles—and mine—came about, Mr. Wyndham.
They say that he had been gambling."

"Gambling?" he echoed. "I knew that your father
enjoyed a good game of cards now and again, but I
assumed that he'd been done in by the war like so
many others. Without cotton to mill, what chance did
he have?"

I shook my head. "Papa had taken large sums of
money from the business. He mortgaged the mill.
There was nothing to fall back on when the hard
times came, no money to settle the accounts. The
attorneys told me that he must have gambled it all
away."

I wanted to add that I would never credit this, that
there had to be another explanation, but I hadn't even
a negligible amount of proof and not the slightest
hope of finding any. There was compassion in
Matthew Wyndham's dark eyes, but I wanted more. I
wanted to hear him say that Ben Dalton wasn't the
type of man to gamble away his fortune and leave his
only daughter penniless and alone.

"I had no idea that things were so desperate," he
finally said.

I sighed. It was a hopeless sound.

Mr. Wyndham cleared his throat and promptly

changed the subject. "You have been introduced to
my daughter, Miss Dalton?"

I decided to put aside my questions about the child
until I knew more of her situation.

"Yes, she seems . . . bright."

"She is a timid thing. I think you will discover that
she is willing to learn, though what she is most in
need of now is a companion, someone to whom she
can look for guidance. I daresay that you shall be able
to fulfill these needs."

"I shall certainly try."

When Mr Wyndham turned to the door to signal the
conclusion of our interview, I rose and as I ran my
hand over the table top, a wood sliver bit into the
tender flesh of my palm. I pulled a handkerchief from
my sleeve and dabbed at the crimson drop of blood
that had formed.

"What is it?" he asked, taking my hand and turning
it palm up.

"A sliver of wood," I replied. "It's only just pierced
the skin."

I drew my hand away shyly as we examined the
tabletop together. Carved into the smooth, varnished
surface were two splintered initials, "JW". I surmised
that it was the handiwork of one of the more
irreverent Wyndham students, but the look that
overtook Mr. Wyndham was positively black, as if
some horrible obscenity were scrawled there.

"I shall send someone up to see to this before you
begin with Susannah's lessons," he assured me. "I
might have known it was my brother's work. He has
been ever the thorn in our side. You may count
yourself lucky, Miss Dalton, that this is the only
wound you shall receive at Jason Wyndham's hand.
Others have not been so fortunate."

I could feel the enmity that Matthew Wyndham had
for his brother. Its vehemence sent a shiver through
me. Soon, though, the cloud had passed and once

again he had a pleasant look for me.

"I shall be making my regular monthly tour of the estate on Friday," he told me. "I think it would be an excellent opportunity for you to become better acquainted with the grounds, and who would be a better guide than I? Do you ride, Miss Dalton?"

"I do, indeed."

"Splendid. I shall send a maid up to fetch you on Friday afternoon at one. You will be ready?"

"I shall. Thank you, Mr. Wyndham, for all that you've done for me."

"It is a pleasure to have Ben's daughter here with us."

I felt insignificant in this house, and it was a new feeling for me. The classroom was far too large for only the two of us, I discovered, and when I spoke, my voice echoed off the walls, unnerving me. Equally vexatious was the fact that Susannah had been inattentive all morning. She had stared out of the window for nearly as long as I had been speaking.

"I know that this all must sound overwhelming, but we shall take up your lessons slowly at first to determine how far you have already progressed. I understand that your mother had been tutoring you herself. Susannah?"

Her attention was clearly elsewhere. I looked out of the windows to see for myself what had so captivated her. There was no one below in the gardens, no movement save the swaying of a delicate, purple lilac hedge in the wind. The child must have been daydreaming.

Tension had been steadily building in me, and the patience I had exhibited thus far eluded me now. "Susannah! It is only common courtesy to give me your attention while I am speaking. I see that certain areas of your education have been sorely neglected."

My quick temper had gotten the better of me, and I

soon found that this was not the way to deal with the child. Susannah turned around to face me, and her eyes narrowed, glinting amber. She pouted her little mouth, and with one great shove pushed the stack of books before her off the table. They slammed to the floor at my feet. To say that I was taken aback by this would have been an understatement, but I restrained my anger and calmly bent down to retrieve the books and returned them to the table. I spoke to her in a reserved tone.

"You've not answered my question. Was your mother tutoring you?"

The child rose and met my eyes haughtily.

"I've had enough lessons for one day, miss."

With that, she turned and left the room. I stood there, incredulous. I had never before felt so out of control. I began to wring my hands and pace a small section of the floor as I went over the episode in my mind. I had been rash. Anger was not the way to deal with a sensitive child, but another part of me fumed, determined not to let this spoiled child get the better of me.

"You mustn't worry yourself. It was only a squall and will blow over sooner than you think. It's often this way with her."

Mrs. Garen was there in the doorway, her arms full of a tray of tea things.

I sank down into my chair. "Oh, Mrs. Garen, I'm afraid I've gotten off on the wrong foot. Where do you suppose she's gone?"

"Off to her room, I expect. She'll pout for a time and then reappear, our little ray of sunshine once again."

She glided into the room and set down the tray. I was so preoccupied with my thoughts that I was barely aware of her movement until she pressed a cup of tea into my hand. The steaming brew revived me.

"Here now. I thought you might need some refreshment. I could do with a cup myself."

She settled herself into the chair recently vacated by Susannah and poured for herself. "Do have one of the currant cakes, Miss. It's Mrs. Black's special recipe."

"I've not much of an appetite. Has Susannah always been this way? . . . difficult, I mean."

"Oh my, no. Mama's little darling, she was, and always with a smile for you. The two of them were inseparable. I've been thinking as how maybe it was a bad thing, they're being so close. When her mama died . . . No, I don't want you to be worrying. My missy Susannah, she warms up slow but she'll take to you soon enough, just wait and see if it isn't so."

"I hope you're right, Mrs. Garen. I hope you're right."

My room was more than I had expected. It was dominated by a testered bed with a yellow floral counterpane and matching hangings. Along one wall were a marble-topped vanity table with mirror and a wardrobe, and across the room was a fireplace, its mantel also of Italian marble. A comfortable reading chair stood next to the bed, and on the far wall were french doors with a balcony view of the formal gardens at the rear of the house.

Seated at the vanity table, I wound my ash blonde hair into a smooth coil and set the porkpie hat of rice straw at a jaunty angle on my head. I thought that the veil of rose-colored net shadowing my face made me appear older than my twenty-two years, and I rose and stepped back from the mirror, pleased with what I saw.

The smart mauve riding habit was part of a trousseau assembled for a marriage that would never be. My vanity would not allow me to part with these new gowns, though, which had been designed for me by a French couturier. Convention might have called for mourning wear, but these new gowns were as

vital to me as a soldier's armor. Papa would have
understood. Clothed in a Paris creation, I retained
some of my dignity. Without them I was another
pitiful charity case. Pushing my shoulders back, I
gathered up my doeskin gloves and went down to
meet Matthew Wyndham.

He stood there, balanced with a foot on the bottom
stair and a hand on the baluster, rhythmically
slapping his riding crop against his thigh. He was a
more dashing figure in his riding clothes, I decided.

"Good afternoon, Miss Dalton," he called, sighting
me on the landing.

He touched his forelock with the tip of his riding
crop and went ahead to open the double doors. I was
somewhat ill-at-ease as I descended the stairs, but
when he led me out onto the drive and I saw what
fine horseflesh the Wyndham stables had to offer, my
disposition improved. Mr. Wyndham was soon
astride a proud Morgan, while the groom held for me a
coal black mare with white stockings. As he gave me
a hand up, the boy whispered, "Her name's Gypsy,
miss."

"You've brought Gypsy then," Mr. Wyndham said,
and then to me, "I hope she suits you, Miss Dalton.
She's more spirited than some might like."

"We'll be fine," I replied and hoped it would be
true. I'd not been riding in years. Gypsy was obliging,
though, and once in the saddle, I studied the
surroundings and was soon at ease.

The countryside was breathtaking. Away from the
house the forest was thick with spruce and hemlock,
towering on either side of the road and casting long
shadows across our path. At the base of these trees,
highlighted by filtering rays of sunlight, were lacy
ferns and spring wildflowers.

"You are pleased with our humble estate?" my
companion wondered.

"By no means humble," I replied, "Wyndcliffe is

every bit as grand as Papa described it in his letters."

"Your father wrote to you often about us?"

"Yes. He loved to visit here, and I can see why now. We wrote to one another once a week faithfully. I would write about frivolous things mostly: the parties I attended and the people I met. He would describe the places he visited and all of the wonderful things he saw. When his letters came it was as if he were right there in the room speaking to me—except at the last. He must have been feeling out of sorts; his last letters were so distant."

My voice trailed off. Matthew Wyndham's brow furrowed as he digested all that I had said, and when he spoke again, it was as my tour guide.

"The Wyndham land extends north another mile or so beyond this road and east to the ocean."

"A great deal of land."

His chest was puffed with pride. "As you will see, it sustains a good many people."

There was a very real chill on the air now in the shade of the forest. Ahead was a clearing, and to my surprise in it was a large castlelike structure. It was in no way comparable to the size of Wyndcliffe but dignified in its own way. It had crenellated battlements and walls of gray stone with fine leaded windows set in them.

"What is this place?" I asked in a hushed voice.

"Chandler House. It was built not long after the main house as a wedding gift for my great-aunt and her husband, whose name was Chandler. It has been home for all of the Chandlers since. Now it belongs to Aaron Chandler, a cousin and the family attorney. He lives here with his sister, Rachel."

"It reminds me of some ancient castle," I said. "Do they keep archers on the battlements in the event of an attack or merely spill cauldrons of hot oil down on unwanted visitors?"

He threw back his head and laughed heartily. "As

their liege lord I should be indignant at either prospect. I assure you we are quite safe.''

"As you say, milord.''

"You're of much the same humor as your father, did you know that?''

"Cut from the same cloth or so I've been told. I'm afraid that I'm not as well-rounded as Papa was, though. It never ceased to amaze me that at one moment he could be discussing economics with his political cronies and in the next you could find him in the kitchen with the cook, discussing the proper way to roast the goose.''

Mr. Wyndham nodded in agreement. "He was an intriguing man, conversant on many topics. His favorite, though, was you.''

"Oh?''

I raised an eyebrow, as curious as any woman with an ounce of vanity as to what my father had said of me. Mr. Wyndham noted my curiosity, smiled a crooked smile, and spurred his horse up the drive toward Chandler House. I did likewise, and as I drew up beside him, he dismounted.

"Aaron has some papers for me to sign. It won't take more than a few minutes, and it will allow you to see the interior of the house.''

"I'd like that,'' I admitted.

I held out an arm, but instead of handing me down, he put his hands on my waist and lifted me from the saddle. I felt his eyes on me, and, uncomfortable, I looked away to the upper floors of the house as he set me down. The draperies of one window drew quickly closed; someone had been watching us and did not wish to be seen himself. This did not disconcert me as much as Mr. Wyndham's scrutiny. Why did he study me so, a hard edge to his gaze as if he expected to strip away my mask and see something ugly beneath it?

And then he was himself again. Taking my arm, he led me up the flagged walk and rapped on the door.

There was a loud creak when it opened, and I laughed to myself, it even sounded like an old castle.

"Good afternoon, Kathleen," Mr. Wyndham said to the girl. "Would you kindly tell Mr. Chandler that I am here?"

"Yes, sir. Please come in."

She bobbed a curtsey and hurried off to find her employer, leaving us alone in the spacious entry hall. I looked about while we waited, admiring the blue and gold Gobelin tapestry which hung down from the second floor balustrade. There was a high-backed chair in Gothic style set against the wall and, of course, the obligatory suit of armor.

"Well, how do you find Chandler House?" Mr. Wyndham wanted to know.

"As I had expected."

"Matt?"

We turned to the man who had come in with the maid at his heels. "Good afternoon, Aaron," Mr. Wyndham said. "I'm here about those tenant leases."

"Yes, of course."

I thought Aaron Chandler a serious-looking fellow: lean and bespectacled, his thin lips twitching as if he were uncomfortable in the presence of his cousin.

"Aaron, this is Miss Adrienne Dalton. She is staying with us at Wyndcliffe . . . to tutor Susannah."

He took my hand as if he were in a hurry, and I could not help but notice how his eyes were darting from Mr. Wyndham to myself behind his spectacles. Mr. Wyndham offered him a rather perturbed look, which only served to further upset him. "Yes . . . well . . . we should take care of those leases. Kathleen, see that Miss Dalton is made comfortable until we return. All that is required is a few signatures," Mr. Chandler said to me, "we won't be long."

The two men disappeared into the study, leaving me to feel as though I'd come in in the middle of a three-act play. I couldn't ascertain the plot and was only vaguely aware of the relationship between the characters.

"Would you like to sit in the parlor, miss?" the girl asked. "I can bring you some refreshment."

"Thank you, no. I'll just wait here," I said and perched myself on the monstrous Gothic chair.

"Yes, miss," she replied, looking a trifle unsettled as she left me.

I was becoming quite piqued. What was it that put everyone around me on tenterhooks? A footfall above startled me back onto my feet, and when I looked up at the second-floor landing, I saw a woman at the head of the stairs. She bore more than a passing resemblance to Aaron Chandler, though compared to her Aaron was but a pale shadow. This must be Rachel Chandler, I surmised. She descended slowly, a delicate white hand flowing down the rail beside her. Her dark hair was caught up in a caul of black net shot with green thread to complement her emerald taffeta gown. Watching her, I was possessed by an unflattering amount of jealousy. The woman bore herself with pride and assurance, and there was no expression on her face to distract one from her nearly perfect features.

"Good afternoon," I said.

Her reply was but a slight inclination of her head, and as she glided by, I could not miss the unfriendly slant of her eyes.

Before I could collect my thoughts, Mr. Wyndham had emerged from the study, followed by his cousin, who was calmer now.

With the appearance of Matthew Wyndham, Miss Chandler came to life. Her green eyes sparkled vivaciously as she flitted around him and flashed a well-practiced smile.

"Matthew, I had no idea you would be paying us a call this afternoon."

Matthew Wyndham's dark eyes perused the

woman with slow relish as a connoisseur might admire a great work of art. I felt suddenly no more than a spectator in the room.

"This is not a social call, my dear, but estate business."

"Ah," Rachel sighed, conjuring up an air of melancholy, "I am hurt. But I shall forgive you if you promise to be more attentive to your poor cousin at the reception next week. I've a new gown especially for the occasion, you know, and I'd hate to see it wasted on your stuffy politician friends."

"She's kept the seamstress busy all week with alterations," Arron noted.

"Give a care to those 'stuffy politicians,' Rachel," Mr. Wyndham said. "They can turn into most useful allies. I should think that you'd be anxious to meet our guest of honor, Mr. Hannibal Hamlin."

Rachel looked wholly unimpressed, but I had taken a sudden interest in the conversation. There was to be a reception at Wyndcliffe next week in honor of Mr. Hannibal Hamlin! The man was only the state of Maine's most illustrious politician. Having been engaged for a time to a politician, I was well aware of the man's reputation. He had served as vice president under Mr. Lincoln during his first term, and might now have been president himself had things turned out differently during the convention in 1864.

"Will he speak?" I asked Mr. Wyndham before I realized that it was not likely that I'd be attending this function.

He seemed pleased by my enthusiasm, and Rachel Chandler shot me a venomous look.

"He's agreed to speak on behalf of our own Republican candidates."

"I hear simply everyone has been invited," Rachel said, capturing his attention. "You must be exhausted by all the preparations. You really do need a wife, you know, to handle these things for you. Your stepmother is getting on in years and surely not able to handle all the details these functions entail.''

I was incredulous. Such enormous talent was wasted here in the Maine woods; the woman ought to be on the stage. I would not have believed it possible to convince anyone that Felicia Wyndham was a withered old woman anxious for retirement, and yet Aaron Chandler watched his sister's performance fair to bursting with pride, and Matthew Wyndham grinned at her like a callow youth.

''I shall certainly take your suggestion into consideration,'' he replied. ''Now I am afraid that I've neglected to make the proper introductions.''

Mr. Wyndham took my arm and drew me into the circle of conversation. ''Rachel Chandler, I should like you to meet Miss Adrienne Dalton. You might remember her father, Benjamin Dalton, who has visited us at Wyndcliffe from time to time.''

''A pleasure, Miss Dalton,'' Rachel said, though the coldness in her voice indicated otherwise.

Mr. Wyndham did not release my arm, and I found that it gave me a sense of security. But this small gesture wrought only displeasure in Miss Chandler, whose sharp green eyes snapped from one to the other of us lest she miss any subtle innuendo. *Mon Dieu!* Why did everyone about me fancy that I had designs on Matthew Wyndham? He was a man to be admired, a man much like my own father, but no more in my eyes. This woman was growing fast intolerable, and with my confidence restored and the devil at my elbow, I thought I'd give Rachel Chandler exactly what she expected to see.

I peered up through the dark fan of my lashes and captured Matthew Wyndham's eyes, distracting him with the hint of a smile. I sensed that only just in this instant did he begin to realize that I was more than Ben Dalton's little girl.

I had his full attention while he spoke to Rachel.

"Miss Dalton is . . . staying at Wyndcliffe . . . to tutor Susannah."

I was heady with the feeling of power. How easily I had disconcerted him; I'd never have thought it possible.

"But you are so young," Rachel said to me, "to be teaching. Why, you must hardly be out of the nursery yourself."

Beneath their veiling, my gray eyes narrowed. "Perhaps that is why I have no trouble recalling those lessons in deportment that many an 'experienced' lady forgets," I replied.

Before Rachel had an opportunity to parry these remarks, Aaron jumped in to smooth things over. "Matt was very much impressed by Miss Dalton's education. She attended an exclusive young ladies' academy in Paris, you know."

Rachel only raised an eyebrow in reply, turning a most unpleasant look on her brother. He seemed to shrink visibly. I was grateful to the timid Aaron for making my situation appear less desperate than it was in actuality. I feared that I could not gracefully brook further condescension from Miss Rachel Chandler.

"We must be on our way," Mr. Wyndham said, "we've the whole of the estate to cover this afternoon."

We made our farewells and went out. Rachel followed and stood on the threshold, arms folded over her chest, missing nothing. When we reached the place where our horses were tethered, we were well out of earshot, and Mr. Wyndham chuckled. "By God, you're your father's daughter, without a doubt!"

He lifted me easily into the saddle and continued. "I must admit that she had you cornered at first like some frightened mouse, but you certainly proved your mettle."

He patted my hand and swung up into his own saddle, still amused.

"I will apologize," I said to him, "if you think I was out of place."

"Nonsense. It is the only way to handle her."

And that was the end of it.

Mr. Wyndham urged his mount ahead, and I barely had time for a backward glance. Rachel had not moved from her outpost in the doorway and watched us with cold eyes. I was sure that it was those same eyes that had watched us from the upstairs window when we arrived, and with only slight regret I realized that I had made an enemy at Chandler House.

I eased Gypsy into a canter, still contemplating Rachel Chandler who, despite an inexcusably coarse manner, was able to artfully weave her spell over a man and bewitch him with her beauty. A woman with such abilities had little to fear from me. Mr. Wyndham was not immune to her charms. His attention to me had only been a part of the game, but then she had not been as amused as he. I was disquieted, full of nervous energy and the need to prove myself somehow. When we had ridden inland for some distance and reached a valley of tall grasses, I saw my opportunity.

"Might we let the horses have their head for a bit?" I suggested.

"If you wish. Captain has been headstrong this afternoon. Perhaps a good run is what he needs."

He used his riding crop to point off in the distance.

"Do you see that stand of trees at the far end of the field?"

I said that I did.

"Among them is a spreading oak. I shall meet you beneath it."

Again he touched his forelock with the tip of the crop and was off. I prodded Gypsy with my left foot and clamped the toe of my right boot hard behind my calf as the mare galloped off. If I had been in a normal

frame of mind, I would never have raced a strange
mount on untested ground, and I might have
remembered that I had been told that white-
stockinged horses often had too much spirit for their
own good. As it was, these thoughts did not come to
me until after the brown streak of a frightened hare cut
a path directly in front of Gypsy, who quite naturally
bolted, her forelegs pawing the air. I prayed that she
had been well-trained to the sidesaddle as I struggled
to keep myself from being unseated. The mare tried
repeatedly to rid herself of me before I was able to
collect her.

Gypsy jigged fretfully for a while, but eventually I
was able to soothe her with a calm voice and take her
in a slow gait to the spreading oak where Matthew
Wyndham was waiting. The rush of blood in my ears
surmounted all but the incessant pounding of my
heart. My face was flush when I met him.

"How did a young lady from Boston become such a
horsewoman?" he wanted to know.

"It was foolish of me to race an unfamiliar mount. I
hope I've not upset your mare."

"You cannot be held accountable for a rabbit in
your path. I thought you would surely be thrown. So,
Miss Dalton, I repeat my question. Wherever did a
city girl learn to ride like that?"

"My grandparents had a country house in Oakham.
I spent many summers there and learned to ride
almost before I could walk."

With that I dismounted, but the tip of my boot
caught in the stirrup and sent me tumbling headlong
into the tall grass. "What is it they say? 'Pride goeth
before a fall.' "

We laughed together, and Mr. Wyndham knelt
down to help me to my feet. With a firm hold on my
arms, he pulled me upward and when we were face
to face, he hesitated. I dropped my eyes shyly but felt
his on me all the while. I had behaved like a foolish

child for the entire afternoon, and this is where my actions had led me. I had played my game with Mr. Wyndham in order to taunt Rachel Chandler, and I thought that he had understood, but had he really?

He did not release me yet, but studied the planes of my face.

"Adrienne?" he whispered as if there were something he wished to impart to me.

There was on the breeze the ring of laughter. It was distinctive laughter, full of derision, and I knew that I had heard the sound before. We clambered to our feet to see from whem it had come. At the crest of the hill was a horse and rider. Having made known his presence, the tall man turned and rode away before I could see his face. Mr. Wyndham, though, must have seen him. His expression was most unpleasant, and he uttered a curse.

"Damnation!"

3

The afternoon sun was waning and the wind had turned brisk when we returned to the stables. The grooms saw to our horses and we separated, Mr. Wyndham stopping to have a talk with Lucas Pagett, his farm manager, while I began the walk up to Wyndcliffe. On any other occasion I might have stopped to admire the artistic arrangement of the gardens, the neatly trimmed yew hedges and border of pastel flowers, but now my every muscle ached. The last few miles of our ride had left me in pain, though I would never have had Mr. Wyndham know it. I entered the house and haltingly maneuvered up the stairs, fighting stiff limbs every step of the way. By the time I reached my room, I had unpinned my chic little hat and, entering, tossed it onto the vanity table, fully intending to collapse onto the bed. Instead I was met with the melody of my carousel and Susannah, with elbows resting on the bureau, watching as the ponies went around. I was irritated that the child had such a lack of respect for my privacy. The music stopped and Susannah reached to wind the mechanism.

"Don't touch that!" I shouted.

Susannah looked up, and with eyes wide, she bolted
from the room. I was immediately sorry, but far too
tired to think of a way of remedying the situation at
present. I shed my jacket, dropped down into the
vanity chair to pull off my riding boots, and then
unbuttoned my blouse. Pouring the tepid water from
the ewer into the washstand basin, I washed, wishing
I could wash away the ache in my limbs. What I
needed now, desperately, was a steaming bath and
the ministrations of Lottie to rub me down with
liniment, so that I might sink between the bedsheets
and forget my aches. I stared blankly out of the french
windows and sighed. Below the terraced gardens I
could see the stables, and I thought of Gypsy. No
doubt the horse was receiving better treatment than I.
I wondered if I would ever stop feeling bitter at what I
had lost.

I had only just finished changing my clothes when
there came a knock at the door and a young woman
let herself in.

"I'm Brenna McKeon, miss. I've brought up a
dinner tray for you and Miss Susannah . . . in the
classroom."

"Thank you, Brenna."

"Yes, miss."

She wore an apron over her faded calico. She had a
pretty face with a pale complexion and an abundance
of dark hair which was escaping its pins. I felt quite
suddenly ashamed of my selfishness. This girl could
have been but a few years older than I, and yet her
enormous brown eyes had a depth which foretold
experience that I could only imagine. Her hands,
which she was now wiping on her apron, were
cracked and red, nails broken.

"You must be old Mr. McKeon's daughter," I
guessed.

She nodded.

"And the boy, Timothy, is your son?"

"Yes, miss," she replied.

"He is a handsome lad."

"Thank you for saying so, miss."

Brenna bobbed her head and slipped out, leaving me disoriented. I wanted to go on talking with her. There was an ethereal quality about her that fascinated me. I began to wonder about Brenna McKeon, who did not appear to have a husband yet had borne a son, whose position in life had aged her beyond her years. I remembered the girl's rough hands and looked down in my lap at my own white ones, so carefully manicured. I recalled the worn cotton dress and compared it to my own gray cashmere. The experience left me with an unpleasant feeling as if I had seen things for the first time as they really were.

The meal was palatable, but I had no appetite. Across the table, Susannah's dinner was not any better received. The child twisted her fork back and forth, pushing the food across her plate, consuming nothing.

"You seem to have lost your appetite, Susannah," I said. "I must confess that I feel the same. Your father took me on a tour of the grounds this afternoon, and at each farm we visited, the wife bade us taste a new recipe."

There was no response from the child.

"How did you pass the afternoon?" I wondered.

"Reading."

"And what were you reading?"

"*Alice's Adventures in Wonderland*. Papa brought it back on his last trip to Portland."

"How very thoughtful of him."

"Oh, he never chooses gifts himself. He has no time for shopping. He has someone pick them out for him."

I winced inwardly, not wanting to face how close the remark had struck at my own childhood memories.

"And how do you know this?" I asked her.

"Mama told me so," she replied matter-of-factly.

What an odd thing to tell a child, whether true or not.

"So how do you find *Alice's Adventures*?" I was suddenly anxious to change the subject.

"My favorite is the Cheshire Cat. Did you ever wish you could disappear, miss?"

"Yes. I suppose everyone has felt that way at one time or another."

"I do."

"Just think how much your father would miss you if you should."

There was a long pause before Susannah replied. "Mama would miss me. I miss her."

I looked up at the child, wondering if at last she had decided to face reality. I knew that if I was to make any progress, I should have to tread lightly.

"I know how you must feel. I miss my father terribly sometimes."

"He was here," she said to me, "at Wyndcliffe."

"Yes, but how did you know?"

"I heard them talking, and I remembered his name. He was a nice man. He brought me a sack of horehound candy once. He's dead now, isn't he, miss?"

"Yes, he is. Susannah, would you like to tell me about your mother? My father said that she was very beautiful."

"She was the most beautiful woman in the whole world. Everyone thought so, but Papa most of all. He named one of his ships after her, you know . . . the *Nora Jean*."

So the graceful ship that had carried me here had been named for Matthew Wyndham's wife. I'd not have guessed it from his dispassionate tone as we had discussed the sale of the vessel.

"She would read to me every day," Susannah continued, animated now. "Even when she was sick and Dr. Fletcher said that she mustn't leave her bed, she would call for me and we would read together. In the spring, she would pack a hamper and we would have a picnic in the garden. On her birthday, we would spend the day with Grandfather Talbott at Longfield. He would let me pet his horses and feed them carrots and sugar lumps. They tickled my hands when they ate the sugar. I miss him, too."

I was overwhelmed. This was the most conversation Susannah had offered me thus far. It was as if a dam had burst and the memories of her mother spilled forth unchecked. I was hopeful for our relationship all at once, yet still cautious.

"Your grandfather died?" I guessed.

"No. I am not permitted to see him any more. He and Papa had a terrible fight. I don't understand. It must be like Mrs. Garen says, 'grown-up reasons and not for the likes of me.' "

"Your father knows what is best for you," I assured her, though this time I was not sure of it myself. What reason could Matthew Wyndham have for depriving the child of her grandfather?

Sleep was long in coming that night. I lay there in the darkness, unable to put to rest the questions in my mind: about Matthew Wyndham, a most unfathomable man, and about Susannah, who had far too many worries for a child of her years. I had just drifted off when a tugging at the bedclothes startled me awake. A small white face hovered close to me in the moonlight, with dark eyes wide and staring.

"Mama? Mama?"

"Susannah?"

I raised myself up and saw that the door joining our rooms was ajar. The child clambered onto the bed and threw her arms around me, sobbing.

"Mama, I knew you wouldn't leave me!"

When I called her name again, she did not reply, and I realized only slowly that Susannah had been sleepwalking. I held her close to comfort her and stroked her hair.

"Hush, child. Everything is all right."

"Don't leave me again, Mama. Please!"

"I won't. I won't leave you."

Lifting her small frame into my arms, I carried her into her room and tucked her beneath the quilt, running a hand over her forehead to wipe away the strands of hair, damp with perspiration. She tossed fitfully, caught in the throes of her dreams, and I sat down beside her bed, feeling helpless. I crossed my arms over my chest against the chill night air and waited, until at last the child settled into a peaceful sleep.

Though I had not been able to sleep at all a short time ago, I found myself overcome by exhaustion and went back to the warm comfort of my bed. Perhaps I did not want to admit to myself that I was frightened, frightened by the complexity of this child and by my own inability to help her. Perhaps I was only succumbing to the hopelessness as I slipped into a deep sleep.

Was it a dream? Eerie piano music floated on the air as I roused myself to consciousness and tried to discern whether it emanated from inside my head or out. When I was satisfied that I was no longer dreaming, I lifted myself up and threw aside the bed-clothes. My first clear thoughts were of Susannah. Had she been sleepwalking again and wandered off somewhere?

Blue moonlight spilled in through the french windows as bright as daylight and I could see without the aid of a lamp. Surely enough, Susannah's quilt lay in a heap on her bed. She was not beneath it.

My heart began to beat faster as I went for the

chamberstick on my mantel and struck a match to it. I grabbed a paisley shawl from the vanity chair where it lay and threw it over my shoulders. Candle in hand, I padded out into the hall and past the main staircase. Every door was shut and all was quiet, save that haunting melody and the tall case clock in the foyer below, which now chimed twice. Ahead was the great oak door that closed off the east wing, protecting the source of nocturnal concert. Mrs. Garen had pointed out that this part of the house was unoccupied, but such was not the case now. I knew that Susannah could not play the piano, yet perhaps the music had attracted her, too. I wrapped my free hand around the doorknob, wholly expecting to be stopped there, but the lock clicked and the door creaked open.

A rush of cold air swept past me and the candle guttered low. I drew the shawl close about me, and as I crossed the threshold into the east wing, the temperature dropped measurably. There was carpeting beneath my bare feet but its nap was worn and the floral pattern was faded beyond recognition. I followed the hall past several open doors and paused at each to let the candle's light illuminate the room. Some were empty, but most held furnishings in hollands. The flickering candlelight danced over the dustcloths, animating them and causing my heart to start again and again. Gooseflesh broke out up and down my arms and I wished that I had taken the time to find my dressing gown. Perhaps I needn't venture much farther. Just ahead the hall turned sharply, and as I rounded the corner, the music grew louder.

"Susannah!" I cried in a hoarse whisper. "Susannah, are you there?"

I held the candle at arm's length, peering down the dark hall where I thought I spied a figure. All at once I gasped, stifling a cry as I clamped a hand over my mouth. There in the shadows floated the outline of a

woman in a filmy shroud, her long, pale hair flowing
over her shoulders. I stood paralyzed, not daring to
advance or retreat. I was reminded of the Wyndham
ghosts my father had joked about in his letters. Was
this one of them?

My mind raced, wondering at the possibilities. One
thing was certain. The apparition stood between me
and the source of the music. It was my duty to find
Susannah. If the child was indeed sleepwalking, some
harm might come to her. I drew a long breath and
held it as I stepped forward cautiously. I shut my eyes
unconsciously against the vision, expecting that when
they opened again, the figure would have vanished. It
had not. It floated as it had before, ethereal yet
unmoving, only now I smiled at it. The "ghost"
smiled back. I might have laughed out loud had I not
still been trembling. The specter had been nothing
more than my own reflection in a watery mirror
hanging over a console table at the far end of the hall.
I felt like a child who had been dared to spend a night
in the graveyard and had come out the next morning
unscathed. It was a wry amusement, at my own
expense, but I did not dwell on it. Susanna was still
missing.

There was only one room remaining at the end of
the hall, the tower room. It was circular, with long
windows facing the sea. I heard quite clearly the
pounding of the incoming tide against the rocks. Its
rhythm blended with the intense strains of the piano
sonata.

From my spot in the doorway, I felt the warming
waves of heat from the fire blazing in the grate. In the
center of the room was a grand piano. An ornate
candelabrum stood atop it, and the golden aura of the
candlelight beckoned, yet I ventured no further into
the room. Seated at the keyboard and diligently
working at the complex sonata was a man I immediately recognized. It was the man who had accosted

me on the *Nora Jean*. Instinct told me to turn away,
but my limbs would not respond. Irrepressible
curiosity held me there.

I studied him as he played. It was he, and yet he
was so unlike that other man at this moment. Such
diversity there was in his expression as he played! His
music was charged with the vehemence of his
emotions. I was left breathless by the rage of which
this music foretold, and yet, too, I sensed anguish. I
trembled. It was because of the cold, I told myself. He
played from memory, for although the sheet music
stood before him, his eyes were closed. He was carelessly attired. His waistcoat hung open, the linen shirt
beneath unbuttoned for comfort's sake. His frock coat
was tossed on a nearby armchair. His riding boots
were mud-spattered and would surely ruin the
expensive carpet beneath his feet. He was so different
from the swaggering, forward man I had encountered
on the deck of the *Nora Jean* that I wondered if they
could truly be the same man. He raised his hands
from the keys, and the silence disturbed my reverie.
He had seen me then, and I turned to start back down
the hall.

"No, wait, don't go," he called.

I hesitated and he was beside me in a few strides.

"After an evening of hard drinking I see a good
many of our Wyndham ghosts, but I've not touched a
drop all night, so how shall I explain you, my dear?"

Cautiously he ran the back of one hand along my
cheek. I flinched at his touch and withdrew a bit.

"Oh, so you are real," he said with a mischievous
grin.

He took a step backward then and threw up his
hands. "I've no wish to be slapped this evening."

His deep-set eyes were surveying me in a far too
familiar manner, and I pulled the shawl up around
my shoulders, clenching it to my breast.

"You!"

He bowed in a derisive fashion. "Jason Wyndham, at your service."

I knew that my mouth was agape, yet I tried still to preserve my dignity. I wasn't sure whom I had expected him to be but certainly not a Wyndham, not brother to Matthew.

"I don't believe I've had the pleasure," he went on.

His every word seemed to taunt me.

"As I remember it, upon our last meeting you were not much interested in introductions," I snapped.

"Then I fear you misunderstood. I am very much interested."

"Well then, I am Adrienne Dalton, Susannah's governess."

The very word set him off and his resonant laughter broke the quiet like a clap of thunder. "The governess? I'd not have guessed. You are not attired like any governess I've encountered," he said as he rakishly took stock of me with his eyes. "I thought they'd all been turned out of the same factory, clad in drab mouse brown and spectacles."

He watched my visage darken and no doubt suspected that I was perilously close to striking him again. He cleared his throat.

"I mean no offense, Adrienne, but you are a superb actress. You had me convinced that you were off to France. Schooled in Paris, indeed!"

Suppressed anger was causing me to tremble uncontrollably, and I wondered why I continued with this man. I tried to keep my voice even. "I am happy to have amused you, sir, but you are distracting me from my purpose. Susannah is not in her bed. I am sure that she has been walking in her sleep, and I must find her before some harm befalls her."

He pursed his lips. "I see. Then I shall accompany you, of course."

"That will not be necessary."

"Ah, but it is. Susannah is my niece, and I am at

least as concerned for her well-being as you are."

"As you wish," I replied coldly.

I started back down the hall at a brisk pace, not caring whether or not he followed. I felt his eyes on me every step of the way, though he did not attempt to converse further.

On the main floor, I made a cursory check of the library and the drawing room before coming upon Jason Wyndham again in the foyer. I was growing more distraught with each moment that passed. His facade of indifference slipped away then.

"You mustn't worry yourself. We'll find her."

Just then there was a crash of shattering porcelain from the kitchen. We exchanged glances and fairly ran there to find Susannah in the pantry, shame-faced and awaiting discovery, the remains of one of Mrs. Black's pastry trays at her feet.

"Susannah, those were for the reception!"

"I'm sorry, miss, truly I am. I was hungry and everyone was asleep—"

"Sorry won't mend this platter," I chided, bending down to gather up the pieces of porcelain, "and there will be more work for Mrs. Black. You shall apologize in the morning."

"Yes, miss."

Jason Wyndham chuckled to himself throughout my censuring. Susannah looked up now for the first time to see him. She looked puzzled. "Uncle?"

He nodded and bent down to her. "So you remember me, then? You were just a tiny thing when I went away."

"Of course, I remember you."

"I'm glad, but let's not lose sight of the fact that your midnight venture has scared poor Miss Dalton nearly out of her wits. You'd best limit your pantry-raiding to the daylight hours."

She giggled and threw her arms about his neck.

"When did you come home, Uncle?"

''This afternoon. Now let's help Miss Dalton clean up this mess, and then it's off to bed with you. We shall talk in the morning.''

We removed all traces of mischief from the pantry and trudged back up the stairs, single file. I saw Susannah back to bed with a warning that she stay there and returned to my own room by way of the adjoining door, without thinking that I had left the hall door ajar. I laid my shawl over the vanity chair and looked up to see Jason Wyndham in the open doorway. Advancing warily toward him, I put the door between us. I moved to shut it, but he did not step out of the way.

''Will you come join me in a brandy, Adrienne? It's just the thing to help you sleep.''

''Good night, Mr. Wyndham.''

He took a step backward, and I closed the door and as an afterthought, bolted it shut.

4

It was a cloudless day, a warm breeze soughing through the pines. The landscape was verdant. Salt air and fragrant pine mingled to make a heady perfume. I had been at Wyndcliffe more than a week and already felt accustomed to the routine of the household. I had taken to walking the grounds with Susannah after our morning lessons, and today it seemed a wise choice as preparations were going on throughout the house for the political reception that Mr. Wyndham would be hosting this evening.

With Susannah in tow, I set a rather brisk pace, striding across the lawn to the headland. It was a narrow finger of the rocky cliff, which rose up at the land's end and jutted out into the water, creating a point of interest on the coastline. I judged it would be the best vantage point for miles. On a clear day such as this, it might be possible to survey the entire Wyndham estate. I felt the drag on my arm as though Susannah were resisting but surmised that I was simply moving faster than her legs could carry her.

"Come, Susannah. I'd wager that we can see the ships in the harbor from that point of land."

"It's called the Widow's Walk," she replied in a curiously small voice.

"Widow's Walk? Do you mean like a captain's walk on the rooftop of a house? It does sound more ominous, though."

"It was named on account of one of our ancestors. Diana Wyndham was her name, I think. Her husband was a ship's captain. He was lost at sea and she went mad.

"After dark each night she would go out to that point and wave a lantern to guide him safely home. One night she disappeared. Some say her captain came to take her away with him, but most say that she lost her footing in the darkness and—"

By now we were well out onto the peninsula. Susannah recited the tale as if it had been told to her a hundred times before, and I was admiring the view of Wyndham Harbor. When she stopped so abruptly, I turned my attention to her. She had a stricken look, her face washed of color.

"Yes, Susannah?" I prompted, wondering why she had gone silent, as if she were suddenly frightened by her own ghost story.

"They say you can see her still out here on some nights, waving her lantern."

I took her face into my hands. "That's not the sort of story that a young lady should be telling. You'll only excite yourself. Such things are nonsense."

I looked around for something to which I could divert Susannah's attention. "There's a marble bench there near the point. Shall we sit and rest a moment?"

She shrugged, concentrating on the toes of her black kid boots. I took her hand to firmly lead her to the bench, and then went to the cliff's edge and looked down. Far below, the ocean playfully lapped at the sharp rocks. If someone were to fall from this height, death would be a certainty. Still there was an exhilaration for me on the edge and I tarried there, feeling the enormity of the elements all around.

The sudden pressure of a hand on my arm unbalanced me and just then I imagined my body lying broken and lifeless on the rocks. I managed to steady myself and turned around quickly to be met with Susannah's small, pale face. She stared up at me, her eyes strangely bright. What a preternatural expression she wore!

"Come away, miss! You mustn't ever go so near the edge. You might slip and fall."

She tugged at my sleeve and made me follow her away from the headland. There had been an anxious few moments when I'd seen Susannah's feverish expression as I'd turned to her. I thought then that she might have intended to push me, but no, it could not be. She only wanted to warn me away from the precipice. She had been overexcited by the ghostly tale of the Widow's Walk. I took it as my duty to discover who was relating these stories to her and put a stop to it. It was no wonder the child was plagued by nightmares and walked in her sleep.

When we were safely on the lawn once more, I sought to question her, but she let go of me and darted across the lawn toward the rear of the house. At length I found her in a desolate corner of the gardens, kneeling in a bed of daffodils, neatly snapping them off at the stem to make herself a bouquet.

"I don't think you ought to pick any more flowers," I said. "The gardeners have done their best so that everything will be presentable for the reception tonight."

"These won't matter. Mama planted them. They were her favorites."

"You've enough of them. Come out of there now before you dirty your pinafore."

"Yes, miss."

We crossed to the central section of the formal gardens where stood a double-basined fountain, its jet sending up a geyser of water that splashed down over the stone embellishments like a dozen tiny waterfalls. Less than a hedgerow away, I heard Felicia Wyndham as she gave last-minute instructions about the care of her own special rose garden to the groundskeeper. I tried to steer Susannah in another direction. We avoided Mrs. Wyndham whenever we could, but it was too late on this occasion.

"Susannah! Where did you get those flowers?"

The child straightened her back, ready for battle.

"The bed by the east gate," she replied.

"You are a wicked child! You know that you are not to touch anything in this garden."

I felt my heart thud.

"No doubt you've ruined the design somewhere with your willfull mischief." She paused as if contemplating an effective punishment, then held out her hand. "I'll have those flowers. We can use them in one of the indoor arrangements."

"No, you can't take them!"

Felicia snatched for the bouquet, but the child was quicker and stepped out of her reach. So she turned on me.

"You are responsible for this. I told him that it was ludicrous to put a spoiled child in charge of a spoiled child. You can rest assured, Miss Dalton, that my stepson will hear of this."

"Susannah told me that the flower bed had been planted by her mother and was of no importance—"

The groundskeeper, a burly man, cut in on the conversation. He was meek, despite his size. "That's right, Mrs. Wyndham, if you don't mind my sayin' so. That patch is set apart from the rest. Missus Nora, God rest her soul, she dug it all up herself and planted it as she liked. Mr. Wyndham told us we wasn't to disturb it."

"We shall see about that!"

The tone of Felicia's voice made it clear that she

wished to restore him to respectful silence, but he went on in spite of her.

"Miss Susannah, she picks the flowers and puts them on her mama's grave. I watched her myself, I did, many a time."

Susannah dropped her head so that it was impossible to read her expression. I felt a rush of relief, though, as the situation turned around, and I placed myself between Felicia and the child.

"I'm certain that Mr. Wyndham won't mind if these few flowers are left out of your floral arrangements so that Susannah might put them on her mother's grave."

Felicia turned on her heel and stomped off toward the house, muttering to herself, "Her mother planted them, did she? Mistress of the house, digging in the dirt like a common laborer—"

The groundskeeper set off in the opposite direction, also muttering, "Hateful old woman, no respect for the dead—"

I breathed a relieved sigh and turned my attention on Susannah, who looked positively cherubic with a slightly bewildered expression and her arm full of vivid gold blossoms. I could scarcely have missed, though, the malevolent look the child had cast after Felicia.

"Had you truly intended to take those flowers to the graveyard?"

Susannah nodded vehemently.

"Well then, would you mind very much if I walked along with you?"

She said that she wouldn't mind, and so now it was her turn to lead. She took me by the hand.

"It's not far. Come this way."

The Wyndham family cemetery was in a sheltered valley a short distance south of the stables. The path was well-traveled but steeper than I might have expected. When we had descended more than half of

the way, I turned back and was met by a magnificent
sight. Wyndcliffe loomed larger than life above us,
shimmering silver as the sun reflected on its granite
walls. I could think of no finer view the Wyndham
ancestors could hope to admire throughout eternity.
Susannah went ahead now, through the wrought-iron
gate which creaked in protest as she passed. She
dropped down in the grass beside one of the newer
headstones. I followed her in solemnly, taking stock of
the score of headstones scattered around a central
mausoleum, the Wyndham name carved into the
granite over its double gates. In his letter to me,
Matthew Wyndham had offered to bury Papa in this
place, but I had politely declined. I had wanted him to
rest beside my mother in the cemetery in Boston.
Now I almost wished that I had assented. Then I
would have been able to come here, as Susannah did
now, to hold my one-sided conversations with him
and remember a happier past.

Susannah carefully removed a withered bunch of
wildflowers from the vase at the base of the
headstone as I read the inscription. "Nora Talbott
Wyndham, beloved wife and mother, 1838-1865 . . . a
gentle soul."

The bouquet of daffodils seemed to give a sunny
glow to the shaded grove, and I smiled at the loving
way Susannah cared for her mother's final resting
place. The grass here was trimmed neatly and the
grave bordered by smooth pebbles, the kind one
could find along the seashore, all lined up in a row.
Each was unusual in some way, as if careful thought
had been given to each choice. Some were striated,
others sparkled with feldspar, while still others were
of a soft rose color. I knew that the child must have
given much thought to the arrangement.

"I come here every day when the weather is warm
enough," she said, sensing my eyes on her, "but now
things are different."

"How is that?"

"Before, I could go out in the mornings very early. They wouldn't have liked me to be out alone, but no one noticed if I was back by breakfast. But now that you're here—"

"Did you think that I wouldn't allow you to come here?"

"No, but you're like the cat, miss, the one who lives in the stable loft. You're watching, always watching me with those sharp eyes."

I knelt down beside her. "I don't want you to think of me as a jailer. I am your teacher. It is important that I help you grow into a gentlewoman so that you may take your proper place in society. Your father is an important man, Susannah, and I think you know that this is what your mother would want for you."

"I know, miss."

"It is my duty to watch over you, and a lady is ever mindful of her duty. Your father, the servants, and I as well are concerned for your welfare. Imagine what might have happened if I had not been there to lead you back to your bed when you were sleepwalking. You might have fallen over something or down a flight of stairs."

"I do not walk in my sleep," Susannah said, most emphatically.

"But you came to my bed, calling for your mother. You must have had a nightmare."

She jumped to her feet, growing defensive. "I did not!"

I remembered too late that oftimes sleepwalkers did not recollect their nighttime excursions, and it only served to confuse and upset them if they were reminded of what they themselves could not recall.

"I'm sorry," I said.

This seemed to satisfy her, and as she stood there, arms crossed over her pinafore, rocking on her heels, her face took on an animated look.

"Do you like our family resting place, miss?"

I should have been suspicious at once of the child's erratic mood, first argumentative and then amiable.

"I do," she went on, "I've explored it all, looked at all of the markers. Some are hard to read, though. The letters are all worn away. Do you see those three stone angels beside Mama's stone? They are my brothers: Matthew, Jonathan and Edward."

I examined these markers. All three had been still-born sons, the last laid to rest only three months before Nora's own death. Perhaps she had died of complications. No one at the house had spoken of it. Susannah continued with her tour, seemingly unaffected.

"Godfrey Wyndham has a marker that looks like an open Bible, and then there's the plaque for poor Diana.'

"She is the one—"

The child's head bobbed. "The widow of the Widow's Walk. Her papa put up a plaque for her in the mausoleum. This way, miss. I'll show it to you."

I was growing uneasy at this sojourn among the long-departed Wyndhams, but felt that I must humor Susannah. She swung open the tall iron gates, and we passed into the dank twilight of the mausoleum. Susannah took hold of my hand, maneuvering easily, and pressed it against the coolness of a wall. I felt the chiseled indentations but my eyes had not yet adjusted to the half-light.

"There it is. Can you read it, miss?"

The air was close, and my throat constricted.

"No, Susannah. Please, I—"

"It says, 'Diana Wyndham, 1771-1791. She does not rest here. Look to the sea, to the caress of the tides, the gentle froth of the waves, for in them she lives.' "

The words came into focus, and I followed as Susannah read. It was a touching monument to the long-dead woman set down by a loving father, now

long-dead himself, but the words as Susannah read
them came out sounding like some eerie, twisted
poem. I feared that I was becoming light-headed
breathing the bad air, for the child's voice sounded
hollow and was growing fainter. It was not until I
heard the chink of the metal gates as they closed that I
realized that she was gone. The child was a
will-o'-the-wisp. "Susannah, where are you?"

Against my will, I looked once around the vault to
the open chamber where stood several stone coffins.
Surely enough, the child was nowhere in sight. I
shuddered violently, sprang to the gates and pushed
outward. They held fast. Blood rushed in my ears like
the crashing of waves on the shore. It fairly deafened
me as I shook frantically at the bars, calling after my
charge. I could see her now, running off and already
halfway up the hill path.

"Susannah! Susannah, come back!" I cried out.
"The latch is stuck!"

I was loath to turn back into the darkness for I could
hear skittering noises on the flagstones beneath my
feet. The cry of a seabird somewhere overhead sent
me into near hysterics, and in one last effort I pushed
my full weight against the gates. They swung open
wide to send me sprawling into the tall grass, blinded
by the daylight. On my feet again, I stumbled across
the yard to the nearest way out and rushed without
direction into the thick of the grove as if demons were
at my heels. I was oblivious to the straggling undergrowth that tugged at my skirts as I ran. When at last I
stopped to catch my breath and orient myself, I
realized that I could no longer see the hill path nor the
cemetery clearing. I must have come out and headed
in the wrong direction, I decided. A clearer head
prevailing now, I turned toward the sound of the surf.
I could follow the coastline back to Wyndcliffe, of
that much I was sure.

What could have made Susannah run off that way? I

wondered now. Had she frightened herself by reciting the engraving on the cenotaph in the mausoleum, the same way she'd been frightened when she related the tale of Diana Wyndham to me earlier out on the Widow's Walk? I sensed not. The condition of her mother's gravesite told me that Susannah was a frequent visitor to the place; she'd admitted as much herself. It wasn't likely she'd be frightened by the surroundings. Why then had she run off? I hesitated to speculate, perhaps because I already knew the answer, and it was most unpleasant to face. When I'd called after Susannah as she was retreating up the hill path, she'd turned back, and I thought I saw her smile before she went on, as if locking me in the mausoleum was what she had intended all along.

I looked down in dismay at the rents in my coral poplin skirt, which had caught on the brambles and low branches, and the lace cuff that was separated from its sleeve. The bile rose in me, but I swallowed it down. How was I to deal with such a child? Where had she gotten off to now? It was likely that she had run home to escape my wrath, but then again she might have doubled back to see what outcome her mischief had wrought.

"Susannah?" I called out and then again, louder, "Susannah!"

I lifted my skirts, walking at a more cautious pace to prevent further damage to my gown. So enveloped was I in the contemplation of Susannah's punishment that I was not aware of the break in the trees nor the wheel ruts and matted grass beneath my feet that indicated a wagon path. I did not hear the approaching horse's hooves until the great black stallion had issued a guttural neigh and reared up on his hind legs perilously near me. The rider cursed as he collected the reins.

"Damn, woman, are you dreaming? You've

spooked my horse. Easy, Cerberus, easy."

When all was again calm, I looked up at the rider. It was Jason Wyndham.

"Adrienne?" he sounded surprised. "What brings you into this part of the wood alone?"

"I'm sorry if I've upset your mount," I apologized, drawing near to admire the magnificent Arabian stallion.

The horse had a wild look in his eyes, but I held out a hand to him, stroking his muzzle in the way of an apology.

"Such a proud animal and yet such an awful name. If I recollect my Roman mythology, Cerberus was Pluto's three-headed dog—"

"You surprise me, Adrienne. I had no idea you were so well-read. Cerberus, as it happens, was guardian of the gates of Hell, and as such a fitting name for the Devil's companion, wouldn't you say?"

I was entirely perplexed, but Jason Wyndham seemed not to take notice.

"Have you misplaced your charge once again, Adrienne?" he asked, baiting me.

I could not decide which made me the more angry, the way he made sport of me or his flagrant use of my Christian name. The latter left me feeling sullied, and I did not like it.

"No, of course not," I retorted. "We were walking. She—I—"

He had succeeded in confounding me once again and laughed heartily on account of it, leaning forward in the saddle.

"Why don't you leave off trying to teach my niece? I am sure that together you and I can find something you are better suited for."

Through clenched teeth, I let go a screech that made it only as far as the back of my throat and came out sounding garbled and impotent. I would have struck at him, kicked him hard, had he not been astride

Cerberus. I would not risk startling the animal a second time. As it was, I whirled around and stomped off, hoping to put as much distance between myself and Jason Wyndham as was humanly possible.

"I wouldn't advise going off by yourself," he called out, riding until he had covered the distance between us. "There are bogs in this valley. It is dangerous to walk here if you are unfamiliar with the terrain. My dear brother would never forgive me if I left you here to get caught up in the mire. Come on, I'll give you a hand up and you can ride home with me."

"I think not," I replied without a break in my stride. "I shall follow the wagon path until I am safely within sight of the house, thank you."

"You will be soon surprised them, for that trail disappears into the trees over the next rise. It hasn't been used in years.".

He cut in front of my path and held down a hand to me. "I'm afraid I must insist that you ride with me. You have my word that I shall be the perfect gentleman."

I squirmed for a moment or two, wanting to resist yet knowing I should not. I finally accepted his hand, and he pulled me up and across the saddle in front of him, steadying me with an arm about my waist.

"Susannah," I remembered aloud.

"I saw her scurrying into the house when I came out. She knows better than to walk in this part of the wood."

"Then you knew all along that we had been separated—"

His answer to this was a throaty chuckle that sounded uncomfortably close. I felt my face burn as he spurred the horse on but knew I must keep a clear head, for he made every conversation a battle of wits.

"How is it you come riding on this part of the estate if it is so unsafe, Mr. Wyndham?"

The long pause that followed told me that he had

thought me nonplused and hadn't expected the retort.

"Susannah was sporting a most devilish grin when she came home. It reminded me of myself the time I locked my governess in the wine cellar."

I wanted to laugh at this, but the situation was too close to my own recent experience.

"In the wine cellar?" I echoed.

"She had been pilfering bottles of my father's finest port."

"Couldn't you have explained to your father what she was about?"

I turned my head to catch his reply, and he looked at me as if it were the most absurd notion I could have entertained.

"It was a punishment to fit the crime, to my way of thinking. They didn't discover her for hours. It's a wonder she didn't drink herself into a stupor."

I contemplated Jason Wyndham's boyhood as an indulged child, locking up governesses and carving his initials in the schoolroom table, but the silence that followed and the very tenseness of his frame told me that there was more to it.

"I knew when I saw Susannah that she was up to something," he said, at last, "and when you did not return—"

"How very perceptive of you," I said, employing my own brand of sarcasm, "but I would not expect you to be cast in the role of knight-errant."

"Rest assured, my motives were purely selfish, my dear. You are somewhat pleasant to look at and possess a charming wit, as I'm sure you've been told. It would be a shame if you were to decide to leave us on account of a child's mischief."

"I have no intention of doing so," I told him, ignoring his left-handed compliment.

"Good. Now do tell me what my niece was up to."

I would not look back to him and did not reply.

"I should think you owe me that much at least,

seeing as how I came out here after you."

"I did not ask for your help, Mr. Wyndham, nor did I require it."

"You'd have welcomed me sure enough if I'd found you knee-deep in mud and sinking fast."

He was an exasperating man, and it was ludicrous to conduct an argument on horseback, closer to my adversary now than convention would normally allow.

I sighed. "We went to the cemetery that she might put flowers on her mother's grave. She wanted to show me the mausoleum and while I was inside, she—she shut the gates. The hinges must have been rusted. They stuck fast and I had quite a time of it getting out."

The episode was too vivid in my mind still. My words brought it all back again: the ominous, shadowy world of the dead, the closeness of the damp stone walls, the musty airlessness. . . . I found myself suddenly unable to catch my breath, and the greens of the forest and blues of the sky were spinning around like a kaleidoscope. Not now, I told myself, not here. I waited, expecting the stillness to be broken by his cruel laughter. He would not pass up such an opportunity to ridicule me. And so silently I fought off the vertigo and waited for his attack. The gibes did not come, however. He dropped the reins and I felt his hand on my shoulder.

"You're trembling."

My head lagged. "I'm fine, truly."

"Are you certain you are all right? Have you told me all that happened?"

I tried to look at him and told myself that the compassionate expression could not belong to Jason Wyndham.

"Yes," I replied, "It's only that . . . when I was a child, only about six years old, I fell into a dry well on my grandparents' land. I called out until my voice was gone, but they did not come for me till almost nightfall. There were no broken bones, no damage done, but since then I've not been able to bear close spaces. It's foolish, I know."

He looked at me anew. "I am sorry. I'd never have related my own story to you had I known."

He drew a silver hip flask from the pocket of his frock coat and unscrewed the cap.

"This will help," he said, handing it to me.

"No, thank you. I'll be fine when the dizziness passes."

"Just a sip to clear your head."

I acquiesced, hoping that it would indeed slow the whirling in my brain. It was but a small sip and slid down easily enough, but I was then seized by such a fit of coughing and sputtering that he had to steady me lest I slip from the saddle.

"You've never tasted whiskey?" he asked, incredulous.

"Certainly not," I replied, "nor shall I again, although I do believe the dizziness is gone, thank you."

I replaced the cap and handed him his flask.

Since I had first encountered him on the deck of the *Nora Jean*, I was aware that Jason Wyndham ever studied me as though he expected to see something more than was plain to the eye, as though he suspected I had a second self, decidedly more unpleasant than that which faced him, and when at last it might be revealed to him, he could say, "Aha, I knew it all the while." That this particular encounter had left him puzzled was plainly written on his face.

He collected the reins then, and directed Cerberus toward the Wyndcliffe stables at a gallop. When we reached the stableyard, I slid down effortlessly, patted Cerberus and turned to him.

"I would be grateful to you, Mr. Wyndham, if you would not relate any of this to your brother. He would rebuke Susannah severely, I am sure, and it would only worsen the situation. I would like to handle this in my own way."

"We Wyndhams are not an amicable lot. You can rest assured that I will not be having a discussion on any matter with my brother."

I sent him a grateful smile and gave him my hand, playing gracious lady to his knight-errant. "I am in your debt, kind sir."

His eyes met mine and would not release me from their intent gaze. The pressure of his grip on my fingers was almost painful.

"Someday I shall collect, Adrienne," he said fiercely.

5

I rapped my knuckles
against the study door and waited until a disembodied
voice called out, "Come in."

Matthew Wyndham was at his desk, shielded by
stacks of ledgers and paperwork, and was checking
figures in an open book.

"I'd like to speak with you, if I may," I said. "It's
rather important."

He looked up at me but I could see that his mind
was still on the figures.

"I'm sorry to intrude upon you this way. If you are
occupied, I can come another time."

He pushed away from the desk and leaned back in
his chair, tenting his fingers. "No, please come in,"
he told me. "Sit down. I suppose I have been
expecting you."

I perched myself on the chair across the desk from
him and my head tilted to one side as it did when I
was puzzled. Could he have been apprised of
Susannah's behavior somehow?

"You are aware of Susannah's problems, then?" I
guessed.

"Susannah? Why, I—no," he stammered.

"You've torn your skirt," he suddenly noticed, changing the subject.

"We were out walking in the grove behind the house—"

"Leave it with Mrs. Garen and she will have someone mend it for you."

"I don't wish to be any trouble, and it is, after all, my own fault. If I hadn't wandered off the path—"

"Nonetheless, I insist."

I began again. "About Susannah . . . I believe that she is having more trouble adjusting to her mother's death than anyone has realized. She misses her terribly, and it is affecting her behavior. I think—no, I *know* that she resents my intrusion into her life."

Mr. Wyndham took in all that I related to him, betraying little of what he was thinking. In the end, though, he looked perturbed. "She has said something to you? Something to upset you?"

He lifted his muscular frame from the chair and went to the windows, gazing out over the fine-trimmed lawns. "I have allowed her far too much freedom and that is where the trouble lies. She will adjust to her mother's death in time, as we all have."

"She feels very much alone in her grief, sir," I noted.

"And you believe I should speak with her?" he said, coming back to the desk.

"I believe that what Susannah needs is to have some pleasant memories to cling to. So much of what she has now is morose: memories of death, a gravesite to visit. Why, the very mention of her mother's name brings out long faces and a shaking of the head. She needs to remember her mother as the woman she was when she was alive.

"I understand that Susannah's grandfather resides not far from here. She has mentioned him to me, you see. I thought that if we were to visit him in the house where her mother lived as a child, Susannah would have these pleasant remembrances to help her shake off her grief.''

Matthew Wyndham took his seat. His jaw clenched tightly. ''I'm afraid that what you suggest is impossible.''

I was undaunted by his reaction, which appeared to leave no room for discussion. ''Susannah has explained to me that there is bad blood between the two of you,'' I said boldly, ''but whatever quarrel you have with your father-in-law surely cannot be more important that Susannah's well-being. I speak from experience, sir. As you know, I have of late become well-acquainted with grief, and I believe that the child needs the company of her grandfather. She is quite fond of him.''

He slammed his ledger book shut, seeming to have lost his patience all at once. I was startled.

''She is but a child,'' he flared. ''What can she know of these things?''

I pushed myself back against the cool leather of the wing chair, hoping I might disappear into it. Once again I had overstepped my bounds. Waiting now, I barely breathed.

He sighed heavily and looked for a moment as if he might confide in me, but only shook his head. ''He is a bitter old man and will poison the child's mind. I'll not have him turn my own daughter against me.''

I sensed a hesitancy in him, despite his harsh words. He was considering the proposal whether he would admit it or not. Recklessly, I proceeded with my argument. ''I shall be there with her to set a balance to things. I would not ask this of you, Mr. Wyndham, if I did not think it most important to your daughter.''

And then the corners of his moustache turned up.

''I wonder if Susannah will grow up to be as much like me as you are like your father, Miss Dalton. You are certainly blessed with his powers of persuasion.

All right then, I shall send word to Longfield that the
two of you request an audience with Franklin Talbott.
I shall not, of course, be accompanying you.''

"Thank you, sir.''

"There is one condition I must impose, however.
You must never allow him to be alone with the child,
and if he shows any signs of delusions, if he should
say or do anything out of the ordinary, you are to
bring Susannah home at once. Do you understand?''

I said that I did.

The study doors slid open with such a crash as to
remind me of thunder. As they shuddered in their
track, Felicia Wyndham stormed between them and
marched to her stepson, spilling the contents of her
lace apron onto his desktop in a flurry of precious
rose petals.

"Just look at what that awful child has done! I will
not have it, do you hear me? She ought to be whipped,
and if you don't see to it, I may do it myself!''

Mr. Wyndham rose slowly. "Calm yourself, Felicia.
I am sure that in your distress you did not realize that
you have interrupted the discussion Miss Dalton and I
were having. I take it all of this has something to do
with Susannah, so if you will begin again—''

Mrs. Wyndham did a half-turn to include me in her
tirade, pointing an accusing finger. "She is not worth
her salt. She has done nothing to discipline the child;
in fact, I believe that she encourages her to run wild.
This very morning she took the child's side against me
. . . and in front of the groundskeeper.''

I met her insults with a venomous stare and rose to
meet my accuser. Mr. Wyndham came between us.

"It accomplishes nothing to assault Miss Dalton. If
you will kindly explain what has happened.'' He
brushed the petals off of his paperwork.

"Explain, why I'll do better than that, I'll show you.
Come along with me.''

He followed her out, with me close at his heels. My

mind was working feverishly, and I feared I already knew what mischief Susannah had wrought. My worst fears were realized when Felicia Wyndham led us out into the garden, and with a perverse sort of pride showed us her precious rose bed, now a cluster of thorn bushes. The head of each bloom had been snipped off and the petals crushed in the dirt.

The only sound came from me as I drew a sharp breath upon gazing at the carnage. The violence with which the act had been carried out frightened me. It was difficult to imagine Susannah capable of such intense, destructive emotions, and yet I knew it must be so. Matthew Wyndham seemed unaffected by the sight except for a slight twitch at one corner of his moustache.

"You are quite certain that Susannah is responsible for this?" he asked.

Mrs. Wyndham grew a trifle nervous under his scrutiny. "No one actually saw her. Easton was in the potting shed and I was busy inside, but after this morning—"

"Then you are not sure?"

"Well, no."

I turned away from the ruined flower bed.

"It was Susannah," I said in a low voice.

I felt weak, almost sick at my stomach, and left them to rest myself on the long bench across from the fountain. I was confronted with the memory of the child's face when she had touched my arm on the Widow's Walk. There had been a wild, unworldly look about her. I was beginning to believe her capable of, yes, capable of any violence.

In a matter of seconds Matthew Wyndham joined me on the bench. "Miss Dalton, Adrienne, please forgive my stepmother's atrocious behavior. You must understand how precious that rose garden was to her. I suppose she thought of it as the only part of this house that was truly hers.

"Since my father's death, she has been painfully aware of her impotent position in the household. Perhaps she thinks I may turn her out, though she must know that my father's will protects her in that respect. She was not born to this kind of life, as you may have noticed, and so feels an extra amount of pride in calling herself mistress. Your own natural gentility must intimidate her and thus cause her to behave in so unforgivable a manner."

I barely heard him, so intent were my thoughts on my charge. But I could not believe that, given the enormity of Susannah's problems, he was seeing to my well-being first. He seemed to have a total disregard for his own child.

"I bear Mrs. Wyndham no malice," I assured him. "It is Susannah's problem to which I must address myself."

"She will be punished, of course. And you realize that I can no longer consider any plans for a visit to her grandfather."

Distress was plain on my face. "Oh, but you must. The visit is more important now than ever, don't you see? This morning Mrs. Wyndham made an unflattering comment about your late wife within the child's hearing. It was this that caused Susannah to retaliate. I am sure of it."

"She must be punished," he insisted.

"Undoubtedly. She owes Mrs. Wyndham a formal apology and some sort of redress, but to deprive her of the very thing that may improve her state of mind would be a serious mistake."

He paused to consider. "I shall think on the matter and give you my answer later in the week. As to Susannah's punishment, you may tell her that after this evening's reception, she is to be confined to her room for one week, excepting lessons in the classroom. She is also to apologize to my stepmother, and furthermore, she is to spend half an hour each day working with Easton in the rose bed until it is returned to its former state."

"If I might say so, Mr. Wyndham, you ought to be the one to carry the news to her. She is, at present, in need of a strong hand."

He looked at my furrowed brow and laid a hand over mine. The gesture startled me. "Your concern for Susannah is admirable," he said.

I was far less optimistic. "It will be only hollow praise if I am unable to help her."

He patted my hand. "Come then, we shall go to her together."

I was very much aware of his attentiveness to me. Instead of having a reassuring effect, though, it made me uneasy. I supposed that it was because I was beginning to blame him for Susannah's behavior. If he had been there for her to confide in, to depend upon, instead of always occupied with business . . . A wound which I thought had healed long ago stung me anew. These thoughts were not of Matthew Wyndham, but of my own father, and I quickly buried them again.

The scene that met our eyes in Susannah's room was a damning one. Her kid boots lay in one corner, caked with soft earth, such as was to be found in the rose garden, and a pair of shears lay atop her bureau. It was as if she wanted to be caught and punished. In the midst of the scene, Susannah lay fast asleep on her pink floral counterpane looking deceptively innocent.

Matthew grabbed up the offending shears and examined them. For a moment his look was so menacing that I feared he might strangle the child while she slept, but this soon passed and he was his stoical self once more. He laid aside the shears and sat on the edge of the bed to wake his daughter.

"Susannah?"

Her dark eyes popped open almost immediately,

causing me to wonder if she had been asleep at all or
only lying there, waiting. At the sight of her father,
she threw her arms around his neck.

"Father, you've come to see me!"

Matthew Wyndham disentangled himself and put
the child's arms at her sides. "You know very well
why I am here, young lady."

Susannah looked much older than her seven years
as she surveyed first her father's expression and then
mine. I was poised in the doorway not sure quite
where I belonged in all of this. I had no trouble
reading the question in the child's eyes, asking if I had
betrayed her action in the graveyard.

"How could you destroy Grandmother Wyndham's
roses?" her father asked. "You know how she prizes
them."

"She's not my grandmother," Susannah said, under
her breath.

"Curb your tongue, Susannah, else you shall find
yourself in more trouble than you can handle."

She put on a countenance that was suitably contrite
and laid her head in his lap. "Yes, Father, I'm sorry."

"It was a wicked thing to do."

"She said that it was wrong for Mama to dig in the
dirt and plant flowers," the child explained.

Mr. Wyndham looked to me then, obviously
surprised that my assumptions had been correct.

"I'm sure you misunderstood," he said, "and that
does not in any way excuse your actions. You shall
apologize to Grandmother Wyndham and work with
Easton in the rose garden until the plants are
restored."

"Yes, Father."

"And you shall spend all of next week in this room,
excepting lessons. Do you understand?"

This was harder to take, it seemed. The reply was
barely audible. "Yes, Father."

We left her on her bed, looking very grim. Closing

her door behind us, Mr. Wyndham said, "I hope that will prove sufficient."

I was not at all sure that it would.

"Don't frown," he entreated me, "else you'll crease your brow."

He seemed without a care, having left Susannah's troubles behind the closed door. It was somewhat irritating.

"You've a fine countenance, my dear," he observed, "and it pleases me to look on it."

He tried to capture my eyes but I was intent on the pattern of the hall runner at my feet, and so, finding himself unsuccessful, he shook off his reverie and cleared his throat.

"Until tonight, then," he said and left me.

His words were not significant until I went to my room and found Brenna, laying out my mourning gown.

"Oh, miss, you startled me," she said.

"What is this, Brenna?"

"Mrs. Wyndham sent me up. You're to attend the doings this evening with Miss Susannah."

I was overcome. This was what I had hoped for, but there was so little time to prepare.

"You may put away that awful black dress, Brenna. I have a lavender faille or a blue silk, but which?"

The girl made no move toward the black dress on the bed but continued to sort through the petticoats in the drawer. "I daren't, miss. Mrs. Wyndham was very particular. Said that your gown must be 'suitable.' "

All of the energy that had risen in me drained away like an ebbing tide, and sank into the vanity chair. So Felicia Wyndham was to have her revenge on me. I wondered if the woman had come rifling through my wardrobe or had merely instructed the girl to choose the plainest gown I possessed. I sat there for a long while, considering whether I should cross her, but

finally decided that this was not the time. My own
position was none too secure after the day's episode
with Susannah.

"It will be fine," I said in a tired voice, "and you
may go. I'll manage by myself, thank you."

"Yes, miss," Brenna replied, " 'tis a shame, miss,
with all of the beautiful gowns in the wardrobe."

The door closed silently, and I turned to examine
the gown on the bed. Perhaps it could be altered to
make it more "acceptable" and less "suitable." It was
a black poult de soie with a modest decolletage, and
its skirt was not cut wide enough for a fashionable
hoop. It was hopeless and I slumped back into the
chair. Frustration welled in me, and snatching a jar
from the vanity table, I drew back my arm and sent it
sailing across the room, where it smashed against the
closed door and fell to pieces on the floor. I felt no
release from my emotions.

There was a knock at my door and the doorknob
twisted slowly. Brenna cautiously stuck her head in.
"Are you all right, miss? I heard a racket."

"Yes. I—I dropped a jar of face cream."

She looked from the broken glass behind the door to
me, seated well across the room.

"I'll clean that up right away, miss."

She promptly did so and gave me a look that said
that Miss Adrienne Dalton was turning out to be just
what she had expected.

The ballroom, solarium, and adjoining sitting rooms
comprised most of the ground floor of the east wing.
In the ballroom, several pairs of french windows on
the far wall were opened out, and I could see paper
lanterns casting their weird, colored glow in the
courtyard and gardens beyond. The cloying scent of
fresh-cut flowers mingled with a hundred different
perfumes, masking the more enticing aroma that
emanated from the buffet tables. Before long the ball-

room was filled to capacity and guests spilled over into the adjoining rooms. The sight was dazzling, the women in low-cut, wide-hooped gowns in pastel hues, their jewels glittering in the light of thousands of candles set in the crystal chandeliers overhead.

From my seat in a secluded corner of the room, I watched Susannah snatch a sugary confection from the table. Catching her eye, I beckoned to her. She came to me, wiping traces of icing from her fingers into the fold of her skirt. "Susannah! You'll spoil your dress. Please remember that we are only here so that your father may show you off, and then it's upstairs to bed."

"Oh, miss," she said in a way that pleaded with me not to spoil her fun.

I hoped we would be dismissed soon. I felt decidedly inappropriate: a sparrow in the midst of exotic tropical birds. After this night I would burn the offensive black dress. I drew my skirts closer around me and tried to hide in the corner while Susannah stood silently beside me, her wide eyes taking in all that they could. So intent was I upon becoming a part of the furnishings that I did not see Matthew Wyndham approach until he spoke to me.

"So, Adrienne, how do you find our rustic social life compared to the Beacon Hill set and the beau monde of Paris?"

I rose but took a quick step back against my chair as Rachel Chandler arrived to entwine herself possessively on his arm. She was in white satin brocade with a necklace of emeralds that matched her eyes.

"Not at all rustic, sir," I replied in a meek tone befitting a sparrow.

Aaron Chandler joined us. "Good evening, Miss Dalton," he said.

"Mr. Chandler," I acknowledged, noticing for the first time that he walked with a pronounced limp.

"And Susannah," he went on, "is that a new dress you're wearing?"

The child nodded, auburn ringlets bobbing. "Yes, thank you, Cousin."

"I thought it might be. You are by far one of the prettiest ladies here tonight. I should like it if you would reserve your first dance for me."

She bent her head coyly and made a moue with her tiny mouth. "Father says that I am to retire before dinner."

Aaron nodded. "Young ladies do need their beauty sleep. But I shall dance with no one else this evening."

Her freckled nose wrinkled in amusement.

"May I go and watch the musicians, miss?" she asked me. "I'll be no trouble, I promise."

"If your father does not require you at present—"

"Go ahead," Mr. Wyndham cut in, "but don't stray too far."

"Yes, Father."

Rachel promptly drew Mr. Wyndham into an intimate conversation, leaving me alone with Aaron Chandler.

"Susannah is behaving nicely this evening. It's due to your tutelage, I'll warrant," he commented.

"Thank you, but I'm doubting my worth today. It was not an idyllic afternoon. To be quite frank, she is under probation this evening. I believe she wants to please her father."

"Matt has faith in your abilities, and he is seldom wrong."

"Thank you, Mr. Chandler."

"Do you dance, Miss Dalton? I did promise Susannah that I'd sit out tonight, but I'm sure she'd understand. Perhaps later—"

"I'm not so light on my feet, I'm afraid. In any case I must see that Susannah is put to bed."

I felt a pang of guilt at the lie. There was nothing I

enjoyed more than being whirled across the dance floor, but not tonight and not in this awful black gown.

"You'll miss the rest of the evening, then. I'm sure if I spoke to Matt, he would—"

"No," I said, rather abruptly, "please don't."

I feared that Mr. Wyndham would overhear and I would be made to remain the entire evening. I was tired of pressing myself into the shadows.

"Perhaps it's for the best," Aaron said with a sigh. "I'm not so graceful since I got this."

He slapped his lame leg for emphasis. Rachel turned to him then as if she had followed our entire conversation. "You know that I would dance with you, Aaron, but I've promised them all to Matthew."

She batted her long lashes at me for emphasis.

"You were in the war?" I asked Aaron, ignoring his sister's attempts to goad me. I was in no mood for her games tonight.

"Yes, thought I've no heroic stories to tell. I caught a Confederate musket ball at Sharpsburg. Nearly shattered the bone, the doctor says. I'm lucky to be able to work at all."

"I'm sorry," I said, and then added, "you must understand that if I seem distrait this evening, it is not the company. It's only that I've not been to a social function since my father died."

It was an adequate lie. I did not wish to offend Aaron, but I had to escape.

Soon thereafter, Felicia Wyndham drew near with the guest of honor, Mr. Hannibal Hamlin. I thought him an impressive-looking man: tall and powerfully built, with graying hair and dark, sensitive eyes. I nearly forgot my own discomfort, wishing that I could stay at least long enough to hear him speak. I had heard that he was an eloquent orator.

When first I saw the man at Mr. Hamlin's side, I had to look again to assure myself that my eyes were not deceiving me. As his familiar features grew clearer in my rheumy eyes, the rest of the surroundings blurred, and Aaron had to put out an arm to steady me. There, standing before me, was the fiance I had left behind in Boston, Phillip Landis.

6

Humiliation,
utter and complete humiliation, swept over me. For a
brief moment I thought that he had come for me, but
he was as surprised by my presence as I was by his.
Mr. Wyndham seemed the only other person aware of
what was transpiring and so directed the conversation
away from us that our reunion might be less
conspicuous.

"Adrienne?"

I nodded, unable to move otherwise. I had forgotten
that he was so handsome.

"They told me that you had left Boston but no one
knew where you had gone, and then I got your letter.
You shouldn't have left me that way, Adrienne."

I could not meet his eyes.

"It was the only way, Phillip. Let it alone, for both
our sakes."

"What are you doing here," he wanted to know,
"and in such humble mien?"

"I am the governess."

I could not tell if he was more astounded or
irritated. "Governess? Adrienne, why have you done
this?"

He threaded a hand through his blond hair and then reached out to caress my arm.

"Come outside with me. We'll talk and set things right."

I drew in a ragged breath. If I were to follow him, I would be lost. He was far too persuasive. I did not love him, by God, I did not, but I was weak enough to consider what he offered: the security of marriage, of a comfortable life, all the amenities I could require. I cursed my weakness.

"No, Phillip, there is nothing to be said. This is for the best. You have a difficult enough campaign to face without me to complicate things."

"Whatever do you mean?"

"I am destitute, and there was talk . . . about my father."

"His gambing? Adrienne, every man voting in the election has laid a wager at one time or another in his life." He patted my hand as if I were a child who needed everything explained to her.

I would not let him tempt me, would not let myself listen. I shook my head vigorously.

"I do not love you," I told him. "I have been your friend and you mine. I have admired you and been awed by you, but I do not love you. My father and yours wanted this match to forge a dynasty. What do you want of it, Phillip?"

His brow creased as if my words had been in some obscure language that he could not fathom. "I have a duty to you," he persisted.

"I have released you from your promise. You are free of me."

"This cannot be. This is not right."

"Tell me honestly, Phillip, do you love me?"

His face was washed of color. He did not reply.

"I thought not. Leave things as they are," I told him and stepped back. "Goodbye, Phillip."

I moved blindly through the crowd, looking back

only once to catch his impotent stare. I was angry and sad all at once, and not at all comforted by the knowledge that I had done the right thing.

Matthew Wyndham caught up with me in the outer reaches of the garden, away from the glow of the jewel-like lanterns, where the gaiety of the soiree was only a distant mixture of laughter and music, no more insistent than the pounding surf or the incessant chirp of crickets. He touched my shoulder, and, startled, I turned to face him.

"Oh, Mr. Wyndham. I've left Susannah, but I needed some air."

He took both of my hands in his. "Adrienne, please understand that I had no way of knowing that Phillip Landis would be here. He came with Mr Hamlin's party. If I had known, I'd have seen to it that you were not subjected to this."

"It was childish to run away from Phillip, but I've faced him now, honestly, as I should have done at the start."

His face, edged in shadow, was expressionless.

"You'll go back to Boston with him, then?"

"No," I replied.

"Dare I hope. . . ?" he said, but the words died away.

His arms slipped around me as he sought to comfort me, and I rested my head on his shoulder. There in the darkness everything took on a dreamlike quality, and I was filled with a sense of security that I had not known since I lost the comfort of my father's arms. Thought processes were suspended as I took refuge in his embrace. We did not speak. He stroked my hair and, tipping my chin upwards, kissed me reverently as if the kiss would heal me. The approach of Felicia Wyndham brought me to my senses and I drew away from him. He sent me a questioning look until he heard her seething whisper.

"So she's got her claws in you already, has she? I

knew she wouldn't wait long when there's a fortune to be had."

Mr. Wyndham turned on her. "How dare you? What right have you to meddle in my affairs? You endow all women with your own contemptible motives. And what do you know of Miss Dalton? If she wanted money, she'd never have turned away Mr. Landis. I've not one-half of the Landis fortune."

I slipped away unnoticed.

Below the Widow's Walk, the ocean was alive. The rushing surf carried on it whispering voices, taunting me. Frothy arms reached up into the night sky and beckoned me downward. This was a place on the edge of the world, where life and death met. Little wonder there were legends about this piece of land. No doubt on the morrow someone would claim to have seen the ghost of Diana Wyndham here. That would be a partial truth, at least, for there was a lone figure at the point of the Widow's Walk, clad in black and staring out to sea, head thrown back as if she were daring the sea gods to take her. My hair was wild, having blown free of its coiffure, and it undulated upward on the wind like silver waves in the moonlight. Spindrift floated about and settled on the rocks at my feet. With my soft-soled evening slippers, I could easily slip—

Strong hands pulled me away from the precipice, hard-thewn arms enfolded me. "Never, never go that close to the edge!" a voice told me in uneven breaths.

It was Jason Wyndham. He held me close for a long while. I was chilled from the damp night air and shivered in the warmth of his embrace. He turned my face up to his, puzzled at the placid expression that met him. He could not know that I had released a tangle of emotions to the wind and waves and had drawn back a blissful inner peace.

"No man is worth this. You will forget him."

Did he think that I intended to throw myself on the rocks on Phillip's account?

I might have laughed but I did not. His heart was thumping hard against his chest, his breathing harsh. He had truly feared for my life. The harsh chord of his breathing did not subside, however, and I suspected that it was now my proximity that affected him. And I was not immune to him. He was elegant in his evening clothes, his squared jaw thrown into prominence by the upturned collar. The air around him was redolent of cheroot and whiskey. I felt myself a wild and reckless creature, here among the elements. I was curious; I craved new sensations. Beneath heavy brows, his steel blue eyes glittered fiercely. He was a dangerous man, a devil of a man by all accounts, but a fever had overtaken me. He threaded a hand through my hair, and when his mouth captured mine I did not fight him. I pulled him closer and my hands traveled the hard planes of his back. His lips moved feverishly over my face as I drew a sibilant breath.

"You're a witch!" he declared. "Out here communing with the waves and the water and the moon—"

Reaching up, I wrapped a hand behind his neck and drew him down to me, eager for his kiss. Good conscience was abandoned. He had aroused my senses in a way that no other man had, and like a greedy child, I wanted more. He obliged. I could feel the power in his long, lean limbs, the keen tension of each muscle. His next breath ended in a low growl, emanating from deep in his throat, and he set me apart from him. I looked up, bewildered, and reached out.

"No, Adrienne. If I make love to a woman, her thoughts must be with me alone . . . and yours cannot be tonight."

He turned away and walked back toward the house.

He was wrong! Jason Wyndham had intoxicated me fully. There had been not one stray thought, not even to consider the consequences of this release of myself unto my senses. And now I stood here alone, every nerve raw.

Hot tears pricked my eyes as I crossed the lawn. I could see now that Jason had not gone in but was watching me from a distance. Oh, yes, I told myself, he was a dangerous man.

"I hate her! She's an awful, ugly witch, and I hate her!"

Susannah grabbed the bedclothes into her clenched fist, and I laid a hand over hers and stroked her hair to soothe her, then dabbed at tears trailing down her freckled face with my handkerchief. "You mustn't say such things, Susannah," I told her. "What would your father think if he heard this kind of talk about Miss Chandler?"

She tossed fitfully beneath the counterpane. "I don't care, and I do hate her. After you went away, she told Father to send me upstairs to bed. She wanted to be rid of me so she could have him all to herself."

While Rachel might have been able to beguile many who were older and wiser than the child with her charms, to Susannah she was as transparent as glass. I found it a difficult task to reprimand her for what she'd said when, in all likelihood, her observation was correct. Instead, I chose a different approach. "I thought you understood that you weren't to stay at the reception all evening."

"Yes, but Father would have let me stay a while longer if she hadn't interfered."

I pulled her close, intending to comfort her, but her small frame hung limp as a rag doll. She would not respond to me. With a sigh, I rose up from the corner of the bed where I'd been sitting and moved toward the lamp on the night table.

"I'm much too tired to cross words with you tonight, Susannah. Just remember that in only a few weeks' time you'll have a party for your birthday. No one will send you off to bed then, I can promise you that."

"Yes, miss," she mumbled grudgingly.

With that I blew out the lamp.

"Goodnight, Susannah," I called into the darkened room as I headed for the communicating door.

I heard the rustle of bedclothes and then a hoarse whisper. "I wish she were dead!"

The vehemence with which Susannah gave voice to her feelings sent icy fingers down my spine. I closed the door between us, my head lagging with the heavy weight of responsibility. What could I do to help this child, so lonely and so much in need of a mother's love?

There was no lamp lit in my room, but on this night I preferred it that way. I undressed without hestitation, tossing the offensive black dress, petticoats and all, into a heap in the corner. I slipped into a satin wrapper of soft rose hue, its sleeves edged in Mechlin, and felt my spirits lift almost immediately. Taking in hand my silver-handled hairbrush, I opened out the french windows and stepped onto the balcony. The moon had disappeared behind the clouds, and I felt protected by the night. Below in the garden the lanterns twinkled like colored stars, and the soiree went on without me. I could hear the rich tones of Mr. Hamlin's voice, followed by a swell of applause, and wished I could have heard the speech. Had he given voice to his disillusionment with President Johnson's ridiculously mild reconstruction policies? I wondered. Or had he likened the government to a tinderbox with Democrats and "Radical"

Republicans poised with matches in hand?

I settled myself on the wrought-iron stool and began to draw the brush through my unbound hair, pulling it outward until it slipped free and drifted down around my waist. I wondered about Phillip, who was somewhere down below, making his own speech and shaking hands. I wondered if I was in his thoughts. No, he was the type who would put unpleasant thoughts out of mind, and I certainly would be an unpleasant thought to him now.

Unbidden, my thoughts replayed the encounter with Jason Wyndham on the Widow's Walk, and I flushed at the memory. I did not like to think on what I would do when I saw him next, and I knew that he would not be easily avoided.

Below the balcony, I became aware of the strained whispers of an argument.

"The announcement should have been made hours ago. People are expecting—"

"Expecting what? I've told no one of our plans."

I recognized the voices as those of Mr. Wyndham and Rachel Chandler, and would have withdrawn immediately except that any movement on my part now would have made my presence known to those below. I decided to wait for them to leave.

"I thought we had decided that this would be an ideal time to make the announcement."

"As I've tried to explain to you all evening, I need more time. Susannah was terribly upset by Nora's death. She has had some unpleasant episodes of late. This very afternoon she destroyed my stepmother's rosebed. I know that she is not yet ready to accept a new mother."

I covered a sharp intake of breath with my hand. I had not guessed that a marriage between Rachel and Matthew Wyndham was in the offing.

"Must we wait on the whims of a child?" Rachel

asked, sounding irritated and much like a child herself.

I could sense Mr. Wyndham stiffen. "She is my daughter, and you'd do well to be a bit more tolerant where she is concerned. Try to be kind to her. Speak to her with understanding. If you were to become friends, she might more readily accept you as a mother."

"Accept me? Matthew, this is nonsense. She must be made to understand that you have a life to live. As for myself, I cannot compete for your favor with a child. Now if it were another woman—"

The remark had been made offhandedly but the long pause which followed told me that Rachel was considering the possibility. As I thought on it myself, a chill of guilt crept over me. No, it was not so. Matthew Wyndham's intentions this evening had been to comfort me, no more.

Rachel stepped back, and I could see her below, silhouetted in the red glow of a nearby lantern.

"Or perhaps it is another woman. I did wonder where your thoughts were when you chose such a comely young governess for Susannah . . . or was it for yourself?"

There was an ugly implication in the words, and a long silence ensued, too long. I waited to hear Mr. Wyndham's denial. When it finally came, it was unconvincing. "This is ridiculous, Rachel. What's come over you?"

He moved beside her and touched her bare white shoulder, but she would have none of him. She shrugged his hand away.

"You expect that I should believe you? You'd not be the first Wyndham to behave like a rutting stag. Your father had quite a reputation in that respect, and the whole village talks of your brother's bastard by one of your housemaids. The boy roams the estate in rags."

''Rachel, you go too far.''

''Of course, I suppose I can't fault you for a roving eye. It's only normal for a man who has been without a wife. I shan't let the little tart come between us. Enjoy yourself, but pray do not postpone our engagement on account of it.''

I had dropped the brush onto my lap and was grasping the railing as if I might bend the iron. I was astounded at Rachel's lack of breeding. Yet while I sat there open-mouthed, I had begun to accept the possibility that Matthew Wyndham did, indeed, desire more of me than I'd guessed. He had not denied it, but he was such an upstanding man, so kind, so like my father. The fault was surely in my own demeanor. I must proceed in a more circumspect manner, I decided, for it would do no good to jeopardize my position here.

In the half-light, I watched him raise a hand furiously as if he might strike Rachel, then he clenched it into a fist and recoiled. Without a word, he turned on his heel and left her there. She called after him twice before she collapsed sobbing against the face of a brass sundial.

I was utterly exhausted and did not want to muse on the convoluted thoughts that filled my brain. I felt it safe to withdraw, but then heard a boisterous clapping of hands and calls of ''Brava! Brava!'' which drew my attention back down to that secluded spot in the garden. Jason stumbled out of the hedgerow.

''A fine performance, Rachel,'' he said, ''truly inspired, but you may dispense with the tears. Matt is long gone. I fear you've overplayed your hand this time. My brother will not be pushed to the altar.''

Rachel lifted her head, green eyes wide. ''Jason Wyndham! How could you come back here after . . . after . . .''

Even from my vantage point, I could see her bottom lip quiver effectively as her voice broke off in a sob.

"Don't waste your talents on me," Jason said to her, unmoved by the scene, "and don't pretend you haven't heard that I'd returned. The village is abuzz with the gossip. I spent a few days at the inn, just to stir them all up, before I moved into the east wing. Matthew is, of course, suitably annoyed by my presence."

Jason walked around her slowly and clucked his tongue. "I must say that you've grown more forgiving in these past five years. When I was the lustful fiance, you branded me an unmitigated lecher and canceled the nuptials."

"How could I possibly go through with the marriage after you—after the way you tried to take advantage of my innocence?"

Jason threw back his head and let go a rude laugh. "You may be many things, Rachel, but innocent—never. I recall, even if you do not wish to, the many times I shared your bed—time enjoyably spent, I might add—before that fateful evening when your brother came upon us and you cried 'rape.'"

Rachel winced at his crude speech, perhaps not so much because it offended her gentility as in fear that he would be overheard.

"I've always wondered how the two of you arranged things so that he would come upon us at precisely the right moment," he went on.

"How dare you suggest such a thing! My brother is a respectable man, he would never—"

"He would do whatever you ask of him. He worships you, though I am sure he does not truly understand you as I do. I wonder how the eminent Mr. Chandler would react to discover that his beloved sister has the morals of a dockside barmaid?"

I did not envy Rachel her position at this moment. I knew only too well how uncomfortable Jason Wyndham could make one with his words. He had no pretensions to gentlemanly behavior whatsoever. To my surprise, though, Rachel turned on him.

"And is he to take your word for it, sir? A man who has been disowned by his family, who earns his living with a pack of cards and brawls in taverns like a deckhand? A man who makes it his business to put his brand on every Irish scullery maid who steps off the boat from Dublin, some of them still clinging to their mama's skirts!"

Her voice rose up and ended on a shrill note. Inebriation notwithstanding, Jason straightened himself and glared at her.

"I've never had to beg for a lady's favors nor force myself where my attentions were unwelcome. We've played at this charade long enough, Rachel. Shall I tell you where five years of contemplation have led me?"

She turned away from him, but he pressed on. "I did not find it hard to credit that a lady in your position would naturally tell her brother that the gentleman in question had forced himself upon her, but I never comprehended why you stood by this 'rape' story and broke off our engagement, not even after my father died and I found out that he had cut me out of his will. Only after many sleepless nights did I realize that the codicil disinheriting me had been drawn up by Aaron only a few days before that nasty episode. Oh yes, the two of you must have plotted and planned in order to extricate you from our engagement. My compliments on a plan well executed."

"It wasn't that way at all," she protested.

He threw up his hands. "Have it your own way. It matters not to me. As I see it, my brother is far more deserving of your charms than I."

It was hard to say whether Rachel felt the full effect of his sarcasm, for by that point she had lost interest in their war of words and, tossing her head at him, she strode off.

Jason's lips curled into an ugly sneer and he reeled, none too steady on his feet. I had little time to digest all that I had heard. Rachel's revilement of Jason's character only confirmed what I had already suspected. He was a profligate and an unrepentant one at that. No doubt he sought me out only to satisfy the cravings of his lascivious appetite. I had guessed that much from the first. But, a small voice within me interjected, why had he come to my rescue only to turn me away if such were the case? I might have followed willingly where he led tonight, without a care for my own virtue, and yet he had rejected my advances.

He was still there in the garden below me, and it was as if his mask had slipped away. He had been grievously wounded, I told myself. His shoulders sagged and in the twilight I could see his pained expression. He looked so much younger now. This was a moment I had never expected to witness. I could see how deeply Rachel had hurt him with her deception. Surely his wounds had not healed in five years, only festered. Emotions that I could not yet fathom welled in me and brought me to my feet, full of the need to comfort him.

Whether he heard the movement above him or merely sensed my presence, he turned and looked upward, and our eyes met. I held his unadulterated gaze for only a second before the mask slipped back into place, and he sent a harsh laugh up to me. But that one second had been his undoing, for I had seen the man behind the devil's mask and would never be deceived again.

7

It was nearly two weeks later
when Matthew Wyndham sent word that the meeting
with Susannah's grandfather had been arranged. In
the meanwhile I had had to deal with a new bout of
the child's sullenness, a direct result of her father's
neglect. Mr. Wyndham had been preoccupied with
business problems of late, spending most of his time
at his office in the village, and was unable to give
Susannah the attention that I knew she craved. The
message he sent regarding the proposed visit
reiterated his earlier warnings about the old man's
eccentricities, but I thought this was precisely what
Susannah needed at the moment, in any case.

It was a hazy, still morning in August when we set
out at last. We were to be driven by one of the grooms
in an open landau to Longfield where we would
luncheon with Mr. Talbott and then return to
Wyndcliffe by late afternoon. We had not yet left the
drive, though, when our progress was halted by the
approach of Jason Wyndham astride his black
stallion. He was especially stylish in a buff-colored
coat and trousers. His dark curls were tousled over
his forehead, and he sported a raffish grin.

"Hold up, Tom!" he called to the groom. "Where are you taking the ladies this morning?"

"Longfield, sir."

"Longfield, eh? I haven't seen old Franklin Talbott in years. Would it upset your plans overly much, Miss Dalton, if I were to accompany you?"

Before I could think to reply, Susannah cut in excitedly, "Oh, please do, Uncle! We're going to see Grandfather Talbott. It will be such fun, and it's all Miss Dalton's doing! I told her that Father was mad and wouldn't let me come, but she made him agree. I've promised to be on my best behavior."

"And that being the case, Susannah, where are your manners?" I asked. "A young lady should never behave in so forward a manner."

She slumped back onto the seat. "Yes, miss. I'm sorry."

I hadn't meant to be sharp but I did so want the day to turn out well, and Jason's presence could only distract me from that purpose. Susannah had been delighted with me for having wrought such a miracle, but now I feared that this outing might, after all, prove to be too much excitement for her.

My motives were not entirely selfless in all of this. While I was by no means ungrateful to my benefactor, his actions during these past weeks had made me feel as if I were not so much a governess to Susannah as—to borrow Felicia Wyndham's words— an "orphaned waif" that Matthew Wyndham had taken in. Something in my nature rebelled against the very idea of this, and I needed to prove that I could be a help to Susannah.

Jason regarded me, still awaiting reply to his request. I could not put him off without appearing ill-mannered.

"Do as you will, Mr. Wyndham," I said at last.

He promptly dismounted, tying his horse's reins to the stone post in the drive. No sooner had he taken his

place across from Susannah and me than the landau
jerked into motion, and we were at last on our way.

Though he feigned an interest in the scenery, I could
still feel his eyes on me. Vanity told me that I must
present a fetching picture in my dotted white
mousseline, adorned with dark green ribbons and
bunches of wildflowers, the whole worn over a
stylish half-crinoline. Today I could take refuge in my
appearance, knowing that I had nothing of which to
be ashamed.

"You look particularly lovely this morning, Miss
Dalton," Jason mentioned politely and then turned
his attention on his niece, who was busy making a
verbal list of all the things they must see at Longfield.

I felt somehow slighted by his compliment, by its
formality. His whole manner, in fact, was distant,
almost gentlemanly. To my chagrin, I found that I
missed the honesty of his overt gaze. Perturbed by my
own emotions, I endeavored to concentrate on
something else.

The ocean was becalmed, reflective as glass. The
day would be hot, for there was no breeze to stir the
heavy air. I removed my gloves lazily and began to
fan myself with them. We were not long out of the
gates when I witnessed a strange sight. Before us an
overturned dory was being propelled across the road
by three pairs of legs, clad in worn trousers, feet bare.
As we passed by the odd craft, Jason called for Tom to
hold up.

"What's this?" he called.

The dory rolled over into the tall grass, revealing
three scruffy lads, the smallest of whom I recognized
as Brenna's son, Tim.

The tallest stepped forward with arms akimbo. A
red kerchief was tied around his slim throat.

"Cap'n Sean O'Hanlon at yer service, Mr.
Wyndham, sir, and these be my mates: Kevin
Donnelly and Tim McKeon."

Jason scratched his chin thoughtfully.

"I see, and where are you bound, Captain O'Hanlon?"

"We plan to be makin' our maiden voyage out to Bishop's Rock, sir. Me and the boys come upon this old dory up on the rocks near to a fortnight ago. Pretty banged up she were, too. We mended her, give her a fresh coat o'paint and christened her the 'Belle of Ireland.' She be a fine vessel fer the likes of us, sir."

"You're all able seamen then?" Jason wondered.

Tom let go a rude snort, and then, reconsidering his position, let his head drop, pretending to examine the leather straps in his hands. O'Hanlon paid him no mind.

"Aye, sir. We been weaned on tales o' square-riggers. Me da sails with the Wyndham Lines on the China run, and Tim here, his gran'sir claims he was born in the riggin'."

Jason nodded, and affected an expression to show that he was suitably impressed with their credentials. "Carry on then, captain, and mind keep the wind at your back."

"Aye, sir."

Jason sent the boys a mock salute as Tom snapped the reins, and we set out again.

I lost all interest in the surroundings and had missed most of Jason's exchange with the would-be sailors. Something else had captured my attention. I knew now why young Tim's eyes had unsettled me when first I had seen him. They were Jason's eyes. With both of them before me, I could see the resemblance. Suddenly Rachel Chandler's ravings beneath my balcony on that night of the reception did not seem so hysterical. Jason *did* have a bastard son at Wyndcliffe, a son by Brenna McKeon.

"Uncle Jason, are those boys going to take that tiny boat all the way to Bishop's Rock?" Susannah asked.

"I expect so. It's a calm enough day, and with two

mates manning the oars, they should have no trouble."

She shivered at the thought of such adventure, so far beyond her own reach. "How exciting! They must be very brave."

We had turned westward heading inland where the terrain was gentler, but the heat was more intense. My color was heightened by that which I could not erase from my thoughts. I hoped my flush would be attributed to the heat. In fact, I no longer felt so crisp and confident. Perspiration had formed in the valley between my breasts and began to trickle downward, making a damp place on my bodice. My stays were restricting my breathing and creaked audibly as I moved to keep them from digging into the soft flesh of my sides. Making use of my gloves, I fanned myself all the more.

"Are you in some distress, Miss Dalton?" Jason inquired, ever polite.

"I'm afraid I find the climate more unfriendly than usual this morning."

He nodded sympathetically. "The heat is unbearable. There'll be a storm by evening, though, for relief. All the signs point to it."

He leaned back, adjusting himself into a more relaxed position. "How thoughtless of me, Miss Dalton. I had forgotten that you are a newcomer to the area. Shall I describe some of our landmarks for you?"

"Father took Miss Dalton for a tour of the grounds weeks ago," Susannah informed him.

Jason raised a single eyebrow. "How considerate of him. Then I must endeavor to highlight the less apparent aspects of the Wyndham estate," he said, unable to completely conceal the acerbity in his voice.

"For example, the farms you see on either side of you are part of the estate. They are barely above sustenance level now, I fear. The soil is not rich, but under the proper management, the acreage could produce considerably more.''

"You do not approve of Mr. Pagett's management of the land?'' I surmised, feeling at last that we were in concurrence. My own meeting with the farm manager had left me with the feeling that he was not to be trusted.

"He is hardly qualified. Our tenants are not slaves, although such a comparison is inevitable under the present circumstances.

"Seth Newell farms these acres,'' Jason went on. "He's had to send his sons out with the fishing fleet while he and his wife work the land just to pay the rent and keep a roof over their heads. My brother runs his shipping company at the expense of these farms.''

I was surprised to hear Jason speak on any subject with such fervor, but for Susannah's sake I sent him a warning glance. The child should not be exposed to such criticisms of her father.

"As a Wyndham yourself, I should think you capable of effecting a change where the farms are concerned,'' I reasoned.

Jason smiled as if he had been waiting for those words. "Alas, thanks to my father's wisdom I am a Wyndham in name only, persona non grata, you might say. I have no claim upon any family holdings.''

If he had expected to see a look of astonishment on my face, then he was disappointed. I gave him no measurable reaction, only met his eyes directly.

"I see, and since you would not benefit from any improvements that might be made, you do not feel compelled to offer free advice to your brother. You feud with him at these people's expense, it seems.''

Jason reacted as though he had been smartly slapped. "I do assure you that my brother would not welcome advice from me on any subject and would hardly be inclined to follow it.''

I sighed. ''Reasonable men are always willing to listen to reasonable ideas.''

''There comes a point when a man believes that money is reason and the lack of it—insanity. Believe me on this score, my brother sees people as rather insignificant when compared to the black figures on a balance sheet.''

''I cannot believe it.''

Again came that insolent smile that he wore so well. ''That is because, Miss Dalton, you are struggling under the idealism of youth.''

I turned abruptly from him to end the discussion. What response could there be to such a comment? Indeed, why should I apologize for my youth?

''Are we nearing Longfield?'' I asked Susannah, noticing that she had begun to crane her neck.

''Oh yes, miss. It's just over the next hill.''

We passed a sturdy stone fence, and then a stretch of white-painted fencerow sprang up on either side of the road. Beyond, a mare and her foal frolicked in the pasture. They were Morgans, a short-legged, muscular breed. Ahead was a collection of out-buildings, foremost among them a long, low stable, and nearby a schooling ring.

''Mr. Talbott raises horses?'' I asked.

I had expected a quiet country house, not a working horse farm. This was a pleasant surprise.

''The best horses,'' Susannah boasted.

''I'm sure you're right,'' I agreed, smoothing her locks with a gentle hand.

I could not help but be pleased with the sunny disposition that this visit was bringing out in her. Not wishing to break the spell, I touched the ring on its chain around my neck for luck. I had of late begun to think of this gift from my father as a magical charm. I hoped its power would prevail on this day.

The house looked friendly enough. Of mellow red

brick with green shutters, it stood in the shade of half a dozen beech trees that sheltered its facade. As the landau rocked to a halt, a horseman came up behind us in the drive and waved a hand in greeting. Susannah turned, kneeling on her seat and swinging her arms wildly in reply. "Grandfather, Grandfather, it's Susannah! I've come for a visit."

I watched carefully the man who drew nearer the carriage now. He was astride a chestnut Morgan, whose regal disposition would rival Jason's Arab stallion, but Franklin Talbott controlled the mount easily. He was a smallish man, stout, and with a wisp of white hair over each ear. He had keen eyes and did not seem at all to be the eccentric old man that Matthew Wyndham had led me to expect. When he dismounted, Susannah sprang from the carriage to be at his side. Jason descended next, in order that I might take his proffered hand as I alighted. He did not release my hand at once, but drew me closer to him and said so only I could hear, "I must apologize, Miss Dalton, for the unpleasant tone with which I addressed you earlier. It was inexcusable, and I beg your forgiveness."

I looked up at him, certain that his horse must have thrown him and kicked him in the head while they were riding this morning. Only a brain fever could cause such a change in personality. I acknowledged the apology with a nod, for I had no time to discover what his game was.

"Talbott's horses are the best in the state," Jason informed me. "He raises several breeds, but his preference is the pure Morgan. He's a zealot on the subject. I hope you shan't be bored."

"It's been five years, my boy. Never thought to see you back in these parts again, not after old Jonathan gave you the short shrift, and that—"

Mr. Talbott seemed only then to realize my presence and cleared his throat. "—that . . . other business.''

I knew instinctively that ''that other business'' involved Rachel Chandler's ugly insinuations.

''You're staying at Wyndcliffe then?'' he asked Jason.

''I'm homesteading in the east wing, squatter's rights, you know.''

''Good for you.'' Mr. Talbott slapped him heartily on his shoulder. ''Good for you.''

I could make an educated guess by studying Mr. Talbott's amused expression that anything that would upset the routine at Wyndcliffe and thereby Matthew Wyndham would conversely delight him.

''And now, sir, before we are accused of ignoring her entirely, may I introduce Miss Adrienne Dalton, Susannah's governess.''

Mr. Talbott took my hand into his firm grasp.

''It is always a pleasure to meet a beautiful young lady.''

''Why, thank you, Mr. Talbott. Susannah has told me so much about you.''

''Has she now? Susannah?''

He turned just in time to see her offer a carrot, which she had purloined from the Wyndcliffe kitchens and carried here in her pocket, to his horse. ''Here now. Don't do that, Susannah, else you'll spoil him.''

She let the horse finish his treat before marching purposefully to her grandfather's side. ''Can't spoil children enough. You told me that, Grandfather. Well, Archimedes is four years old and that means he's still a child.''

''That unfortunate adage was meant for grand-daughters, not horses, you little minx,'' he said, tousling her curls.

She responded by throwing her arms around his middle and looking up at him through the fan of her dark lashes. ''May we go in the house now? I haven't said hello to Nanny Gresham yet."

"You go on ahead. I believe she has a plate of sugar cookies waiting for you. We'll be along shortly."

We all watched as, with a proud carriage, Susannah ascended the steps to the front door and then disappeared. "She's got more than her share of Talbott blood, I'll wager," her grandfather said, well-pleased.

A fleeting twist of sadness crossed his features. It was clear to all that his thoughts were of Nora, his daughter. When he sighed, it was a weary sound despite his smile. "Let's go in, then. Edith will have lemonade for us in the parlor."

Edith Gresham was Mr. Talbott's widowed housekeeper, a sweet-faced woman who, it became apparent, took care of him with all the loving care of a wife. She was of the class of servant who spent so many years in a household that they became a part of the family. In fact, Susannah responded to her as if she were a grandmother. I found her to be a gentle soul and extremely perceptive where Susannah was concerned.

At the onset of the visit, the child had hovered very near her grandfather's chair but when finally the conversation ceased to hold her interest, she silently wandered off.

I soon discovered that Jason had been accurate in his observation that Mr. Talbott was outspoken on the subject of his profession, but I could not help but think that in Boston gentlemen would never discuss something as indelicate as the breeding of horses when ladies were present. I myself was not offended by such discussion; it would be ridiculous to be so in spite of social custom, but the conversation had reached a level beyond my interest. The gentlemen were discussing the merits of crossbreeding the Thoroughbred and the Morgan—an idea to which Mr. Talbott was vehemently opposed—when I realized that Susannah was gone. I chided myself that had I not been socializing, I could have kept a closer eye on her. Nervously recalling Matthew's apprehensions about this visit, I sought out Mrs. Gresham.

"No need to worry yourself, Miss Dalton. I know just where she'll be."

True to her word, Mrs. Gresham led me to an upstairs bedroom where Susannah was sitting in the center of a testered bed, stroking the wool hair of a worn rag doll. She wore the same expression that she had on the day that she and I had visited her mother's grave. It was a bewildered look, as if she expected to find all of the answers in the doll's stitched face. She did not hear us come in, nor was she aware of us as we watched her.

It was a sunny room with its floral-patterned carpet in pastel shades of green and pink and a delicately crocheted bedcover and tester to match. In one corner stood a tall etagère stacked with a child's playthings: a doll's house, a tiny Sèvres tea service on a tray, and a family of china dolls. This had been Nora's room.

Above the mantel hung a portrait which I sensed did not belong to this room. At first glance, one might have mistaken the woman for a child. Her face was heart-shaped, framed by a halo of golden curls. The limner had sensed her timorous nature, for it was etched forever there in her doe eyes. "It hung over the parlor mantel once," Mrs. Gresham explained when she noticed me examining the portrait, "but after she died, he couldn't bear to see it there day after day, reminding him. I brought it up here."

"She was beautiful."

"Yes, like the first rose of spring, she was. The portrait was done on the occasion of her seventeenth birthday, just before she married and went to live with *him*."

My concentration was still on the face that seemed to be staring back at me. There was a fey look in those eyes, and I wondered if even at that early stage Nora had known she was not long for this life.

"He comes in here sometimes," Mrs. Gresham went on, "and just sits in that chair over there, staring up at her. It comforts him, I think, as it does the child."

I looked over to Susannah, now curled up asleep on the bed. The housekeeper shook her head and crossed her arms over her chest. "Poor angel. It grieves my heart to think of her growing up in that house that her mama hated so."

I cocked my head, thinking I had misunderstood. There was so much I did not know about Nora Wyndham. "Mrs. Wyndham was not happy at Wyndcliffe?"

"I stayed with her when Susannah was born and for the little ones she lost. Sometimes at night she would wake up crying and shivering. 'Take me home, Nanny,' she would beg me. 'Take me home where it's warm.' "

"She must have been very ill," Adrienne surmised.

"Heartsick," Mrs. Gresham replied. "You live in that house, Miss Dalton. Can you feel it? . . . the coldness?"

"I'm accustomed to large houses and the drafts."

The older woman smiled politely. "No, dear, not the drafts, the 'coldness' . . . a family with only four walls binding it together, not love nor warmth. It's not a healthy atmosphere for the child, Miss Dalton. You will take care of her for us, won't you? See that her spirit is fed as well as her mind?"

"Of course. I will do all that I can for her."

Mrs. Gresham patted me on the shoulder. "Good. Now let's see about our meal, shall we?"

When the time came for us to leave, we congregated in the drive to say our goodbyes, and Mr. Talbott drew me away from the others. "Miss Dalton, I have been meaning to thank you for arranging this visit.

Matthew and I are much too stubborn to come to terms over our differences and poor Susannah finds herself in the middle."

"I feel that her well-being is very much my responsibility, Mr. Talbott."

"I know that you have been made to promise to keep a watchful eye on my granddaughter while she is here, and you have done well. I don't want to leave you with the impression, however, that I am a doddering old fool. No matter what my son-in-law believes of me, I would never hurt Susannah. She is too young to know the truth, and I would gain nothing by telling her that Matthew is responsible for her mother's death."

My mouth dropped open in astonishment. Matthew Wyndham? As I thought on it, I realized that my father had never mentioned how Nora Wyndham had died. I had merely assumed it had been some illness. No one in the household had ever mentioned the circumstances of Nora's death, and it certainly would have been indelicate for me to inquire. But now Mr. Talbott was implying that Matthew was responsible—

"I'm afraid I don't understand," I told him, under my breath.

"Oh, my dear, you look so mortified! Of course, he did not *murder* her, but her blood is on his hands just the same. He did not understand what a fragile creature she was. He was callous and cruel, and she withered in his grip."

His eyes narrowed with those words, but in the silence that ensued, he looked old and wistful, as though his strength had drained away. I wondered at his logic, saying that Matthew was responsible for her death simply because he did not understand her.

Just then Jason approached them and sent the briefest look to me which made me think that he had overheard at least a part of our conversation. How much did he know of all of this?

"I am sorry to steal Miss Dalton away from you, sir," Jason apologized, "I know how difficult it must be to give up the company of such a lovely young lady, but if we are to reach Wyndcliffe before the storm breaks—"

"Yes, yes, of course. Susannah, come here and say goodbye to your grandfather."

The strong northeast wind was making mare's tails of the wispy clouds that blew in from the ocean and brought a much-needed relief from the heat. The rusty sky looked harmless enough, but the grumbling offshore left no room for disagreement; there would be a storm by nightfall. Jason's prediction had been accurate. Tom had raised the top of the landau in anticipation of the foul weather and was waiting for his passengers at the far end of the drive, his team of bays tossing their head anxiously.

We crossed the drive slowly, promising to return soon for another visit. I noticed that even the leaves on the beech trees shuddered at the portent of the violent storm to come.

It had been a pleasant afternoon, I decided, but the high point of my day came when, after we had waved our last goodbyes to Longfield, Susannah squeezed my hand, and with an earnest look in her dark eyes, thanked me for bringing her here.

My companions rested quietly much of the way back to Wyndcliffe, leaving me to ponder the mystery of Nora Wyndham. I could not get the melancholy face from the portrait out of my mind. I still did not know how the young woman had met her death, and without that piece of information, I could not discern how much truth there was to Mr. Talbott's allegations that Matthew was responsible. I could understand his need to find someone to blame for Nora's death, but a real connection was unlikely. I wondered why he had chosen to voice his accusations to me. Was it because he felt that I needed to know that Matthew Wyndham could be a cruel man for Susannah's sake or for my own?

I had been absently watching the landscape until I felt something being pressed into the palm of my gloved hand. Jason closed my fingers into a fist around a copper penny. "That's for your thoughts," he said. "I've never seen a woman look so pensive."

I might have told him, so curious was I about the whole affair, but I glanced at Susannah, her head resting against the seat cushion, and saw her eyelids flutter. I looked back to Jason and smiled. "Another time, perhaps," I said, returning the coin.

The carriage jolted to a halt, seemingly at the same time as we heard the call for Tom to hold up. I was thrown nearly into Jason's lap, and Susannah bolted upright, eyes wide. "What was that?" she asked.

Jason released the latch on the carriage door just as the O'Hanlon boy whom we had encountered on the road that morning reached for it from the outside.

His clothes were sodden and clung to his skin, dripping to form a puddle at his feet. He shivered, perhaps not so much from the cold as from the same fear that shadowed his face. He gasped for breath before he began.

"Mr. Wyndham, sir, you got to help! We was out to Bishop's Rock and made it as far back as Whaleback Ledge when she started to come apart. Kevin and me, we knew we could make it to shore, but Tim, he ain't such a strong swimmer. We had to leave him on the ledge and go for help."

Jason did not hesitate but jumped down beside the boy. "Damn!" I heard him say, and I did not like what the look on his face told me. "Whaleback's a half-tide ledge."

I leaned out the carriage door. "What does that mean?"

"When the tide comes in, the ledge is submerged,

and the way the storm is blowing in off the water—''

He did not finish his sentence but turned to Tom. ''See the ladies home and send Donnelly and some of the men down here.''

He turned to go, and as an afterthought called back, ''And have someone contact my brother.''

Jason sprinted off after the boy, who had already started back in the direction from which he had come.

Tom lifted the reins, but I called to him to wait, and leaving my gloves and bonnet on the horsehair seat, I stepped out of the landau with the carriage blanket over my arm. ''I have to see if I can help, Tom. You go on, and do as Mr. Wyndham says. Susannah, you go home with Tom. Tell Mrs. Garen what's happened and go to your room and wait for me there.''

''Yes, miss.''

I followed the path Jason had taken. It wound its way downhill, and I could see him below on the beach. He took off his coat and boots and followed the O'Hanlon boy out onto a rocky peninsula where Kevin Donnelly awaited them anxiously. Jason dove headlong into the churning water and within seconds surfaced. The Donnelly boy pointed to a place offshore. Jason's long arms began to . draw him seaward; he was swimming toward the place where, God willing, Tim would still be waiting, high and dry.

When I reached the shoreline, I was no longer able to see Jason in the water and found myself saying a silent prayer for both of them. It was a long wait. I paced the stretch of sand against the wind, which had intensified and was tossing a salty spray at me. I picked up Jason's coat, full of his spicy scent, dusted the sand from it, and moved it, along with his boots, to a grassy place where the encroaching tide could not reach. I searched the horizon again and again, focusing my gaze on each frothy whitecap, but the nearly landlocked cove was a poor vantage point. When at last I heard the boys shouting from where

they waited on the rocks, I breathed a sigh of relief.
There was Jason, struggling out of the water and onto
the rocks, with Tim in his arms. While he wearily
crossed the rocky barrier separating him from the
beach, I noticed that Tim was limp and still. Without
giving myself time to think, I spread the carriage
blanket on the sand and knelt down beside it to wait
for them.

"Adrienne?"

Jason was startled to see me there but wasted no
time in laying the boy face down on the blanket. He
began to pump on his back to push the sea water out
of him.

"It's all my fault, sir. He ain't gonna die, is he?" the
O'Hanlon boy wailed.

Beside him, Kevin Donnelly folded his arms over
himself, shaking with fear and cold. Jason looked up
from his ministrations for only a moment. The sleeves
of his linen shirt clung to his arms, and, annoyed, he
tore it from his back, tossing it in a heap on the sand.
"Kevin, you and Sean go up and watch for your father
and the other men. Send them down here. Go on
now!" he ordered.

The boys scrambled up the hill, spurred by the
urgency of Jason's voice. When they were out of
sight, Jason rolled the lifeless Tim onto his back. His
face was tinged blue, and at the sight of it, a sharp
breath caught in my throat. Tears pricked the corner
of my eyes as I watched Jason tip back the boy's head
and begin rhythmically breathing into his mouth. He
worked tirelessly, but I could not bear to look at the
boy, who was so still. I focused my attention on Jason
instead. For the first time, I noticed the twisted knot
of flesh on his right shoulder. It was a substantial scar,
smooth tissue pulled over what must have been a
gaping wound. I wondered about its origin.

Jason put his ear to Tim's chest and listened. At last
he turned away and dropped his head in his hands.

He reverently wrapped the boy in the blanket and, getting to his feet, faced seaward. "If only I'd come along sooner. He tried to make it to shore but he wasn't strong enough."

I was remembering Tim from our brief meeting this morning. His eyes were so wide, full of anticipation of the great adventure, those unusual blue eyes. I groaned, realizing only now what I had discovered this morning, that this boy was Jason's son. I rose to come beside him and laid a hand on his arm. He turned to me. His face was devoid of emotion. Perhaps it was his way of coping, but it so disconcerted me that I lost words for a moment.

"I—I'm sorry. I know that he was your—"

His glaring eyes dared me to speak the word but I could not. I feared his wrath. He pulled his arm from me and turned away. Why should he not admit it —even now?

There was a bansheelike wail, and I looked upward to the crest of the hill. Mr. Donnelly, the estate manager, was holding his son fiercely, relieved to see that the boy was safe from harm. Brenna, though, had broken away from the two stablehands who were restraining her. She ran headlong down the hill path, arms flailing, and threw herself over the still form beneath the blanket.

"Mother in Heaven, not me baby! Not me baby!"

I stood by helplessly as the woman screeched and sobbed into the wool blanket. I wanted to comfort her but I had no words of comfort, so I stood there, numb. Jason had retrieved his clothes and dressed, looking much the worse for wear. He faced off against the burly stablehands who came on the scene now. "You fools! What made you bring her here?"

"She was up at the house when word came 'bout her boy. Couldn't talk her into stayin' behind nohow, Mr. Wyndham, sir."

Jason shook his head at them as Matthew

Wyndham joined the group. He, too, was surprised to see me among them. When his gaze fell on Brenna, mourning over her son, he became very pale and his lips pressed into a tight line. "What happened here?" he asked in a low voice.

Jason moved into his brother's line of sight, facing him almost defiantly. "The boys rowed their dory out to Bishop's Rock. They'd repaired it themselves before the trip. On the way back in, it stove in. They beached it on Whaleback Ledge and swam to shore. Tim didn't make it."

Mr. Wyndham heard the story stoically, only the rapid movement of his dark eyes indicating that he was taking in all of what went on around him. "And Miss Dalton and yourself?" he asked calmly.

"We were returning from Longfield when the O'Hanlon boy stopped us to ask for help."

Storm clouds forced an early twilight. The wind was whipping the foamy sea into a frenzy and lightning cut a jagged line across the sky just before the sharp crack of thunder sounded. It startled me to attention. We couldn't stay here much longer. "Mr. Wyndham," I called, "I'll see Brenna back home, if it's all right."

"Thank you, Adrienne. It would be kind of you."

Gently, I eased the exhausted Brenna to her feet and urged the woman to rest her head against my shoulder. She sobbed inconsolably against me the whole of the way back to her tiny cottage. It was no more than a hovel really, but more than most had. This must have been Brenna's remuneration for having given birth to a Wyndham child. It was clean and well-ordered, to be sure, but I was appalled at the cramped, meager quarters. A faded drape strung on a rope separated the corner where Brenna slept from the rest of the room. There were four mismatched chairs which might have served better as firewood, and a battered oak table, lovingly polished to a bright sheen. A fire blazed in the woodstove against the damp chill that had blown in with the storm.

Outside, under the shelter of a makeshift lean-to, old Daniel McKeon planed pine boards smooth and hammered on, heedless of the weather. Word of his grandson's accident had reached him even before Brenna and Adrienne arrived, and he was busying his gnarled hands with the practical work that had to be done, making a box for the boy to be buried in. His lean frame was more stooped than usual, and I thought when I saw him how old and tired he had become.

Brenna sat silently at the table, her dark hair in wild disarray, her back stiff and her red-rimmed eyes never straying from the cot across the room where Tim had been laid, still wrapped in the carriage blanket.

Before leaving, Mr. Donnelly had told me that he had sent for a woman from the village who would prepare the body. Mr. Wyndham had requested that that much be done for the boy. Brenna looked as if she hadn't heard. I took him aside then to voice my worries about Brenna. "She was so distraught, Mr. Donnelly, and now she just sits there. I don't know what to do for her. Couldn't someone send for Dr. Fletcher?"

"The family's doctor? We couldn't ask him to come out on a night like this just to tend one of the house-maids because she's grieving."

My look made it plain that I thought him heartless. "Don't misunderstand. I feel the woman's pain. My son was out there as well. It might just as easily have been him lying there. She'll be all right, miss. These girls are made of stern stuff. Give her time."

"Just the same, I'd like to stay with her a while longer."

"As you please, miss," he told me, though his irritated expression made it plain that he thought I should tend to my own responsibilities. "You can come back with the rig that brings that village woman."

"Thank you, Mr. Donnelly," I said, seeing him to the door.

I went to the barrel in the corner where the fresh water was kept and filled the teapot. Brenna had not stirred from her spot, and I wondered if I were doing any good at all here. Why hadn't I gone back to Wyndcliffe with Mr. Donnelly? I decided, though, that what kept me there in that damp cottage, with the rain seeping in through the roof and making puddles on the floor, was Brenna's haunted expression. She seemed to have withdrawn into herself, and I truly feared that she would go mad.

When the tea had finished steeping, I brought it to the table in two battered cups. I sat down beside Brenna and laid a hand on her shoulder.

"Please, Brenna, drink this. It will warm you."

The door banged open and Mr. McKeon shuffled in, his clothing sodden with rain water, despite the shelter he had made for himself outside.

" 'Tis done," he said. "You still here, missy?"

"I didn't think Brenna should be alone. You're drenched, Mr. McKeon. You ought to get out of those wet clothes and have some of this tea yourself."

"I've me own brand, miss," he said, reaching into the cupboard for his bottle of precious Irish whiskey. He filled a cup for himself and poured a generous amount into Brenna's tea. " 'Twill help her sleep," he told me, "she needs to sleep."

"Please drink the tea, Brenna," I urged her again.

She did not respond. I took a moment to reflect and then began anew. "I can't presume to know what it's like to lose a child, there can be nothing worse, I'm sure. I saw Tim just this morning. He was with the other boys, and they were so proud of the repairs they'd made on their dory. He was a brave little sailor.''

Those last few words brought forth a flood of tears from Brenna, and then she began to rave.

'' 'Tis his fault, all our grief. I curse the Wyndham name! If he'd been a father to the boy, me Tim would be safe yet, not a-layin' cold on his cot.''

I knew that there was no reasoning in her words. They were only the ravings of a grief-stricken mother. Jason had done all that he could to save the boy's life.

''Damn his eternal soul! May he never know a moment's happiness for all the grief he's laid on me! Me poor baby, me poor Timmy!''

Together old Mr. McKeon and I managed to get Brenna to drink her whiskey-laced tea, and it soothed her into a deep sleep.

The boy was buried in a quiet corner of the village cemetery, and there was soon erected over the spot a stone marker, far too costly to have been purchased by the McKeons. It read, ''Timothy McKeon, born in the year of our Lord 1859, laid to rest on August 8, 1866,'' and beneath this a single line which read, ''A brave little sailor.''

8

It was not yet eight o'clock and the morning sun streamed in the french windows, making dust motes in its beam sparkle like tiny snowflakes. It was a peaceful morning but for the sharp "kee-ah" of a lone seabird somewhere nearby, and as I plaited my heavy hair and pinned it in a coil at the back of my head, I contemplated Susannah's birthday gift. There would be a celebration this evening, and as we were to have no lessons today, I had planned to go to the village in search of something suitable.

Since the day of the outing to Mr. Talbott's farm more than two weeks ago, Susannah had become an amenable creature. She had, I think, developed a fondness for me by then. I was her protector, her mentor, and she was awed by the changes I could effect on her behalf. I believe that she thought me capable of working any miracle, and I feared I could only disapoint her in the end.

This fear became a real possibility when we went to breakfast that morning. As it was a special occasion, we were to have our morning meal in the dining room, though we would still be by ourselves. The family rarely gathered together for breakfast.

Susannah looked about anxiously. "Where is Father this morning, I wonder?"

"Has he not come to wish you a happy birthday yet?"

She shook her head.

"I'm certain he'll be down presently," I told her. "He worked very late last night, you know."

"Yes, miss," she replied, buoyed by my assurances.

I needed to speak with Mrs. Garen about my trip to the village, and so, after settling Susannah down to eat, I left her, promising that I would return soon. I found the housekeeper exercising her authority over the kitchen staff.

"Hurry with those trays, girls. There's plenty to be done when you've finished here."

Mrs. Black, the cook, crossed her arms over her ample chest, brandishing her wooden spoon like a weapon. She did not take kindly, it appeared, to Mrs. Garen's infringement on her territory.

"Mrs. Garen," I called, "have you seen Mr. Wyndham this morning?"

"Believe he's gone to his office in the village, miss," she said, without taking her eye from the idling kitchen maids.

So he had no intention of spending the day with his daughter. He hadn't so much as wished her a happy birthday. I was annoyed.

"Did he mention when he would return?"

"I believe he was saying something or other to Donnelly about a ship behind schedule and some lost cargo. Told me as how he might be late."

He wouldn't miss tonight's celebration, I assured myself. Susannah was so looking forward to this party.

"I'll be gone this afternoon, Mrs. Garen," I told her.

"You will see to Susannah, won't you? I'm going down to the village. It's a fine day for the walk."

"Walk? My good heavens, miss, the mister'd never hear of it. We'll have one of the boys drive you."

"I don't wish to be any trouble."

"No more trouble than I'd see if I let you walk the two miles to the village. There'll be a rig waiting for you in the drive at noon, if that's all right."

I said that it was. It was not that I did not appreciate the kindnesses that Mr. Wyndham accorded me, but since overhearing the ugly accusations that Rachel Chandler had made regarding my place here, I felt that each time I was given a special privilege, I was looked upon by the household with a jaded eye. The sidelong glances of the servants were not lost on me.

Still staring at my shoes, I turned to leave and nearly ran into Jason, who was leaning on the door jamb. I stopped short as he took a bite from the crisp apple in his hand. He was ever turning up unexpectedly. There was a long pause as we stared one another down.

"Good morning, Miss Dalton," he drawled.

"Whatever are you doing in the kitchen?" I asked sharply, transferring all of the annoyance I felt this morning to him.

"Wherever there's food, Mister Jason won't be far away. You can be sure of that," Mrs. Black called.

"Especially if you're at the stove, Mrs. Black," he retorted.

I went off down the hall, my thoughts occupied with the problem of what to say to Susannah about her father. I needn't have worried, for Susannah was at the moment occupied with a more pressing irritation. I returned to the dining room to find Rachel Chandler there across the table from Susannah, whose cheery disposition had become decidedly less gracious.

"Well, it's Miss Dalton. I understood that you were free of your duties this morning."

"I am," I replied curtly, pouring myself a cup of tea. I had lost my appetite all at once.

"I thought it would be nice for Susannah and me to spend her birthday together," Rachel announced.

So she had decided to take Mr. Wyndham's advice after all. But as I watched her, I noticed that her smile seemed to have frozen in its most dazzling state. She was twisting her ring around her finger, and her usually sharp eyes had a blank look in them. Perhaps she really did love Mr. Wyndham, I decided. What else would force her to say that she wanted to spend the day with Susannah when every part of her seemed to rebel at the thought?

Susannah's eyes pleaded with me to save her from this woman whom she so despised, but I thought that if Rachel were sincere, then the best course for all concerned would be for Susannah and Rachel to become friendly.

"Where's father?" Susannah asked, her voice squeaking.

"He had business in the village," I explained. "Mrs. Garen told me that he sends his best wishes to you, though, and . . . of course he promised to be home in time for your party."

I was not a good liar by any means, but it would not have helped if I had been. Susannah did not believe me. She pushed away her breakfast plate and slumped in her seat. I came up behind her and laid a hand on her shoulder.

"You can show Miss Chandler all the flowers blooming in the garden," I suggested.

"She's seen the garden."

"Well, then, she can help you make a birthday bouquet for yourself. Only this time, please stay out of the rosebed."

The corners of the child's mouth turned up. "No more roses for me, I think."

She smiled at Rachel then, and I wondered what she was up to.

"Father would have taken a rod to me for spoiling the roses if it weren't for Miss Dalton," Susannah began, with the most cunning look in her eye. "She asked him to spare me, I'm sure of it. Father always listens to her, just the same way he listened to Mama."

Rachel blanched. The remark had done the intended damage. I was shocked that an eight-year-old child would have the presence of mind to set Rachel and me against one another, but I would not be manipulated.

"Perhaps you oughtn't have been spared," I told her, "if you've not yet learned your manners. Now if you have finished your meal, you may take Miss Chandler upstairs to the classroom and show her your sketches."

I turned to Rachel. "The child has shown quite a talent for drawing. You must see the pictures she's made of her grandfather's horses."

Rachel's mouth was creased in a tight line. Her eyes were bright and her expression seemed to say that she would not be bested by a child nor humiliated by a governess.

"Yes, Susannah, why don't you show me the classroom and the nursery as well? There is so much of the house that I've not seen, and I'll need to be familiar with it when your father and I are married, dear."

Susannah sprang to her feet and her chair rattled back and forth on two legs on the highly polished floor. She looked bewildered and stricken. Had the thought never occurred to her?

"Married? You can't live here! Mama won't allow

it!'' she screeched.

As she ran out calling for her mama, I could see all of the progress I had made with the child unraveling before my eyes. I turned on Rachel. ''What a foolish thing to say!''

Rachel was stunned by the child's outburst and paid me no mind.

''You had no right to tell her about your marriage plans,'' I went on. ''She was not ready for such news. It's only been a year since she lost her mother, and she still grieves. She cannot share her father with anyone yet. She will adjust, but you must give her time.''

''Matthew said that—but I thought that he—of course we shall give the child time,'' Rachel conceded, before the callous tone that was part of her nature crept back into her voice, ''but sooner or later I *am* going to marry Matthew Wyndham.''

After Rachel left, I went to look for Susannah and found her in her room curled beneath her quilt, fast asleep, or so it seemed. Her small face was tear-streaked and she would not respond to me, so I decided that perhaps it would be best to let her rest. I could explain things to her later, and that would give me time to ponder the matter. What could I say to cheer her? Later, as I prepared to leave for the village, I went in to check on her again and found her still asleep. I was mercifully spared.

And so with gloves in hand and a wide-brimmed English straw hat to shade my face from the sun, I went out to the porte cochere where, sure enough, a carriage was waiting. A driver sat patiently up on the seat, reins in hand. I did not recognize him, for a slouch hat shadowed his face and a tattered coat made his stooped figure undistinguishable. I cleared my throat, but he made no effort to hand me into the rig. I managed on my own.

"Good afternoon," I called to him.

"Afternoon, miss."

I settled back onto the seat, and he snapped the reins, setting the carriage in motion. The heat from the sun spread a tingling sensation over me, and I reveled in its warmth. The sky was as vivid a blue as my gown, and the summer breeze fluttered the ribbons of my bonnet. There would not be many more days such as this. Maine summers were all too short.

"It would have been a lovely day for a walk," I thought aloud.

"Wouldn't advise goin' off by yourself, if you don't know your way. Could get lost—"

Something in the gravelly voice sparked a glimmer of recognition in me. I thought it odd that he kept his head lowered so that his face was in shadow. I leaned forward to try and see him better but to no avail.

"I've not seen you in the stables," I said. "What did you say your name was?"

"Didn't. It's . . . Jenkins. Don't get about much. They keep me busy sweepin' up and shovelin' manure."

I wrinkled my nose and settled back on the seat, turning my thoughts to the gift I would purchase for Susannah. I'd thought perhaps a book of poems and some hair ribbons, but it looked now as thought whatever the gift was it would not lift her spirits.

The rig turned off of the main road and was jostling along a narrow, wheel-rutted path, edged on either side by black spruce and balsam with dense undergrowth. I knew that something was amiss. The main road led straight into the village. There was no need to turn off.

"Why have we turned off?" I asked, my voice full of trepidation.

"Shorter this way, miss."

I knew that it could not be. I had sensed something unusual about this man when I first stepped into the carriage. Who was he, and what did he want? I examined my options. We were perhaps half a mile from the house. If I leapt out and was lucky enough not to break a leg in the fall, I might outrun him, but it was not very likely. I would have to wait and see what all of this was about. I spent the next, long minutes on tenterhooks, until the carriage came to a halt in a clearing.

"Why have we stopped here?" I asked.

I was sure that my voice gave away the hysteria rising in me, despite my efforts to appear calm. The trees about me seemed to dip and sway. I must not faint now!

"I thought perhaps you might enjoy a picnic repast before I take you into the village."

The voice had changed. It was now a polished baritone. The man jumped down from his seat, tossing the filthy overcoat and hat into the bushes.

"Jason Wyndham!" I cried.

"At your service."

He bowed graciously, brushing off his light-colored coat and adjusting his crimson silk cravat. I sprang to my feet. The straw hat floated off my head and down my back, its ribbon catching at my throat. I knew that I should have been furious at this prank but I could not help the hysterical laughter that escaped from me. It came partly out of relief that I was free of the bogeyman. A smile twisted on my lips.

"Shoveling manure, were you?"

Impulsively, I threw my reticule at him, and he put up his hands in defense. I looked around for something else to throw. Finding nothing, I jumped down and, picking up the discarded rag of a coat, rolled it into a ball and sent it sailing his way. The hat soon followed.

"How dare you pull such a prank? Do you know that I very nearly jumped out back there? I could have been hurt."

My tirade perhaps would have been more convincing had I not followed it with a fit of laughter.

"My apologies," he said, touching his forelock in mock respect as he began to advance on me. "Do you know, Miss Dalton, that this is the first time I have heard you laugh. I do believe I like it."

"Enjoy it while you can, for when I stop laughing, I may wring your neck."

I took the offensive bravely, but he grabbed my wrists and a slight shove sent me bottom-first into a mossy bank. He fell on top of me and pinned my arms to the ground. To feel his hard body so close was intriguing, and though I knew I should extricate myself, curiosity held me there.

"And so, Mr. Wyndham, now that you've kidnapped me, what are your plans?"

He bent his head down until our faces touched and then kissed the tip of my nose, my eyelids and the column of my throat. When at last his mouth closed over mine, he released my arms and instinctively they wrapped around his neck. And then he eased himself away, proffering his hand so that I might raise myself up.

"Spend the afternoon with me, Adrienne," he said. "Mrs. Black has packed a picnic hamper. It's chicken, I think, and I've brought a bottle of our best Bordeaux from the cellar."

"Mr. Wyndham, I do believe that you are the most unconventional man that I have ever met."

"*Mr.* Wyndham is a title reserved for my illustrious brother. You must call me Jason."

He rose and took my hand, pulling me to my feet.

"Well then, Jason, why couldn't you have invited me on this picnic this morning in the normal fashion?"

"My reputation has preceded me in your case, I'm afraid, as well as my own rash actions. You'd never have accepted me if I'd behaved in a conventional manner."

Perhaps he was right on that score, perhaps it would have been wise to refuse him still, but I did not.

"I accept your invitation as it stands, then, though I may come to regret it."

He kissed my hand and laid it over his arm, reaching for the picnic hamper under the carriage seat.

"Never. I promise you that."

Without speaking, he led me through a break in the dense thicket. We followed the traces of a precarious path that led seaward and then along the high cliff face, finally stepping through a cut in the angular rocks. We had to stoop in order to pass, and when we reached the other side, my mouth dropped in astonishment. The meadow was a riot of color, sheltered on three sides by the rocky cliff face and fringed with orange lichens. It was a place of protection where no human being should be, I thought as Jason spread the blanket on the soft moss beneath our feet. I settled down to admire the unobstructed view of the ocean and the horizon where the robin's-egg color of the sky met the turquoise water. The sea was placid today, the gentle waves churning up a lacy foam.

"However did you come upon this place?"

He had produced two stemmed crystal glasses from the hamper and was struggling with the cork of the wine bottle. It dislodged with a loud pop.

"My mother came upon it years ago on one of her walks. She first brought me here when I was a child. We would come for picnics when my father and brother went into the village. I used to think it was a magical glade—you know, the place where fairies came to dance by moonlight."

He handed me a glass and filled it. "You are the only other person who has been here."

As he raised his glass to mine, the crystal rang out, and I smiled up at him. What was it exactly that I had disliked about him? That he had flouted convention and dared to be honest while those about him hid behind their mask of gentility? While I basked in the warmth of the sunny meadow, listening to the tinkling song of a winter wren somewhere deep in the woods, I could only believe that somehow this man had been terribly wronged by those around him. It was what he had intended.

"I hoped that I might convince you that I am not the villain you suppose me to be, Adrienne," he said.

"I never thought—" I began, but could not go on. I did not want to lie to him. He would not believe me anyway.

"You heard the worst of it from Rachel that night on your balcony."

"I did not mean to eavesdrop."

His hand found mine. "You heard the truth of it at least. That's more than most will ever know, and now you know me for the fool that I am."

"You were wronged," I said in his defense. "There's no shame in that."

Was it the sweet wine that caused the warmth that spread within me, or the fact that his hand was now covering mine? "It must have been an awful time for you," I went on, and curiosity spurred me further. "Might I ask you a question . . . about what I heard?"

"What is it?"

"If—" I tried to phrase my thoughts delicately "—all of it happened the way Rachel said, wouldn't her brother have insisted that the two of you be married as soon as possible . . . to spare her from shame?''

I blushed, unable to meet his eyes.

"One would expect so," he replied.

"And no one questioned this?''

"At the time, no one knew about the changes in my father's will except Aaron, so what possible motive could there be for Rachel's bizarre actions? She was born for the stage, as you may have discovered. That night she meekly followed Aaron into my father's study, looking disheveled, her bottom lip aquiver. She claimed that I had forced myself upon her and that she could never consider marriage to me—under any circumstances. Oh, it was effective, I can tell you," he said, disgust plain on his face.

"But your father, he must have know what they were up to.''

"Undoubtedly. All of it amused him greatly. I could see it on his face when he sent for me. He was laughing at the Chandlers in their righteous indignation and at me for being fool enough to fall into their trap.''

"There's no way you could have known," I insisted. "What manner of man must your father have been to have done such a thing to his son?''

"He was a tyrant, no less, who ruled this little kingdom of his despotically, as if every tide awaited his approval before advancing on the shore. If he found a thing that did not fit his view of the world, he would alter it until it did, and if he could not alter it, he would destroy it lest it offend his eye. Even his own son, if he would not be molded, must be crushed so as not to taint Jonathan Wyndham's world. That night was his triumph, the final destruction of his son's respectability.''

Jason's knuckles went white as he clenched the neck of the wine bottle. He swiftly poured himself another, downing it in one swallow. It seemed to settle him. The firm set of his jaw slackened.

"Let's not spoil our afternoon," he said in a gentler tone. "I am anxious to know all there is to know about you, Miss Adrienne Dalton."

I busied myself with emptying the hamper and setting our luncheon on the blanket. "Where do you come from? You're no ordinary governess, not by the looks of you. I thought at first you might be a fortune hunter, come after my brother and his riches—"

The pause had come so as to make a question out of the statement, but I ignored it. There was no reason for him to trust me yet.

"Your brother and my father were good friends. It was their businesses that first brought them together. The Wyndham Shipping Lines carried cotton for my father's mill before the war and the blockades. When Papa died and the debts were discovered, your brother offered me a position."

Jason nodded slowly.

"My father died while visiting here," I went on. "Your brother felt responsible, I think, for not having paid closer attention to the health of his guest. It's nonsense, of course. Papa had had a heart condition for some time."

"Your father died at Wyndcliffe?" Jason said, surprised at the revelation.

"Yes. He visited here often and had a room on the third floor. It was a restful place away from his troubles in Boston."

"I never guessed that Matt and your father—but that explains why he treats you more like a house-guest than an employee."

He seemed pleased with the discovery, but I lowered my head, my face flushed with color.

"I have thought lately that perhaps I should never have come here. Oh I've been treated well—too well, and I'm eyed suspiciously in all quarters on account of it.''

Jason sliced a wedge of cheese for me and took one for himself. ''And did that politician, Mr. Landis, spurn you when he discovered you'd lost your fortune?''

I shook my head. ''All of Beacon Hill knew of Father's gambling. I couldn't marry Phillip, not honorably.''

''Gentlemen are bound by honor, my dear, but it has been my observation that ladies are spared such hypocrisy. Whatever your father might have done, it would not have tainted you. On the contrary, I should think you'd be the martyred daughter to all those self-righteous Boston blue bloods.''

Jason leaned back on his hands and drew up his long legs, studying me.

''You're a brave woman, Adrienne,'' he said, ''throwing away a chance at a life of ease and the man you love to uproot yourself and settle amongst the Wyndhams. We're mostly vipers, you know.''

It sounded like a warning, and this from the man who'd wanted me to see that he was not a villain. I was feeling wretched at this close scrutiny of my life. My gaze drifted out onto the horizon again, and I let the waves lull me back to quiet complacency. I began to voice my thoughts aloud. ''It's not brave to run away. I just couldn't bear the whispering, 'That's Ben Dalton's daughter. He gambled away her inheritance. Poor child hasn't a penny to bless herself with.' I had to get away from all of them.

''He didn't do what they said, though. He was an honest man, a good businessman. He was so pleased when I told him that I'd agreed to marry Phillip. At last he would have a son, someone to run the mill after . . . but now he's gone and the mill's gone and so is Phillip.''

My chin dropped onto my chest. Jason lifted it so
that he could look into my eyes, and his voice was
cold.

"Did you love your Mr. Landis so much, then?"

"He was a charismatic man. Listening to him speak
could overwhelm you. I admired his ideals, and it
made Papa so happy to see me on his arm."

"But?"

"I did not love him."

"How do you know?" he asked. "What do you
know of love?"

"I shall know it when I find it," I told him with all
the naiveté of youth.

He only smiled. "So you'd have married this fellow
just to please your father?"

"I couldn't hope to please him any other way, don't
you see? No matter what my accomplishments or
what kind of person I'd grow into, I could never be
the son who could take over in his stead."

I traced the rim of the empty wine glass with my
finger and set it on the blanket.

"I'd have served him as well as any son," I said,
more to myself than to my companion. "Lord knows
I'd watched Papa for enough years to learn how the
mill was run. When I went over the accounts with his
clerks at the last, they said that I had a surprising head
for figures considering that I was a woman."

I realized, too late, that Jason would certainly think
me foolish for such an unheard-of notion. I knew it,
and still, when I looked up to meet the astonishment
on his face, it stung me. He was strangely silent as we
began the meal in earnest. I was hardly aware of what
I ate. For me, at least, the food seemed as tasteless as
sawdust. This was no affront to Mrs. Black's culinary
talents but my own preoccupation with the pregnant
silence. When I could stand it no more, I said to him,
" 'Tis I who've spoilt this lovely afternoon. It was

selfish of me to go on about myself."

"Don't be ridiculous, Adrienne. I've just now been trying to find a way to approach you about this matter of your father's gambling. It's upset you, I know, but you mustn't be ashamed of him. I myself am an inveterate gambler; it's in the blood. Your father was only a man, no more, and men do have their faults. You'll come to realize that sooner or later."

He poured himself another glass of wine and insisted that I have another as well. "It's said that whoever plays deep loses either his money or his character. Take heart in the fact that your father lost only his fortune. I, by contrast, come out a winner more often than not, and half the county will vouch for my lack of character."

I took a moment to digest all that he had said. "You told me that you hoped this afternoon to convince me that you weren't a villain. If that was your intention, why do you revile yourself so?"

"Perhaps when faced with it, I'm not proud of the man I've become," he said matter-of-factly.

His mask had slipped again, and it pained me to see what he really thought of himself. "Surely you've plenty to be proud of."

It was then that I realized how little I knew of Jason Wyndham save the unpleasant gossip that his very presence seemed to generate. What were his accomplishments?

"You are a war veteran," I said, grasping at straws. "That is surely something of which you can be proud."

Jason drew himself back, honestly surprised. "Wherever did you get such an idea?"

A warm flush spread upward from my throat to the roots of my hair. "The scar on your shoulder—"

He raised one dark brow. "I was given to understand that young ladies did not notice such things."

He paused to watch as I tried to hide my embarrassment by tending to the domestic chore of clearing away the remains of our lunch.

"But since you have noticed, shall I clarify matters for you?" Without waiting for my reply, he went on. "I was shot while making my escape through a bedroom window, by a jealous husband. Imagine my surprise to have been caught—"

"In flagrante delicto," I finished for him.

He nodded and formed a wry smile. "Exactly, my dear."

I did not know how I knew, but I was certain that he was lying. With a firm set to my jaw, I sat back on my heels. "I would think that a cuckolded husband would have taken closer aim at his intended target. A wounded arm would only insure that you were not able to send any love letters to his wife."

I raised a brow in blatant imitation of his own style, and he howled with laughter.

"You do delight me! Just when I am convinced that I am dealing with an innocent child, you tell me you'd like to have managed your father's mill and then deal me repartee worthy of the most cosmopolitan drawing room. What would my pious brother think of his daughter's governess now?"

I did not know what this comment was meant to signify, and my eyes darted nervously beneath their lids. He took hold of my hands. All at once I was lost in the depths of his gaze.

"You must tell me truly, for I need to know. Which are you, Adrienne, vixen or virgin?"

His grip on my hands was firm, almost painful, and it distressed me that I lost so much of myself to him when he came near. The wild spirits in both of us fused into one overwhelming maelstrom when he touched me, drawing me downward, away from all sensibility. I closed my eyes against it, and the world stopped its crazy spinning. Slipping free of him, I moved to the far corner of the blanket.

"Were you with the Twentieth Maine at Gettysburg?" I asked, in far too animated a way. "What a brave lot, to have held their line when they were outnumbered three to one and then assemble a charge so fierce as to cause the enemy to throw down their arms and surrender."

He avoided the question. "How is it you are so well informed about the war effort?"

"I was away at school in Paris, but I made Papa send me the newspapers. I read every line. Any news from home was welcome."

He gave me a curt nod. I was no closer to having the truth from him. I reached to pluck a few harebells from nearby, and as I rolled the thin stems between my fingers, the pale blue flowers twisted and nodded. Silence proved to be the best course of action. Before too long, Jason's hand began rhythmically tapping on the blanket. His eyes were rheumy, looking through me to see things that, I realized too late, would have been best forgotten. A sheen of perspiration glared on his forehead. I leaned toward him.

"So it is true. Were you with the Maine regiment at Gettysburg?"

He shook his head vigorously to deny it and yet he said, "Why is it so important for you to know? Why call up old ghosts?"

There had been brief moments since I met him when it was as if every emotion he experienced was written plainly on his face for me to see. I was mostly pleased at this ability to see inside him, but in this one instance, I felt his pain at the memory of the tragedies the war must have wrought. His sorrow was my sorrow, and I could no longer be afraid of him. I edged closer and took up one of his hands, examining the long fingers so well suited to the keyboard. I pressed the flower I had been toying with into his palm.

"A lady's token for a brave soldier," I told him. "You needn't say any more. You've more than accomplished your purpose here today."

He took up my hands as if he might draw strength from me and met my eyes. His own were as cold and clear as blue glass.

"I left home after that messy business with Rachel," he began, "and enlisted with a unit of the Massachusetts Cavalry. I was with Captain Magee's Second Company at Baton Rouge."

"Louisiana?"

"Yes, and you mustn't feel you've let me down if you are unable to recall our exploits. It was not one of the major campaigns of the war."

I was ashamed to have drawn him into this and could only hope that by recalling his nightmares, he could be healed of the inner wounds that I knew troubled him.

"You were wounded at Baton Rouge?" I guessed.

"No. Our boys were bottled up in the swamps just holding off the Rebels from Baton Rouge and New Orleans. We tried a couple of runs at Vicksburg in Sixty-two. That was the key, you know, to open up the river. But then those Rebels knew that, too, and fought us off with all they had. I hadn't any liking for swamps myself, so when the opportunity presented itself, I volunteered to carry dispatches from General Banks to General Grant, who was upriver at Grand Gulf and on the move toward Vicksburg."

"Did you meet General Grant, truly?"

My eyes were bright with excitement as I listened to his tale, and he laughed at me in the same way he would laugh at Susannah when she amused him. At this I drew back and turned a skeptical eye on him.

"Jason Wyndham, if you are building castles in the

air, I swear I'll box your ears.''

I coiled my arm for the attack, but he caught it.

"Have a care, else I shan't continue with my story. I did meet General Grant. In truth, I had little opportunity for conversation with him or his staff but managed to make it known that there was no pleasure for a cavalry officer mired in the bayous.''

"And then what happened?''

"I found myself reassigned to General McPherson's cavalry escort and on the march to Vicksburg.''

Once again his eyes stared past me, watching what only he could see.

I resettled myself with a rustle of skirts, and the movements seemed to waken Jason from his thoughts. "Two weeks later, I was knocked from my horse by a Confederate minié ball at Champion's Hill. I never even saw Vicksburg.''

"Who'd have thought such a little thing could do such damage?'' he said, indicating the size of the ball by a gesture with thumb and forefinger.

I remembered the mass of scarred flesh and winced.

"When our boys went off after Pemberton, they left a brigade to guard the wounded, and the doctors set up a hospital in an abandoned farmhouse. The fall from my horse left me unconscious, and when I awoke it was after dark. I was too weak to raise myself up and could only lie there, waiting and listening. The air was full of moaning and crying, pleading and praying. There were so many dying men. It was all evening and half the night before they got to me. That night will haunt me forever.''

An odd quiet settled in, and I wondered whether he would go on. As if he'd read my thoughts, he said, "Don't ask any more of me, Adrienne. It isn't something you should hear. Too many men went home less than men, too many never made it home.''

I nodded.

"No one at Wyndcliffe knows any of this, though, and I'd prefer to keep it that way."

"But you should be proud, and I know they would be, too."

"Just the same, I would appreciate your confidence."

I was perplexed by this need of his to show everyone only his worst side. At least he had not shut me out, I told myself. I agreed to be silent.

He drew me into the circle of his arms. "Besides, after I'd recuperated at any army hospital in New Orleans, I stayed on there with my trusty pack of cards and damn near bankrupted our boys in blue. More true to form, wouldn't you say?"

I laughed in spite of myself.

"Now let's walk on the beach for a while, shall we?"

9

"Open that case as well, Brenna.
We shall have to search through everything until we
find a proper gift. Oh, how could I be so selfish? The
whole afternoon and not one thought to Susannah!"

There was a rustle of tissue paper. "How about
these lace handkerchiefs, miss? They was packed
with a pair of evening gloves, appear just-bought to
me."

"Yes, put them aside. They'll have to do if we can
find nothing else."

I stopped the frantic search long enough to watch
Brenna, who was eyeing with wonder each item she
drew from the trunk: a silk parasol with ivory ferrule
and carved handle, half a dozen pair of kid gloves for
all occasions, elaborate collars and fichus of tulle and
lace and Swiss muslin, an army of fans lined up in a
row like toy soldiers, shawls and scarves of every
hue. All of these things I took so much for granted
that I had to wonder what Brenna found so extraordinary.

"I'm grateful for your help," I said to her. "I
haven't any right to be taking up your time, especially
with Susannah's party tonight."

"Don't you be givin' it another thought, miss. 'Tis a pleasure to be out from under Mrs. Garen's eye, and I'll be back before I'm missed."

She repacked my things in the case with the utmost care, then disdainfully touched the sleeve of her own faded blue cotton dress as if to regain a hold on reality. Something within the folds of material in the case caught her eye, and she drew it out.

"How's this, miss?"

She had drawn out a long scarf of Nile green silk, sprigged with gold flowers. I shook my head.

"Not for the child, but you may keep it for yourself if you like."

"No, miss, I couldn't."

"Of course you could and you shall. It never suited me, but just look how well it goes with your complexion. I insist that you have it."

"Thank you, miss. It's the finest thing I've ever seen."

"It is I who must thank you for rescuing me from Mrs. Wyndham. I'm sure she'd have had more than a few words for me about my 'unladylike' behavior."

Brenna tittered into her hand. "Caused quite a stir, I can tell you, when you and Mister Jason come strollin' in, your clothes all damp and rumpled, and Missus Felicia standin' right in the hall to receive you."

I only wished to put the whole scene behind me. I had taken a long hot bath, but this reminder made me shiver in my wrapper.

"Our timing was a bit unfortunate, wasn't it?" I said.

"I nearly tumbled down from the landin' when that devil of a man told her you was only walkin' on the beach all of an afternoon and diggin' for clams. Oh my, miss!"

"And me come home with nary a clamshell to show for my pains."

Brenna's laughter built to a crescendo, but all I could manage was a weak smile.

"And her callin' him a liar and him tellin' her she weren't nothin' but a nosy old bitch and that his affairs weren't none o' her damned business."

I moaned and rolled my eyes. "Brenna, your language! Must you recall every detail?"

"But he did say it, miss, sure as I'm standin' here."

"All I can say is thank heaven for your quick mind, telling her that Susannah was calling for me when all the while she was asleep in her bed."

"I knew you'd like to have run off, the way you was standin' there, all white-faced and weak at the knees."

"I'm not one for facing the consequences, and that's the truth of it. I suppose I shall be in disgrace now. Is walking on the beach unacceptable behavior for a governess, do you suppose?"

"Can't say as how much of anything would be acceptable if there was Mister Jason involved," she replied.

I chose to ignore her remark, and looking up at my bureau, noticed the music box. The carousel with its tiny carved horses all painted in gay colors would be the ideal gift for Susannah. I sprang to my feet and grabbed it as if it might disappear before I could touch it. I held it close and ran my hand over it gingerly, the gilt and paint untouched by time. It had been so much a part of my life. I didn't know if I could part with it, but remembering the joy it had brought me as a child only served to remind me of the child who needed joy in her life now. With a sight, I pushed the precious carousel toward Brenna. "Here is just the thing for Susannah."

Being in disgrace had its advantages. I did not feel so heartily compelled to dress in a demure fashion to please Felicia Wyndham. The scene in the foyer had left me feeling positively wicked, so I dressed in grand Paris fashion. The gown was of cerise-colored grenadine with a deep decollete that revealed a white lawn chemisette. The undersleeves were embroidered lawn as well, the skirt being gathered up by fasteners to display the petticoat beneath. It was the newest vogue. I pulled my ashen hair into a caul weaved of red silk threads adorned with seed pearls. This evening, at least, I was able to leave my vanity table pleased.

Susannah's birthday celebration was, indeed, an occasion. Two long tables had been set up on the front lawn to accommodate a cold collation for the guests. As I passed through the clusters of people, I could sense the stares that went after me. I wished that dusk would come a little sooner to hide me, for I saw now that while the red dress might have gone unnoticed on the streets of Paris, it was causing quite a stir on the lawns of Wyndcliffe. The buzz of whispered conversation hummed in my ears, and I feared that I looked as skittish as a colt who might break and run at the slightest provocation. I did not see Jason until he had swept up beside me and taken my free arm, linking it through his.

"Good evening, my dear. How lovely you look this evening."

At this the buzzing around us grew more frenzied. He squired me toward the rise of the lawn where the family had made a circle of chairs with Susannah at its head.

"Jason," I whispered, "I fear we are being stared upon from all quarters."

"It's you, Adrienne, and your Parisian fashion."

I groaned. "Is it so out of place, then?"

He stopped suddenly and raised my hand to his lips. "It is exquisite, and I am the envy of every man here tonight."

From her seat beside Susannah, Felicia Wyndham was watching us, mortified by our familiarity. A little voice in my head told me to disentangle myself immediately, but my own rebellious nature won out. In spite of my apprehensions, I flashed Jason a brilliant smile.

"Thank you, kind sir, but pray curb your tongue else you shall give your stepmother a seizure."

He patted my hand, putting it back on his arm, and let go a throaty chuckle. "Certainly not without your help, my dear, and no less than the old harridan deserves."

My laughter was brittle, like the tinkling of crystal striking crystal.

"I'm pleased that you found a gift for Susannah after all," he said, noticing the package under my arm. "I was afraid that if you hadn't, you'd never forgive me for disrupting your afternoon's plans."

"It was a lovely afternoon as it turned out," I protested.

"Even though I subjected you to my stepmother's wrath?"

"There is always the chance of thorns when one is gathering roses."

In the corner of one eye, I saw Matthew Wyndham approaching with Mr. Donnelly at his side. They were deep in discussion, but when he saw Jason with me on his arm, a black look came over him. Without breaking the rhythm of his step, he began to clench and unclench his fists. Jason had seen him, too, for his face split into an evil grin, and he turned to me. "Come riding with me tomorrow," he said urgently.

I could see that he was trying somehow to provoke his brother, and I would not have it.

"I couldn't possibly. I'll be with Susannah all day tomorrow."

"In the morning then, before she wakes. I need to

speak with you alone, Adrienne. We'll ride along the
cliffs and watch the sun rise."

"I couldn't," I protested. "Regardless of how I am
treated, I am not a guest in this house. I've already
presumed too far upon your brother's kindness, and
I've only just realized how much."

I pulled away from him. It had never occurred to
me before that my behavior would reflect on
Matthew Wyndham, but as he was the one who
brought me here, that clearly would be the case. As I
watched Mr. Wyndham join his family, meaningful
looks passed between him and his stepmother. Again
I had behaved like a spoiled child, and I was sorely
ashamed. And there was yet another truth to be
faced. I was not sure that I could trust myself alone
with Jason again. He was still standing beside me, and
even now my body betrayed me, responsive to his
touch, my senses intoxicated by him. I was warmed to
the tips of my toes as if I'd drunk one glass of wine too
many.

"I couldn't," I repeated and looked again to Mr.
Wyndham.

Jason followed my eyes and laughed curtly. His
voice was strained, almost desperate.

"If you don't promise to ride with me in the
morning, I shall take you in my arms this minute and
kiss the very breath out of you, and all of them be
damned!"

He would have had no qualms about making a
scene, the hard glint in his eye confirmed it. So I
acquiesced, having lost my taste for infamy.

I could not say that he was pleased with the easy
victory despite his insistence. He regarded me in the
twilight and there was an apologetic look about him.
He did not speak, though. Exactly what did he want
of me? I asked myself. Was I only an opponent with
whom he traded badinage? Or did he want a "partner

in crime'' who would help him strike at the respectability of the Wyndham family? Or perhaps I was to be a weapon that he could wield in his battle with his brother. I had no taste for this last theory, and yet now it seemed the most plausible. I slipped away from him without a word, wanting only to disappear in the crowd of guests for the remainder of the evening.

When darkness settled in, a host of colorful Japanese lanterns were lit and the musicians struck up a lively polka. The platform that had been set up for dancing was soon filled to capacity, and I watched, mesmerized, as the couples whirled across the boards.

"Are you enjoying my party, miss?" Susannah called as she approached on her father's arm.

Her faced was flushed pink, her eyes bright with excitement. This dose of her father's full attention was having a most beneficial effect on her.

"It's a lovely party, dear," I told her.

"Thank you, miss, for giving me your carousel. I shall take special care of it."

"I know you will," I told her.

Mr. Wyndham's dark eyes had settled on my visage and his scrutiny discomfited me. "It was most kind of you," he remarked.

Susannah was fairly bouncing with excitement.

"You won't guess what Father's given me, miss. It's a horse, and she's called Aurora. Father says that I must ask you if you'll teach me to ride like a proper young lady. Will you, miss?"

What a change there had been from the dejected child I'd left this morning hiding beneath her counter-pane!

"I will certainly try my best. I'm not a riding master by any means, but with some assistance from the grooms I think we'll manage."

"Oh, thank you, miss!"

"Yes," Mr. Wyndham echoed, "thank you, Miss Dalton."

"If you please, Father, I'd like to see how they're taking care of my Aurora now."

Mr. Wyndham laughed heartily at his daughter. "Well, I usually leave the management of the stables to Mr. Donnelly, but if you'd like to check things out for yourself—"

He raised a hand to signal Donnelly, who joined us promptly. "Mr. Wyndham, sir?"

"My daughter wishes to see what, er, accommodations have been made for her new mare. If you would be so kind as to show her—"?

The burly man put out a thick hand to the child, the corners of his mouth turning up. "Come along, Miss Susannah. We've set your mare up in a proper stall, we have."

The unlikely pair walked off in the direction of the stables, and Mr. Wyndham said to me, "A few years more, and she'll be a young lady to be reckoned with."

I had to agree. What a pleasing situation this was. If Matthew Wyndham found his daughter so delightful, perhaps he would spend more time with her, and this being what Susannah needed most, she in turn would be more amenable.

"Would you dance with me, Miss Dalton?" he said then.

The musicians were playing a waltz, and I gave him my hand, allowing him to take me onto the dance floor. I followed his capable lead, very aware of the firm pressure of his hand on mine.

"I've you to thank for Susannah's progress," he said. "I'm aware of the time you devote to her."

I was hesitant to take credit for her improvement. "She's a good child on the whole, but her moods are still as changeable as the winds.''

"Mrs. Garen did mention something to me about a commotion this morning. She didn't seem to know the whole of it, though. Perhaps you would enlighten me?''

I was sorry now that I hadn't taken his compliment and gone on to another subject. "It was only something that Miss Chandler said to her," I explained.

His lips made a hard line under his moustache. "Go on," he prompted.

"It was nothing intentional," I lied. "As I've said, Susannah is still unsettled and the slightest upset—"

"Don't offer your protection where it's not deserved," Mr. Wyndham insisted.

His expression had hardened, but his hand moved over mine in such a way as to assure me that his displeasure was not directed at me.

"Now tell me what my cousin said to upset the child.''

I did not want to go on with this but I could not simply refuse to reply.

"She only made mention of your wedding plans," I said at last.

His eyes grew dark and he stopped mid-step on the dance floor.

"She had no right! The child is not ready for this. We have discussed it.''

All around us people watched their host for a hint about what was transpiring.

"Susannah will adjust, I think, if she must.''

My voice soothed him somewhat, and I urged him on in his steps before we disrupted the others. His eyes never left me as we swept across the boards. I decided that he must be memorizing my every feature or trying to read my thoughts. Nearby, seated at a small table, I saw Jason keeping company with a whiskey bottle. His eyes were not on me but on his brother, and hatred shone in them, bright and fierce.

Mr. Wyndham's arm tightened around my waist, and he pulled me nearer.

"Adrienne, if I thought—"

He stopped mid-sentence and shook his head. "The truth of it is I'm not sure myself anymore if I'm doing the right thing."

I could not acknowledge his words. I let them go as if his comment had been no more unusual than an observation about the weather. I was surprised, though, by the hesitance in him. He was always so sure of his course that I suspected he was never plagued with doubts, as we mere mortals were. He could not be, responsible as he was for the lives of so many people. I guessed then that I had seen a side of Matthew Wyndham that was seldom revealed. It reminded me, surprisingly enough, of something Jason had said earlier that day about my father: "He was only a man, and men do have their faults." And when I began to look upon Matthew Wyndham as "only a man," I was made to realize that there was much more behind his words and actions than I had been hitherto willing to admit.

The strains of the waltz died away, and Mr. Wyndham put my hand on his arm and led me out onto the lawn. I thought he would only see me to a chair, but he took us away from the crowd as if he might have a word with me alone. I was glad of the moonless night and the protection of the shadows.

"Adrienne," he began, "Rachel presumes too far on this score. Despite what she intimates, our fates are not decided, not hers nor mine . . . nor yours."

My heart fluttered in my breast. Whatever was he saying?

"This is no concern of mine, Mr. Wyndham," I insisted.

"Oh, but it is."

I hoped that he could not read my expression by the distant lamplight, for I feared that I had about me the look of a wild thing that had been ensnared.

"I dare presume that I am your friend as I was your father's," he went on.

"Why, yes, of course," I stuttered, "if it is what you wish."

He took up my hands in his. "I wish, dear Adrienne, I wish that you could find it in your heart to think of me more as your dear friend, Matthew, and less as 'Mr. Wyndham, sir.' "

The fates were with me that night and I was spared a reply by Rachel Chandler's arrival.

"So here you are, Matthew . . . and Miss Dalton. I've been meaning to compliment you on your dress, my dear. Wherever did you find it?"

"It's from Worth's in Paris."

"Mr. Charles Frederick Worth? My dear, you do surprise me. I thought it was necessary to have an introduction in order to have Mr. Worth design for you."

"That's true," I told her, "my introduction came through a member of my mother's family." I could not deny myself the opportunity to flaunt my Parisian knowledge. "He is a genius, you know, but rather imperious. He thinks of his clients as canvases and he is the great painter who creates a masterpiece upon them. You must always be pleased with his work, for he brooks no dissension."

"Who would not be pleased with a gown by Worth?"

I took in the comment pensively, thinking of how many of the things in my life I had taken for granted. If I only had them back, I would see them all in a new light: the solid security of our Boston townhouse, my shopping expeditions and evenings at the theater, the sumptuous dinner parties that were so conducive to piquant conversation, which for all its zest was of no great import. Nothing in my life had had much import, in fact, except for the upheaval that followed my father's death.

Nerves had caused my mental digression, to be sure. I did not like this position that I found myself in. Matthew had dropped my hands, at least, and was allowing himself to be mesmerized by Rachel, who was twirling a long strand of pearls around her finger.

"May I ask a favor of you, Miss Dalton?" Rachel said in a sugar-sweet voice. "We shall be spending our honeymoon in Paris next spring, and I wonder if perhaps you could write an introduction for me to Mr. Worth."

"Well—" I said, flustered, "of course, I shall write a letter for you."

In the ensuing moments Matthew's face washed of color and the dark eyes, which had been so entranced, glared at Rachel.

"You go too far," he said, his voice seething with suppressed anger. "No engagement has been announced, no plans have been made, and you have no right to speak as if a marriage between us was already decided on."

In the distance the party went on, the guests oblivious to their host's hushed words. Rachel, however, was speechless and appeared to be honestly frightened.

"I should see that Susannah is put to bed," I said awkwardly, but before I could excuse myself, Matthew's clerk, Mr. Samuels, rode across the lawn to us and leapt from his horse.

"Mr. Wyndham, sir! The *Silver Sky*'s just come in. She's been taking on water, and Captain Powell says near to half her cargo's ruined. He wants to see you right off. The supercargo is in your office now with the manifests."

Matthew turned slowly, his expression solemn. "Thank you, Samuels. Tell him I'm on my way."

He sent one of the grooms for his horse as Samuel remounted and rode off. Rachel caught his arm.

"I've sent Aaron home with the carriage. I thought you would see me home," she said.

He paused, smoothing his moustache before he met her eyes with a blank look. "You should have consulted me before making your plans. That is something you seem to have trouble remembering, isn't it? Donnelly or one of his men will take you home."

"I would be happy to see Miss Chandler home," came an offer of assistance.

It was Jason, and I noticed that although he tried to effect a flippant tone, the set of his jaw was tight and he was glowering at his brother from beneath heavy lids. Matthew did not seem to notice and only waved a hand like a magician who had performed a miraculous feat.

"There, you see, Rachel, my brother will see you home."

Without waiting for a discussion, he hurried off to where a groom held his horse. Once over her astonishment at having been passed between the brothers like a shuttlecock, Rachel fumed, tapping her foot in a frenzied rhythm on the grass. I might have found all of this rather amusing had it not been for Jason. He was obviously drunk and becoming more so as he downed the amber liquid from his glass. He had not acknowledged my presence at all, and this made me uncomfortable. With a suggestive smile, he reached for Rachel's arm.

"Shall we walk, my dear? Perhaps we can yet salvage a bit of this romantic evening."

Rachel hesitated for a moment as if she might indeed follow him into the woods, but when she realized that Matthew had quit the scene and so could not be made jealous, she threw off Jason's hand and spoke through clenched teeth.

"I should rather walk into Hell with the Devil himself!"

She stormed off in the direction of the stables, and when she was gone, Jason still would not look at me. Fury welled in him, and, raising his empty glass, he hurled it to the ground with such force that it shattered, shards flying across the grass.

10

I had decided,
even before the first hint of rosy haze appeared on the
horizon, that regardless of what I had promised Jason,
I would not go riding with him. To think of being
alone with him frightened me. He had such control
over my senses that my very reason was obscured,
and what good could come of that? Yet when the first
fingers of dawn stretched across the carpet, they
beckoned me to the window, and I responded without
hesitation. Pushing aside the draperies, I looked past
the gardens and over the stand of trees to the stables
where I could see him quite clearly, silhouetted against
the weathered boards of the main building. I could
make out the glowing tip of the cheroot he held in his
teeth as he paced before the double doors, but not his
expression. Despite his drunken scene the night
before and the fact that he had all but ignored me for
the latter half of the evening, he had remembered that
we were to ride this morning. I thought to crawl back
under the bedclothes, but I was held there, watching
the way he moved and seeing in those movements a
sense of urgency.

The firm decision I had made flipped over in my head like a tossed coin, and I went to the wardrobe for my riding habit without giving the matter further thought. I pulled out a coffee-colored skirt and tailored jacket of heavy, corded fabric, well suited for a cool morning's ride.

I could hear stirrings in the kitchen as I came down the back stairs, but I encountered no one. I had half-hoped that I might come face to face with some person who could dissuade me from my present course as my own conscience had been unable to. Surely I had convinced myself that what Jason Wyndham wanted was to strike at his brother through me. Why was I going? Curiosity was a strong force, and it compelled me out of the house and down through the gardens. All the while, a childlike voice in my head taunted, "Curiosity killed the cat! Killed the cat!" Why was I going to him?

When Jason saw me coming down the path, he threw down the stub of the cheroot and ground it into the dirt with his heel. I meant to approach him with indifference, but my pulse raced and my breathing was hard. I had fairly run out of the house, fearing he might tire of waiting for me.

"I had begun to wonder if you were coming after all."

"I wasn't," I admitted.

"Yet here you are."

I had no explanation to offer, and he did not ask for one. He turned to swing wide the stable doors.

"I'd not have blamed you," he said.

We rode across the inland fields, taking our mounts lightly over the stone fences. When he stopped along the way to point out the various landmarks, Jason seemed to grow even taller in the saddle, so filled was he with pride. He sounded, in fact, so much like Matthew when he commented on the roadway cleared by his great-uncle or the house erected by some other Wyndham relative that I had to look up to see which Wyndham brother I was listening to.

I followed his lead through the narrow forest paths back toward the coast, where finally we came upon a white clapboard cottage facing the sea at the edge of the trees. It was a modest dwelling, very common in this part of the country, with a peaked roof and twin chimneys. There were tiny-paned windows all around, framed by green shutters, and I thought it a friendly-looking house. I felt sure that we had not come upon it by accident.

"Do you like it?" Jason asked.

"It's a lovely little house," I said, but there was a note of apprehension in my voice. "Who lives here?"

Jason dismounted and came to take the reins from my hand. He tied both sets of leather straps to the bough of a tall hedge and helped me down.

"I hold the lease," he replied. "I've been trying to acquire the house and surrounding property without my brother discovering who the buyer is."

"He would not sell to you, you think?"

He smiled at me indulgently. "I know my brother. If I told him that I needed money for passage to California, he'd write me out a draught and good riddance to me. But if he were to discover that I intended to settle at Wyndcliffe permanently without relying on his good graces, I'd have one hell of a fight on my hands."

"Pardon me if I say that I understand his reasoning. You have managed to build up quite a colorful reputation in these parts."

"Ah, my dear, if half those stories were true—" His eyes twinkled with merriment, and he took my arm. "Come, I'll show you the house."

His demeanor put me momentarily at ease, and I followed him inside. When he led me into the parlor, though, I began to wonder what I was doing here and flitted about the room, first admiring the view, then running a gloved hand along the carved mantelpiece. The furniture was in hollands, and I lifted the corners to get a better look.

"I'll make some changes, of course," Jason explained in rather an anxious way, "to make things more comfortable."

He studied my reactions as we went through the rooms, upstairs and down.

"It is by no means as grand as Wyndcliffe, but one could live comfortably here," he defended, as if he sensed that I found the cottage lacking somehow.

In truth, I was only startled by his sudden interest in domesticity. When we were once again in the parlor, he threw aside the dust cloth that covered the settee and bade me sit.

"I'm going to speak to Matt about a position with the company," he said as he settled beside me. "Nothing prestigious, you understand, perhaps as a clerk. He'd not be likely to resist the chance to have me as an underling."

Bewilderment was plain on my face. "But why? Why put yourself at his mercy? You told me yourself that a deck of cards can supply you with all the money you require. You have a home at Wyndcliffe. It is as much your heritage as your brother's. Can you be happy in this house?"

He took my hands and captured my gaze. "The question is . . . can you?"

So this was it. This cottage, his sudden desire for respectability, all of it had been on my account. I could scarcely believe that I'd heard right.

"I want you for my wife, Adrienne," he said.

Even as he bent to brush his lips over mine, I knew that with things as they were, he could never be happy in this house, working as his brother's clerk.

Jason Wyndham was not a man to live by halves. Did he love me? It was not likely, I had to admit. I suspected that his hatred of Matthew filled up his heart, and so where was there room for me? To examine my own feelings was a painful exercise. While I was in his arms, the wild creature within me dashed itself against my breast, demanding to be heard, and yet I would not listen to its plaintive cry, so full of the portent of unhappiness.

I pulled away from him. The room seemed very still and the mantel clock ticked away the minutes. My hands fluttered to my face to mask the blush that stained my cheeks. "Jason, I can't think—I can't even breathe here!" I cried.

Panic seized me and suddenly I had to get away. Clambering to my feet, I fled the house. I had mounted Gypsy and was off before Jason reached the front steps. I looked back once and was struck by the patient expression he wore. He did not follow at once, for certainly he could guess where I was bound.

Both my gloved hands gripped hard on the bench as I watched a pair of gulls ascend, then swoop low over the water beyond the Widow's Walk. On the mainland in the distance, Gypsy nickered, feasting on the tender leaves of the bush where she was tethered. Jason's horse was beside her now, and I could see him approach, hands shoved deep in the pockets of his frock coat.

"Adrienne?"

He sat down beside me and cautiously took up my hands.

"I'm sorry," I told him.

"I startled you, I know," he said, "but I am a man used to going after what he wants, and, my dear, I've never wanted anything more than this."

His touch was comforting, I had to admit. "There

are so many things about you that I don't understand,
so many things that frighten me, Jason. Last night
with Rachel, you—''

"Last night I was very drunk, and taunting Rachel
was such a pleasant experience, I could not help
myself. I can assure you that I need never so much as
speak to the woman again.''

There was a palpable distaste in his voice as he
spoke of Rachel Chandler. "It is you who concerns
me, Adrienne, only you. If you need time to consider
sharing your life with me, then you shall have it, as
much time as you need, and we will not speak of this
again until you wish to.''

I smiled at his patience, and I thought that he would
take me in his arms again, but he did not.

"I'm glad you've found this bench,'' he told me. "If
you must do your musing out here on the Widow's
Walk, I'd rather you stay away from the cliff's edge.
It's far too dangerous.

"My great-grandfather put this bench out here for
his daughter,'' he went on, trying to fill up the silence.
"Her name was Diana, and she was—''

"The 'widow' of the walk,'' I finished. "I've heard
the story.'' I did not wish it repeated now,
remembering how the tale had both enthralled and
frightened Susannah.

"He could not keep her from coming to this spot,''
Jason continued, "so he put the bench here to keep
her away from the edge. It didn't work out as he'd
planned, however.''

I rose and went nearer to the precipice.

"It's not that the view is so much better here,'' I
began. "I think it's more the feeling of being on the
edge of the world, one step away from disaster, the
exhilaration of a dangerous situation.''

I stepped out still closer to the edge, looking down
on the black rocks that sliced the waves into foam and

spray. My eyes were caught by a patch of vivid green that stood out against the dark outcropping of rock below, and my heart hammered as I recalled Diana Wyndham and her fate. I looked again, expecting some natural explanation to present itself. Instead, I made out pale, white limbs twisted awry. It was indeed a human form, clad in a dress of emerald green and lying broken on the rocks. It was the color that Rachel had worn to the party the night before.

The scream that broke from my lips was wild and unearthly. I backed away from the scene, swaying dizzily. Jason caught my arms. "Adrienne, what is it?"

I managed to utter Rachel's name before clamping a hand over my mouth at the horror of the sight. Jason peered over the edge. His taut jaw was all that confirmed that he, too, had seen the body on the rocks. I was feeling the onset of vertigo, but he gripped my arms hard and shook me to clear my head.

"You must ride to Wyndcliffe and fetch Matthew. Tell him what has happened. I have to go down there."

Later, I could not recall running to Gypsy, nor riding across the lawns, so automatic had been my response. I beat upon the doors with my hands, not bothering about the knocker, until Mrs. Garen opened them and stood back, perplexed.

"Miss Dalton?"

I pushed by her and rested against the newel post at the bottom of the stairs. "Mrs. Garen, fetch Mr. Wyndham immediately, there's been an accident."

"Merciful heavens, not my baby Susannah!"

I was irritated by the woman's inertia. "No, of course not. She's still asleep in her bed. Now please hurry!"

When Matthew appeared on the landing, he was in his shirtsleeves and his waistcoat was undone from dressing hurriedly. His face was still lined with sleep, and I noticed the time on the tall case clock in the foyer. It was not yet seven.

When he had heard my story, he began to issue orders with expediency, and the first was for me. I was directed to wait for him in his study and speak to no one until he returned. I obeyed, and, once alone in that quiet room, a numbness began to creep over me as the reality of the situation presented itself. After her disagreement with Matthew, Rachel had thrown herself off of the Widow's Walk. I felt a certain remorse at having so disliked the woman who was now dead. Somehow, though, I could not reconcile myself to the fact that this Rachel who had taken her own life was the same selfish, scheming woman I had come to know.

Much later, Matthew walked into the study and past my chair almost as if I were not in the room. He sat down at his desk and dropped his head into his hands. Though I could not read his face, he was clearly distraught.

"I'm sorry about . . . your cousin," I said, so that he might be aware of my presence.

"Such a waste!" he said, eyes meeting mine at last.

His face was haggard. "Aaron's taking it badly. He's demanding an inquest. He says that she would never kill herself. Ordinarily I'd be the first to agree with him, but I treated her badly last night. I practically severed things between us. Perhaps that was enough—"

"I don't think Rachel was the kind of woman to let a few harsh words stand in the way of what she wanted," I said boldly. "It could have been an accident."

I was thinking of the times that I had been warned away from the edge of the Walk by Susannah and Jason.

"It is unlikely that Rachel would have walked out there in the dark to admire the view," he said caustically. "It wasn't in her nature to notice the landscape."

"Then perhaps Mr. Chandler is right. Perhaps someone—"

This was a theory that clearly upset Matthew more than suicide. "Who? Who would want to kill her?"

It was a question that would plague the residents of Wyndcliffe as well as the village folk for some time to come, but for now the question lay there, both of us unwilling to speculate.

"First Nora and now Rachel. What will be made of all of this?"

He was thinking aloud and making no sense.

"I'm sorry," I had to say, "but I don't see what this has to do with your late wife."

He sent me a perturbed look as if I must be simple-minded not to see the connection. After a few moment's thought, though, he apologized.

"Forgive me, you could not have known. It's been over a year, and no one speaks of it.

"My wife was a fragile woman. She wanted badly to give me a son, but after three boys all stillborn—"

"She died of complications?" I guessed.

"No. Her health was damaged, it's true, but her mind suffered far more. She was inconsolable when we buried little Edward, and a few months later, we found her dead at the bottom of the Walk. I insisted that it was an accident so that she might be buried in the family cemetery, but—"

I was speechless at the revelation. I could see now what was on his mind. Would it be thought that Matthew Wyndham had driven two women to suicide?

He had risen from his chair and now stood near mine. He perched himself on a corner of his desk and began anew.

"I understand that you have been seeing a lot of my brother."

I looked into his dark eyes for a hint of what he meant. There was no clue. "He has been kind," I replied cautiously. "We are friends."

He clasped his hands together and regarded me earnestly. "My dear Adrienne, when your father died here in my house, I made a promise to myself that I would look after his child as if she were my own. I'm certain that what I am about to say would be no less than your father's own wish were he alive.

"You are a young woman and naive, I daresay, in these matters. My brother is a dangerous man. He would not hesitate to compromise a young lady's reputation if the opportunity arose. As I am responsible for your being here and as I was your father's dear friend, I must take it upon myself to see that you are protected from harm. Therefore I must insist that you avoid any further 'friendship' with my brother, Jason."

I would have protested but I could see that Matthew had only my best interests at heart. Knowing how he felt about his brother, I could scarcely tell him that what there was between Jason and me had progressed far beyond friendship.

"I'm afraid I must have your word on this," he said, sensing my hesitancy.

What else was there for me to do? Jason had, after all, said that I might have time to consider his proposal. I would do as Matthew asked and keep my distance from Jason at least until I had reached a decision. And so I gave Matthew my word.

An investigation was indeed held into the death of Rachel Chandler. To Aaron Chandler's dismay, the jurymen reached a verdict of accident death.

There was a great deal of speculation among those

assembled for the inquest about Jason Wyndham's involvement in Rachel's "accidental death." More than one witness had overheard his altercation with Rachel on the night of Susannah's party and would vow that he had been drunk and in violent temper. The gallery grew so unruly in their speculations that the constable instructed the rabble to quiet down or he would clear the room.

Jason took in all of this impassively. I was amazed at his calm. It struck me that he was the perfect foil for his brother. It was difficult not to draw a comparison between the two men who sat near one another in the meeting room, neither acknowledging the other's presence. Here sat Matthew Wyndham, the forthright, benevolent lord of the manor, and beside him, his dissolute brother, Jason. A curious thought fought its way against my stream of conscience and surfaced. What kind of man would Matthew be if he did not have Jason to be compared to?

For all that it had the air of a three-ring circus, the inquest accomplished little. There was suspicion aplenty but not enough evidence to bring charges against Jason Wyndham for the supposed crime. It would be accurate to say that all those zealous souls present in the meeting room that day believed him surely guilty. All, that is, save one. I would never see him as others did and believed that he must be wounded by their cruel treatment. I could not have imagined that Jason expected no more from these people and, in fact, thrived on their hatred. I knew only that I felt the hurt which should have been his. I wanted to go to him and offer him comfort, but I knew that he would see it as pity. No, I could not go to Jason unless it was to give him my heart.

It was a quarter past eleven by the mantel clock in

the library. Behind the firescreen, the embers in the
grate were fast becoming ash, and the room was
chilly. I set the chamberstick down on the table and
lit the lamp. The yellow glow provided an aura of
warmth, but still I tightened the sash of my velvet
dressing gown, deciding to find a book and be on my
way back to my room where the hearth fire still
blazed cheerily. I was halfway up the ladder that
rested against the wall of books with a likely volume
in hand when the door at the far end of the room
opened. The house had been quiet and dark when I
came downstairs, save a light that shone out from
under the door of Matthew's study. Was it him?

"Jason?" I said hesitantly when I saw that I was
wrong.

He closed the door and crossed to where I was
perched still on a middle rung of the ladder.

"I saw you walking in the hall upstairs—"

"I came down for a book," I explained, holding it
up for him to see.

"I see," he said, clearing his throat, and then
regarded me earnestly. "Adrienne, we have had
barely a word between us in three weeks. There is
something in your manner, as if you've withdrawn
from me."

I did not know how to reply, but then he looked as
though he had suddenly found an answer. "It's everything they said about me at the inquest, isn't it? You
don't believe that I had anything to do with Rachel's
death? By God, I've never cared what the rest of them
thing, but you—"

He was so close, there at the foot of the ladder, and I
reached out to lay a hand on his shoulder.

"You know that I could never believe the lies. I
know you as no one else does, Jason, and you're not
what they say you are."

The words soothed him, and when his eyes met

mine, nothing more needed to be said. He lifted me from my perch down into his arms and brushed his lips against my cheek as if to test my reaction. A breath caught in my throat, and in reply, his mouth turned across mine. His kisses were fueled by an urgency that I only half understood. He ran his hands lightly over the velvet of my dressing gown and caressed the curves beneath it, free now of stays and bindings. The book in my hand slipped from my grasp to slam solidly on the carpet, but the sound could as well have come from some other room for all that I knew or cared. I knew only that I came vibrantly alive in Jason's arms. My hands slid down from around his neck and beneath his frock coat, admiring the hard muscles of his chest, my fingers tracing patterns on the smooth satin back of his waistcoat. While his hands weaved through my unbound hair, his kisses trailed down my throat to the folds of my dressing gown. It occurred to me that someone must have come in to stoke the fire, for the chill had gone out of the air. This wild thought and the sound of a very real footfall in the doorway drew me back to reality. I pulled back from Jason to see that the door, which had been shut, was now ajar. Had someone been watching us?

My face flushed at the thought of some member of the household observing us as I succumbed to Jason's passionate advances.

"We mustn't, Jason," I told him. "I've promised—"

"What is it?" he asked. He was looking into the depths of my eyes but not really listening.

"Someone was watching us just now. I'm sure of it."

He smiled at me in that wry way of his, when one corner of his mouth would turn down rather than up.

"Does it matter? If you fear for your reputation, you need only say the word and I shall announce our engagement, though I daresay such an announcement would in itself damage your good name beyond repair.''

"You overwhelm me, you know, and I still must have time to think . . . clearly," I said. "I must not see you again, Jason, until I've sorted through this muddle in my head. Good night."

I moved away quickly, afraid he might touch me again and hamper my reasoning, but he did not so much as call my name as I took leave of him. I was barely aware of passing Matthew in the hall, so preoccupied was I, though afterward I could recall that the light of the chamberstick had cast an eerie glow on his serious face, his lips pressed tightly together.

Only when I reached the second-floor landing did I realize that I had left the book behind. If I had been restless earlier, I was certainly more so now. I would not be able to sleep and needed that book for company. Surely I could face Jason once more briefly in spite of my dramatic exit. And so I returned to the library.

It was not until I laid my hand against the library door that I heard the furious argument within.

"Stay away from her, do you hear me? I won't have you drifting in and out of here on the wind and doing as you damn well please. She's not one of your Irish whores from the village to be toyed with and then tossed away when you tire of her!"

So it had been Matthew who had been watching us. I pushed the door open slightly and through the crack watched Jason settle himself in an armchair and calmly strike a match to light a long cheroot. At length, he replied. "It's not as sordid as you try to make it, Matt. I've asked Adrienne to be my wife."

"Your wife?"

Matthew's laugh was brittle but utterly cruel, and it was startling to realize how much he could sound like Jason.

''How can you possibly imagine that she would consider such a proposal? I fear, dear brother, that as always your reputation shall precede you. What woman of breeding would consider being affianced to a man whose only source of income is a pack of cards?''

''I am capable of finding suitable employment, with or without your assistance,'' Jason retorted.

''Oh without, surely. And where shall you take her to live? Some squalid room above a dockside grog shop? Or perhaps you'll find a place for her among your other women in the Bay Street whorehouse?''

Throughout the taunting harangue Matthew leaned easily against the fireplace mantel, not bothering to conceal the hatred in his dark eyes.

At the last remark, Jason rose, his every muscle taut, and faced off against his brother. He squashed his cigar into the carpet with the toe of his boot. The air was thick with venom, and I shuddered in my place behind the door. I feared they would soon come to blows, but for these two, words were far more effective than physical brutalization.

''Father was right,'' Matthew sneered. ''You're a profligate, nothing more.''

''I am what he made me!'' Jason shouted. ''Perhaps I owed it to Father to listen to his censures, but I owe you nothing. I don't look for your approval, and I can manage my own affairs well enough without your dictating to me.''

''Then I would suggest that you manage them elsewhere,'' Matthew replied, his voice even.

''Father may have given you the shipping business, the farmlands, and named you lord and master of this estate,'' came the sarcastic reply, ''but kindly remember his most generous bequest to me . . . that I shall always have a place at Wyndcliffe. Now am I to understand, dear brother, that you are evicting me from my own house?''

"Shall we just say that I strongly suggest that you go on extended holiday, preferably somewhere far away, before you get yourself into something you'll regret. I would be more than happy to finance your journey."

Matthew walked to the windows and, pushing aside the heavy draperies, looked out into the night.

"I warn you, Jason, if by some chance Miss Dalton has not heard rumors of your exploits, it can be arranged for her to discover exactly how depraved a life you have led."

"She knows," Jason responded, and I could see that the thought weighed heavily upon him. "I don't understand what your interest is in Adrienne that you should feel compelled to blackmail me," he admitted.

Matthew turned around boldly, his thumbs hooked in his waistcoat pockets. There was a glimmer in his eye that frightened me. And then Jason seemed to understand what this look implied.

"I should have seen it. You brought her here for yourself. I'm treading on Matthew's ground, aren't I? And I shan't have anything or anyone that belongs to you, shall I?"

There was such firm resolve on Matthew's face that a reply was unnecessary. He saw victory at hand. All of Jason's wildest doubts must have been whirling about his head when he saw the satisfied look on his brother's face. I could see that Jason would be defeated by his own self-doubts.

"You've had her already, haven't you?" he asked hoarsely.

Matthew regarded him without pity. "Yes, I have," he replied.

I would hear no more. I was sick and shaking with disbelief and stumbled down the hall, wishing that I were already hiding beneath my bedclothes. Oh, how had I managed to come between these two brothers and what would become of me for it?

Halfway down the long hall, my trembling worsened and the candle in my hand dropped to the carpet, rolling across the wool runner. The tongue of flame licked at the nap, which began to smolder until new flames broke out. I watched for a moment, dazed, before the smell of singed wool revived me, and I began to beat out the fire with my hand. I let out a small cry.

"There now, you've burnt your hand. Come here and let me have a look at it."

It was Aaron Chandler, standing in the doorway of Matthew's study in his shirt sleeves, wire-rimmed glasses resting on the end of his nose at an awkward angle. I must have seemed so startled by his presence that he felt the need to explain. "I was going over some contracts with Matthew. The man has no sense of time. Now let's have a look at that hand."

I let him lead me into the study without speaking a word. He saw me in the chair opposite the desk and tended to the blister that had formed on my palm. Drawing a handkerchief from his pocket, he dipped it into the water pitcher on the desk and wrung it out, carefully bandaging my hand with it.

"I won't pretend that I don't know what's upset you," he began. "I could hear them shouting from here."

He poured me a glass of dark wine from a nearby decanter, and I sipped at it timidly.

"While it is certainly none of my affair, I feel obliged to voice my concern on your behalf. This house, Miss Dalton, is a nest of vipers, and you'd be well rid of them if you left it this very evening."

He paused just long enough for me to observe the unpleasant look on his face. "I curse every drop of Wyndham blood in my veins. This family is a ruthless lot. They will use you if it suits their purpose and toss you aside when you've lost your value."

I listened to him politely, thinking what a change
had come over this heretofore meek man. "But what
value could I possibly be to them?" I asked.

Aaron sat down behind Matthew's desk, folding his
thin hands atop the jumble of papers. "What they
need most now is a son. Their father's will stipulates
that the estate shall pass to the eldest male child. You
understand primogeniture, don't you? If Matthew does
not produce a male heir, all of the Wyndcliffe
holdings pass on to Jason's son, if he should have
one."

"But I understood that Jason was disinherited—"

"His funds were cut off, that's all. If Matthew dies
with no son, Jason's child inherits the whole of it."

I shook my head to clear it. "This is all so confusing.
Why should it matter who owns what after they're
gone?"

"These two men were brought up to believe that
nothing is so important as their land. Its future must
be ensured, and they would do anything to protect it.
You see what happened to my sister and to your
father. Rachel was growing older, past her prime
child-bearing years and no longer of any use—"

The blood had drained from my face and warning
bells were clanging in my head. "What did you say
about my father?"

Suddenly I was alert and interested in his every
word, every nuance of expression. I had always
known intuitively that something was not right about
my father's death and the events that came after.
Whether Aaron had let the words slip out accidentally
or by design, he regretted it now.

"Only that he died on the Wyndham estate, that the
land is cursed."

"I don't believe that's what you meant, Mr.
Chandler. Was there something unusual in my

father's death? Tell me, please. I must know!"

"I am dependent upon the Wyndhams for my liveli-
hood, Miss Dalton, as are most of the people in these
parts. I fear I've said too much already. I only wanted
to warn you away. Of course there was nothing
unusual about your father's death. He suffered a
heart seizure. You knew that. Now please, ask no
more questions of me."

He got up and pushed the stack of papers before
him into his portfolio. "It's very late, and I believe
I've finished my work."

He slipped on his coat, adjusted his glasses, and
made his way briskly to the door. Looking at me once
more, he shook his head. I could see in his eyes that
he was honestly concerned for me. "You should
never have come here," he said and was gone.

Sleep eluded me. Jason's music, emanating from his
rooms in the east wing, was tormenting. It rose on the
air, full of fury and passion before its final explosive
crescendo. When I thought he was finished, he began
anew, but with a piece that was so intense, so moving
that it could only have been his own composition. He
could not hide himself within the bounds of his
music. Each note bared yet another piece of his soul. I
knew then that I had been avoiding the truth all
along. I was in love with Jason Wyndham. It mattered
not what he had been or done, nor what others
thought of him, only that I would be desolate without
him.

I would have gone to him then, but for the memory
of the look on his face when Matthew had confirmed
his worst fears with that blatant lie about a liaison
with me. It was an awful inference, but certainly
Matthew sought only to protect me. He warned me
that he would do so. What hurt me more was that
Jason believed him, did not even question him,

almost as though he wanted to believe. In those blue eyes had been the fatal look of utter disillusionment, and I could not forget it. I knew somehow that even a profession of my love would not be enough to allay his doubts. Jason's hatred of his brother was too strong a thing. I wanted to believe that he loved me, though he had never said the words. Perhaps, I told myself more realistically, I was only the latest prize in the brothers' lifelong competition.

I paced the carpet before the french windows and then threw them open as if the bitter autumn wind might stir my hopes to life as it did the glowing embers in the hearth. I stepped out onto the balcony, and my nightgown whipped at my ankles. I was not aware of the cold. This night I had given up my heart. There was a far more bitter cold and emptiness within.

11

In the fitful dreams
that came to me that night, I was visited by the ghost
of my father. It was a pale, somber version of himself,
shrouded in mist and given to shaking its head sadly
and muttering, not at all the vibrant man my father
had been. Before the wraith receded into the swirling
mists, it spoke to me in a tenuous voice. "It was for
you, all for you."

I awoke with a start, my body damp with perspiration. It had been such a real thing that I had to strain
my eyes in the darkness, searching the shadowy
corners of the room to be sure that it did not remain
somewhere about. When I had been awake for a few
minutes and had a better grasp on reality, I told
myself that such a dream was not surprising. The
encounter with Aaron Chandler and his mention of
my father had triggered it, of course.

Memory of that vivid dream kept my father in my
thoughts throughout the following day. I needed his
counsel more now than ever. In the hours just before
dusk, I found time to go up to the third-floor room
that had been his. It was emptier than when I had

been there before, as I had instructed Mrs. Garen to
box all that remained of his things and send them to
Reverend Mallory to give to the poor. It seemed less
his room now, but surely a vestige of his spirit
remained within these walls where he had breathed
his last. So I sat down at his writing desk and spoke to
him. I opened my heart as I had never been able to do
when he was alive and told him of my fears: of the
untenable situation that existed between the brothers
Wyndham and myself, of the child Susannah, who
grew more dependent upon me as the days passed. I
was only a child myself, I insisted, and needed my
papa here to make my decisions for me. I stayed there
until the shadows swallowed me up, waiting in the
stillness for him to answer, for a ghostly touch on my
arm, but in vain. All that was left of Ben Dalton at
Wyndcliffe, it seemed, were his daughter's memories
and the brass ring.

It was not a particularly important occurrence
when compared with the turmoil in my life, but two
days later when the clasp on my necklace broke, I felt
I was losing yet another piece of my father. I had
promised to wear the unusual ring always as a
reminder of his devotion, and it was a promise I
would keep. So I borrowed Gypsy from the stables
and rode into the village in search of a jeweler.

From the cuff of my riding glove I pulled the slip of
paper on which Mrs. Garen had written the name of
the shop and compared it to a wooden sign swinging
over a door up the street, "Gustav & Son, Purveyors
of Fine Jewelery & Clocks," and below this in smaller
letters, "Watches Repaired."

I returned the paper to its place and dismounted,
tying Gypsy to the post. Though I had no other
engagements, I hurried down the plank walk, for I
could not feel secure until the ring was on its chain at
my throat.

A bell tinkled overhead as I pushed open the door. I walked up to the display case in the center of the room and peered in at the rather modest selection. On a side wall was the selection of clocks, of varying types and sizes, all ticking discordantly and each pendulum seeming to swing at its own rate. It had an unsettling effect on me.

"Excuse me?" I called, hoping to attract the attention of an elderly man at the back of the shop, bent over a table littered with springs and gears, tweezers and files.

"Excuse me. Are you Mr. Gustav?"

When he looked up at me it was in a startled way, as if I were a wraith who had come out of the air.

"Sorry, miss. Lost in my work, I was. Yes, I'm Gustav."

He was white-headed and stoop-shouldered, the latter an attribute of his profession as much as his age. He came to stand across the display case from me and spread his hands to indicate the breadth of the selection.

"What can I do for you today, miss? A locket perhaps, or some fancy earbobs?"

"No," I replied, opening the drawstrings of my reticule and pulling out a folded handkerchief. "I have a chain that needs repair. The clasp is broken."

I laid the handkerchief on the case and carefully unwrapped the brass ring on its necklace chain. He held it up and studied it, a puzzled look on his deeply etched face. The reaction made me wonder.

"You do repair jewelry?" I asked.

"Aye. I can have it fixed for you straightaway."

I was relieved. "Thank you so much. It's not an expensive piece, but it has sentimental value."

Mr. Gustav was soon back at his work table, opening a tiny drawer in his parts cabinet. His hands were steady as he looked through the jeweler's glass and deftly tended his business. "I've seen this ring before," he said.

I arched a brow. "You have?"

He nodded but did not look up from his work.

"I sold it to a gentleman some months ago. Engraved those roses on it myself, I'd not likely forget."

"It was a gift from my father."

"So he was your papa, was he? He must prize you dearly to give such thought to your gift. It had to be a brass ring, he said, though I can scarce imagine why, and he wanted the Wyndham roses engraved on it."

"The Wyndham roses?"

"Aye. They're a part of the family crest brought over from England. All the Wyndham ships fly the crimson roses to identify them."

"I see," I said though I did not. Had my father meant the ring as some sort of message?

"He was nervous as a cat, and in some rush, I can tell you, miss. He insisted that the work be done that very day and then asked me to post it to Boston. Struck me as kind of queer, that. You ought to make him slow down and take better care of himself."

I looked down at my gloved hands resting on the case, fingers locked together. "Papa died only a few days after the ring was posted."

"I'm sorry for your loss. I see why this means so much to you."

He reached out to hook it around my neck.

"There now. It was only a faulty catch. Lucky thing you didn't lose it. But you'll have no more trouble with it."

I touched the spot where it lay and breathed easier, though my mind was now full of unanswered questions.

"Thank you, sir," I said. "How much—?"

The old man shook his head fervently. "Oh no, miss. I wouldn't think of charging you for the repair."

"You're a kind man, Mr. Gustav, and if I'm ever in need of a locket or some 'earbobs' I shall know where to come."

"Aye, indeed."

I walked out of the shop rather blindly, immersed in my own muddled thoughts. I wondered anew about this last gift from my father. What was the significance of the brass ring and why must it wear the Wyndham mark?

I set a swift pace in the direction of my tethered horse, the heels of my riding boots sharply marking my steps on the planking. So preoccupied was I with my thoughts that I very nearly ran headlong into a gentleman. He touched my arm to steady me and I glanced up at him. It was Jason.

He looked down on me, his sharp eyes revealing nothing. He seemed particularly interested in my mauve riding habit and the smart little hat with the veiling.

"Very chic, my dear," he said, "you have a knack for pleasing a gentleman's eye."

His voice was utterly cold and double-edged. There was an uncomfortable pause before I realized that the last time I'd worn this habit was to go riding with Matthew and it must have been Jason's laughter I had heard as he looked down on us that day. Now that innocent scene must have taken on a new meaning for Jason. What must he be thinking?

"I was at the jeweler," I said quickly, "to have my necklace repaired."

He said nothing but picked up the brass ring from where it lay against my skin and turned it over with his fingers. After examining it, he did not let it drop but pulled the chain taut until it cut into the soft skin of my neck. He meant to hurt me.

My voice came out thin and strained. "The jeweler said the roses are the Wyndham mark."

He dropped the necklace and drew something from his waistcoat pocket, comparing it to the design on the brass ring. It was a signet ring with a crest containing the twin roses. He rubbed his hand over it as if to erase the crescented cadency mark that identified him as a second son and pocketed the ring again.

"So it is the Wyndham mark," I said.

"I'm surprised you haven't noticed it before. My brother marks everything he owns."

His words were sharp, and I reacted as if I had been struck, my eyes smarting with tears. "What can you mean?"

"It's all too clear, my dear. My brother has laid his claim to you. It is a lovely trinket, but then I suppose you've earned it."

He turned away, but I laid my hand on his arm. He stiffened at my touch. "Jason, please don't do this. You don't understand, not any of it. We have to talk."

"We've nothing to say to one another," he snarled and stepped into the street just before a heavily laden dray rolled by to separate us.

I watched him change direction and head down toward the docks, where no doubt he would look for solace in the bottom of a glass.

It was a moonless night but there was a comfort in the velvet shadows, in the lull of the advancing tide and the chirping crickets. A cold wind blew in off the water and ruffled the loose tendrils of my plaited hair, causing me to draw my paisley shawl closer around my shoulders. I was all but invisible to anyone who should venture into the garden that night, sitting there on the bench in my gray merino, a prim dress with lace collar and mother-of-pearl buttons. It seemed that at last I was beginning to look my part as governess. I sat very still, but it was a deceptive stillness, belying the turmoil of my thoughts.

I had ridden Gypsy hard this afternoon as I
returned from the village. Through the fields, I'd
recklessly taken the mare over any obstacles we
encountered and half-hoped that I might be thrown. A
broken neck would at least bring sweet peace of
mind. A long evening of contemplation had brought
me no closer to a resolution of my problems. The
brass ring remained another of Papa's riddles. He had
been so fond of games. I felt myself simple-minded as
if I were seeing yet not seeing, as if something were
missing still.

But it was not the ring that brought me out here so
late in the evening. I should go in. I should forget him.
Jason Wyndham was a thoughtless, cruel man who
reveled in tormenting me, and yet for God knows
what reason I loved him, and that love was a strong
thing. Try as I might, I could not forget the man he'd
allowed me to believe that he was. He needed me as
much as I needed him. My memory replayed again
and again the moments we'd spent together, the
tenderness as well as the invigoration of our clashes. I
had to wait for him now and make him hear me. I
could see that he was set on a course of self-destruc-
tion, and I knew that I could help him if only he
would trust me, believe in me.

I was a long time waiting, and it was only when I
had decided that he would not return home tonight
that I heard a horse below at the stables. It was a few
minutes more before his tall figure appeared on the
garden path. I stepped out of the shadows as he
approached.

"Jason, you must let me speak with you." My voice
was full of resolve as I faced him. "You owe me at
least that much."

He staggered toward me and very nearly tripped
over his own feet. "Well," he drawled, "this is a
delightful surprise."

I felt a tingle of apprehension when I heard his slurred voice and saw the hard glint in his eye.

"Out for an evening stroll and whom should I encounter but my brother's charming young protégée. Surely he has warned you against walking alone after dark. There could be any number of scurrilous creatures such as myself lurking in the shrubbery."

He gestured toward the hedgerow. His smile was crooked and the flourish of his hand too broad. He was drunk, and any hope I had of reasoning with him evaporated.

"Perhaps we should talk another time—"

I tried to take my leave but he barred my way with his body, and I shrank back, afraid of the hard look he sent me.

"So you've come to speak with me? I think you must be mistaken. Surely your midnight tryst is with my brother."

I did not like what drink had done to him. Though he weaved on his feet, there was by no means a slackening of his strength. I sensed something animalistic in his movements, as if he were stalking me. I stepped again to pass, and he caught my arms roughly, pinning them at my sides.

"Since you've come, I think I'd like you to stay."

He would not release me, and my arms ached in his grip. "Please, Jason, you're hurting me."

He sneered and moved a long arm around my waist, pulling me to him. With his free hand, he touched my hair, pulling out the pins and combing out the plaiting with his fingers. I waited, not daring to breathe, and hoped that he would give up this game and release me. I hated myself for responding to his touch. He kissed my hair and whispered hoarsely in my ear.

"God, but you're beautiful, too beautiful for him!"

The whiskey on his breath was overpowering, and I

turned my head away, which only made him angrily grab my face in his hand, his fingers bruising the flesh as he turned me to face him again. He crushed my lips beneath his, taking my breath away. His ferocity alarmed me, and when he drew his mouth away, I let out a frightened cry.

"What's the matter?" he snarled. "Is my lovemaking not as gentle as my brother's? How would he feel, I wonder, if I were to damage his goods? Surely he couldn't mind. The merchandise is used, after all."

I was trembling and telling myself that this was not the man I loved but someone else who had taken his form.

"Jason," I pleaded, "please let me go. You're drunk."

I could not look into his eyes, so full of hatred.

"Do I disgust you, my dear?"

My head dropped down, and he lifted my chin so I was made to look into those unforgiving eyes. I shut my own against what I read there. He toyed with the tiny buttons of my bodice for a long while and then in one swift movement tore away half of them with his hand, sending them bouncing on the flagstones. He bent to kiss my skin and I writhed against him. To my surprise, I succeeded in breaking free. I ran, without direction, through the maze of flagstone garden paths, my breath coming in hard sobs, and did not look back until I had reached the low brick wall at the far end of the garden. Beyond this the ground dropped away to the stables at the bottom of the hill. I turned, and he was there behind me.

"Adrienne!"

It was an anguished cry, and as he fell to his knees, I held out a hand and moved toward him, instinct telling me to comfort him despite what had passed between us. But before I could reach him, he struggled to his feet. Savage fury renewed his strength.

"You're like all the rest of them, fancier packaging, perhaps, but a whore just the same! I wouldn't be so repulsive if I were the one with the inheritance, would I?"

He waited for me to reply but I could not. Despair overwhelmed me.

"Say it . . . that you only want Matt because of the money. Say it, damn you!"

"No," I said firmly, summoning all of my courage to meet his eyes, "none of it is true. I want only you, Jason, whether you will believe me or not."

"Liar!"

It must have seemed so easy, in his drunken haze, to silence my lies. He threw out his arm and slapped my face with the back of his hand. So easily done, but he could not have bargained on what happened next. I lost my balance as he struck me and, being back up against the low retaining wall, I fell backward over the embankment.

I was not sure at first of the reality of the situation as I rolled down the hill, tossed like a rag doll. There were alternately flashes of light and sharp pains, which eased only when I lay at last at the bottom of the hill in a tangled heap of petticoats, near the stand of trees that sheltered the stableyard. The stars spun crazily in the night sky, and I dared not move lest the pains return, so I lay still and listened to the rasp of my own breathing. And soon Jason was there. Fear had cut through the fog that alcohol had created in his mind, and he was sober now. He put an ear to my chest, then brushed the tangle of hair away from my face. I closed my eyes against him, still afraid.

"I won't hurt you," he told me. "I never meant to."

He gently touched the place where he had struck me. The jaw was swollen now. He pulled a handkerchief from his pocket and pressed it against a cut over my brow to stem the warm flow of blood. I felt as though I were apart from the scene, watching him tend me, his own brow twisted in pain.

"I love you, Jason," I said.

Still on his knees, he scooped me up into his arms and buried his face in my bosom, sobbing.

"Dear God, what have I done? What have I done?"

There was a commotion in the stableyard but it seemed far away and then a voice cut the air.

"Good Lord, man! What's going on here?"

It was Matthew. Jason settled me back onto the grass and turned just in time to catch Matthew's riding crop as it was brought down across his back. He pulled it roughly out of his brother's hand and tossed it aside, but before he could rise, Matthew, who was smaller though powerfully built, brought a fist up under his chin, sending him sprawling. I wanted to cry out but only a strangled sob escaped. A sharp pain in my side stabbed with every breath.

Matthew bent down beside me and began to speak to me soothingly while he felt my limbs for broken bones.

"You'll be all right, Adrienne. Are you in much pain?"

I shook my head dully, and he drew a clasp knife from his pocket. "I'm going to cut your corset laces so you can breathe more easily."

He hesitated when he saw my torn bodice and sent an ominous look Jason's way before returning to his ministrations. When he had cut through my lacings, the stays eased apart and I thought that a sharp knife was turning inside me. I shrieked in pain. From his place on the grass, Jason groaned, his fists clenched hard against his temples.

Matthew turned on him. "Get out of here, do you hear me? I want you out of my house and off my land.

There's enough of your handiwork here to have you in jail for a good long time, and I swear to God that I'll call the law myself if you aren't on a steamer in the morning!''

Jason took his time in rising and dusted himself off.

''I'll leave but not until Dr. Fletcher sees to Adrienne.''

''I'll take care of Adrienne.''

''It seems you've already taken—'' Jason shot back.

Matthew sent a poisonous look up at him. ''I'd not take a lady without the benefit of marriage, nor would I maul any woman in the brutal manner that you have treated this child.''

He bent down again and lifted me into his arms. My strength was waning and my head lagged against his chest. I could see, though, that Jason was fighting against his torpid brain as he tried to understand his brother's words.

''But you told me you had—''

''You gullible fool! I'd have said anything to keep you away from her.''

With that, Matthew turned and, cradling me in his arms, headed up to the house. I looked back as Jason went to the place where I had lain and knelt down, touching the matted grass. He turned over his hand. It was smeared with blood. His head drooped below his shoulders then and he wept like a child. He had trusted where he should have been doubtful and doubted where he should have believed.

I adjusted the pillows propped up behind me and settled into them, sighing. My breathing was hampered by the tightly wrapped bandage protecting the two ribs I had cracked in the fall. It was no worse than a well-laced corset, but then I did not wear my corset to bed. My head ached and throbbed alternately, and I stared for a long while at the tall, brown-glass bottle of laudanum that Dr. Fletcher had left on the table for me. At last, though, the pressure over my brow relented.

"Evening, miss." Brenna entered with a tray in her arms. "Here's your tea."

Two paces behind her came Susannah, offering a plate of biscuits and strawberry preserves.

"How are you, miss? I thought you might be hungry," she said.

She gave over the plate to Brenna, who was now arranging the tea things on the bedtable, and produced a leatherbound novel, which she handed to me.

"Papa said to bring you this to pass the time."

It was a Jane Austen story—nothing there to disturb the peace of my convalescence. I thanked her.

"I am too pampered," I said. "You shall make me fat and lazy."

"Oh no, miss. We want you to be happy here, and you must get well so I may have my riding lessons."

"I see," I replied, amused.

The child ran off to her own bed, and after stoking the fire in the grate, Brenna said good night as well. I did not want to be alone with my thoughts, though. Questions kept turning over in my mind no matter what I might do to blot them out. They had kept me awake all of last night after the doctor had left me and they plagued me still as I languished in bed all of the day. Why did he—? How could he—? What would become of the both of us now? Logic would not serve me. Logic told me to despise him for his mistrust, his violence, his weakness.

"Can you sit with me awhile, Brenna?" I asked before the door closed.

She peered in around the door, her ruddy complexion sallow in the lamplight. "I'd like to, miss, surely I would, but I have to fetch hot water for

Missus Felicia's bath and then I'm to close up the east wing rooms.''

"The east wing? But those are Jason's—Mr. Wyndham's rooms.''

"Yes, miss. He's leavin' us, and none sad to see him go, I might say. I reckon the mister gave him his walkin' papers after that business with poor Miss Chandler. Everybody knows he done her in.''

I was upright in the bed, a blank stare masking the panic that had overtaken me.

"When, Brenna? When is he leaving?''

"Don't know, miss. Later tonight or tomorrow, most likely. Now you be sure and drink that tea while it's hot.''

"Yes, yes. . . . Good night.''

When the door closed behind her, I threw off the bedclothes and painfully struggled to stand on my own. My muscles were stiff but I ignored them and moved swiftly on bare feet out of the room and through the hall into the darkened east wing. My eyes were accustomed to the dimness by the time I reached Jason's room. There was no fire in the grate, no sheet music on the piano, no trace of him. It was as though he had never been there. I crossed to the tall windows of the tower and pressed my face against the glass. I watched the waves tossed crazily by the wind. Cold drops of rain collected on the outside of the pane, and my warmth fogged the glass. I wiped it away with my hand and saw movement below on the stable path. My eyes strained to make out a tall figure, carrying a portmanteau. Jason!

Without thought or heed to the pain in my body, for the pain in my heart was worse by far, I hurried to my room for my heavy cloak and threw it over my nightgown, running barefoot out into the night.

The rain had slowed to a heavy mist when I caught up to Jason in the stableyard. I called his name twice, and when he turned, I thought I had been mistaken, for he seemed a hard, grim stranger in his slouch hat and gutta-percha cape, the stubble of a beard shadowing his face. At the sight of me, he dropped his bag at his side and we shared a long look.

"Adrienne, you shouldn't be out of bed nor in this rain."

I went to him. The stableyard was a mire from the rain, and the mud was slick and cold between my toes. My sides ached as my lungs strained against the bandage for breath.

"How can you come to me after what I've done?" he asked.

"How can I stay away when it seems you will leave me without a word?"

His fists clenched at his sides. "What words could I have for you? There is no excuse, no explanation. I am what I am."

I stepped closer to stand before him. It was still a comfort to be near him. As I looked up to meet his glazed eyes, my hood dropped back, revealing the bandage wrapped around my brow. He turned away.

"What I have become disgusts me more than you can know."

I laid a hand lightly on his arm. "Jason, please don't. I overheard your argument with Matthew that night in the library. I know what he led you to believe. It was an awful lie, but you must understand that he was only trying to protect me. I don't need protection from you, though, and I shall tell him so myself if you will only come back with me now."

He looked away so as not to be swayed by the pleading look I sent him.

"I cannot. Matt was right to be protective of you where I am concerned. I have deceived you, made you believe that I am something I am not."

My voice was cool and even. "I know what you are.

Who knows better than I?"

I slipped my arms around his waist and laid my face against the slick surface of his cape. He responded instinctively, holding me to him. The air was full of my lavender scent, blending now with that of damp earth and salt air. He caressed me, but when his hands felt the rough bandage beneath my nightgown, it was as though he had touched fire, so quickly did he release me and back away. He had been able to forget for a brief moment all that stood between us, but now it came back to him. His face twisted into an ugly sneer.

"Do you know me, really? Do you know, for example, that I gamble not so much for the money as the amusement? I take money from men who can ill afford it and laugh at their foolishness. I drink until every face I see is hideously distorted. And women? Oh yes, my dear, I have had more than you or I could count, used them and they me, and all this without a shred of Christian remorse. I *am* the devil they say I am. I am not the man you want, and what need have I for such a child as you?"

I looked up at him with hard eyes. "Damn your soul, Jason Wyndham! I know what you're about. Don't think for a moment that I don't. I'll love you no matter what the cost."

A long silence ensued as I held his blue eyes with my own pale ones, daring him to dispute me.

"You are a fool then, for I'm not worthy of such sentiment." His words were full of contempt.

Jason had a lifetime's experience of hiding his emotions to draw on, and it held him in good stead now. His eyes were dark and opaque beneath the brim of his slouch hat, and the distance he'd put between us caused more pain than the dull throbbing in my head or the ache of my torpid muscles. My breath began to come in short gasps. I could stand no more.

"Then I shall live and die a fool! Constancy is all that I have to offer you, and you shall have it, like it or not. I don't care a whit for your brother's high-minded principles nor those of the gossip-mongers who slander you. You are no more evil than any other man, and you needn't lead your life to please any of them. If you must go, then take me with you."

"You don't mean that," he told me, "it's only the spoiled little girl talking who can't abide not having what she thinks she wants."

"I do mean it. You asked me once to be your wife, and I did not give you an answer. You have my answer now, Jason. Take me with you."

He shook his head. "It's too late. I can't deceive myself after last night. If I stayed here, I would only hurt you in the end, perhaps worse than I have already, and if you came with me you'd fare no better."

There was hope in me yet, and to crush it, he took a new tack. "What do you suppose would become of Susannah if she woke to find you gone? She has attached herself to you in the same way she was attached to her mother. She depends upon you, Adrienne."

I thought about what he said and knew that he was right. In my determination to make friends with Susannah, I had lost sight of the fact that what the child really needed was to be encouraged to be independent. Now I felt trapped by Susannah's needs and I had only my own selfishness to blame.

Jason could see by my stricken look that he had convinced me and so went into the stable to lead out Cerberus. I was still in the stableyard when he came out. The rain had begun in earnest and drenched me, though I was oblivious to it.

"Without you here, this house will swallow me up, and I shall become a part of the furnishings," I said, sounding like a lost child.

"You shall never be that," he said and bent down to retrieve his portmanteau, strapping it on behind his saddle before he faced me anew. "You may not have realized it yet, but Matt did not bring you here as a governess. He needs a wife, and you fit the bill."

He checked the saddle girth and stirrups and, as if it were an afterthought, turned back to me.

"You will be better off with him."

I shook my head fiercely. Though I needed all of my strength now, I could not check the hot tears that spilled forth and trailed into the cold raindrops collecting on my face. "I shall wait for you," I insisted. "You'll be back one day."

"No, Adrienne. Go home to Matt. In a few months' time you'll forget me. Matt will ask for you, and he will be the husband your father would have wanted for you."

I knew that in only a moment he would leave me, and there was nothing I could do to stop him.

"No!" I wailed and threw myself into his arms.

"Adrienne," he whispered, his long fingers reaching up to play lightly across the planes of my face and wipe away the droplets of rain mixed with tears. "I swear I never meant to hurt you."

He brushed a chaste kiss against my bandaged brow, but I drew him down to me until I could feel the warmth of his breath on my parted lips. I was desperate to capture and hold some part of him with one last kiss. Jason drew a long, uneven breath, his chest vibrating with emotion, and gave way at last. When his mouth turned across mine, it was hard and demanding, and I responded willingly. Lost in the moment, we touched and tasted, oblivious to the storm that raged around us and Cerberus restlessly stamping the ground nearby. I pressed closer to him, shamelessly using my body to keep him from his purpose. Need of him was so strong in me that I believed there was nothing I wouldn't do to make him stay. But I only enjoyed the comfort of his embrace for a few seconds more before he drew away. I let out a small cry, and he put his fingers to my lips. Disentangling himself, he stepped back. There was a twist of pain in his expression.

"Not another word. Allow me one noble gesture, Adrienne."

He swung into the saddle and looked down where I stood, fearfully still. "Goodbye," he said.

I would not reply.

12

It was a somber young woman who opened out the french windows to brace the winter morning's chill. A mourning dove somewhere deep in the evergreen copse gave out its melancholy call, echoing my lament. My eyes traced a pattern across the horizon where gray sky met gray water and then along the road approaching the house. In a moment, the ritual was ended. I shivered and went in, shutting the doors firmly behind me. I unfastened the buttons of my riding jacket and sat down at the empty dining table to warm my hands over a steaming cup of tea. Jason had been gone for more than a year, yet each morning I would still go out, expecting to see him riding up the drive. Not once did I consider that he might be gone out of my life forever. I could not. I lived a life in suspension, and surely those around me were aware of the change. I moved through the empty days like a sleepwalker. At first I had met Matthew's attempts to cheer me with an unfriendly air, determined to make him the recipient of my bitterness, but I could not long harbor rancor for one who only meant me well. If he had not known what there had been between Jason and me

before this, surely he knew now, and still he was
patient with me and kind. And whether I wanted to or
not, I was healing.

The double doors opened, and Felicia Wyndham
came in. Without a word, she filled her plate from the
sideboard and sat down in the chair that put the most
distance between us. Finally she deigned to address
me.

"Where is my granddaughter this morning, Miss
Dalton?" she asked, without taking her eyes from her
plate.

"We're riding this morning," I explained.
"Brenna's taken her up to fetch her boots."

She spread a generous dollop of marmalade on her
toast and sliced the ham on her plate into neat
morsels.

"Surely you are capable of assisting the child
without bothering Mrs. Garen's girls. If they've not
enough work of their own, I must consider letting one
of them go."

"If you are displeased, I shall see to Susannah
myself from now on," I said quickly and pushed
myself away from the table.

Felicia would have no qualms about dismissing one
of the maids on a whim, I knew that. I was anxious to
quit the room at once, for lately I had not had the
strength to parry her gibes, but before I could reach
the doors she called after me.

"And Miss Dalton, unless we feel that Susannah is
in need of supervision at table, I think it would be
more seemly for you to take your meals in the
nursery."

I studied the carpet wearily. "Yes, ma'am."

When I opened out the doors I very nearly walked
into Matthew. His face was dark with rage.

"Madam!"

I melted back against the paneled wall as he
stormed in. I had never before seen him so incensed.

His shout so startled Felicia that she dropped her
china cup, spilling its contents across the table. She
feigned an impassive air and sopped up the liquid
with her napkin.

"You will apologize to Miss Dalton immediately!"

The woman looked up, her face registering
innocent surprise. "Whatever can you mean?"

"Don't play me for a fool, madam. It seems I must
ever be reminding you who is running this household.
How dare you countermand my orders?"

"Your . . . orders?" she stammered.

He placed both hands flat on the table and leaned
toward her.

"Yes. Miss Dalton is a guest in this house, not some
scullery maid that you may bully about. Her father
was my friend, and I can do no less than offer her the
hospitality of my home. He'd have done the same for
my child."

"You'd not have squandered a fortune at the
gaming tables," Felicia retorted, her voice only a
whisper.

At this, I caught my breath, wondering where she
had gotten her information. Matthew pointed an
accusing finger her way. "That will be quite enough
or, by God, I'll see you installed in some meager
cottage at the far end of the grounds! Perhaps you had
best take your meal in your room this morning," he
added sharply.

She rose, not for a moment losing her dignity.

"I'm not feeling well, as it happens."

She swept out of the room without a second look to
either Matthew or me. I did not feel at all pleased
with this victory. Matthew turned to me and, taking
me by the hands, expelled a heavy sigh.

"How can I ask your forgiveness?"

"This is all my fault," I replied uncomfortably.

"Nonsense. I've allowed my stepmother too much
freedom. She imagines herself mistress of this house

still, but this time she's gone too far.

"My dear, you're trembling," he noticed and folded his arms around me. "If she distresses you, I'll send her away. I swear that I will."

"No," I said quickly and looked up at his face. What was it I saw in his eyes? Curiosity outweighed caution then and I spoke without thinking. "What is it you want of me, Mr. Wyndham?"

"Have you not guessed?"

"Here we are, miss."

It was Brenna come back with Susannah and both not sure what they were seeing. I pulled back abruptly.

"Good morning, Father," Susannah called.

"Good morning," he answered absently and then turned to Brenna. "When you've finished here, bring me a pot of coffee. I'll be in my study with Mr. Chandler."

He went out, leaving three confused souls in his wake.

In a year's time, Susannah had proved to be quite the equestrienne. What had begun as a series of circles around the paddock on leading reins had now progressed to rides across the countryside that lasted most of the morning. Such was this morning's ride, and we did not return to the stables until it was time for the midday meal. I sent Susannah up to the house while I waited for the groom who was to see to our horses.

The stablehands were usually prompt, and so after I had waited several minutes, I tied the reins to the paddock gate and decided to investigate, leaving the horses to stamp the hard ground restlessly, snorting clouds of steam into the chill air. As I swung open the stable door, my nostrils were assailed with the pungent odor of hay and manure. I called out, but there was no one about, neither in the loft nor in the tack room. I went out to the shed, a tiny wooden structure adjacent the main stable which housed tools and gardening implements.

"Is anyone here?" I called.

I stepped inside but could see no one in the shadows. Where had the grooms gone off to? Before I could turn around to come out, I was shoved hard from behind. I pitched forward into blackness.

I struck my head on something, and when finally I regained my senses, I was lying with my face resting on the dirt floor of the shed. I picked myself up, dusting off my skirts, and began to choke on the thick smoke that pervaded the air. The shed was afire!

Pushing against the door, I found that it would not open. What came instantly to mind was the occasion when Susannah had shut me up in the mausoleum. I thought that I had since earned the child's trust, but I knew now that it was not so. I looked behind me. Flames licked upward at the old dry boards, and black smoke churned around the tiny shed. This was no prank.

"Susannah, Susannah, let me out!"

I beat on the door with my fists. The wood splintered beneath my hands, piercing through my gloves, but there was no response. I stumbled toward a slant of light between the upright boards. Pushing my fingertips through, I tried to pry the planks apart. I peered through the crack and while my eyes watered against the smoky haze, I saw the blur of a figure running toward the house.

"Wait, come back!"

I drew in my skirts to keep them from the sparks that the fire had begun to spit forth with popping sounds. Turning away from the flames, I drew a ragged breath. The walls were closing in around me, soon there would not be enough air. Vertigo was upon me, paralyzing me, and I began to whimper as the waves of heat caressed my face. Surely I would die here, this shed my funeral pyre.

But I could not resign myself to such a fate. Desperate now, my mind raced. There must be an axe in this shed, I thought, but I came first upon a spade, which I used as a lever on the door. Pushing on the long handle with all the strength I could muster, I felt the splinter of wood as two planks gave way. I hacked feverishly at a third with the head of the spade, fear supplying my strength, and when the opening was large enough, I squeezed out, stumbling to collapse on the grass.

My lungs filled with clean, salt air, and the cottony clouds above me whirled round and round. When I could, I sat up, coughing to get rid of the awful acrid taste of the smoke.

At long last the stablehands came running and Mr. Donnelly as well. He gave them orders for extinguishing the fire and then questioned me.

"What happened, miss?"

"Someone shoved me in and jammed the door shut," I said.

Though I had made up my mind that that someone was Susannah, I decided not to implicate her until I could speak with her.

"There is a stake shoved through the latch," he observed.

The men's greatest fear was that the stables might catch a spark, but the same good fortune that had seen to my escape prevailed. The winds died and the men soon had the fire put out, dousing the charred boards with buckets of water. The shed looked much less ominous now. The back wall was a few blackened sticks of lumber with a gaping hole, and the door was destroyed, but an afternoon's work would see it repaired.

"Must've been horse thieves," Mr. Donnelly

decided. "We've got a fine lot of horseflesh in these
stables. Half our boys was at dinner and the others
went off to help some old man whose wagon turned
over out on the North Road. Might not have been an
accident, that. Perfect time for thieves to come upon
us. Sure am sorry about this, miss, but 'tis lucky
something scared them away before they could make
off with the stock. Aye, and you might have been
burnt to a cinder in the bargain."

It was sound reasoning on his part, but I knew that
he was mistaken. The figure I had seen through the
crack in the shed had been running toward the house,
not away from it. It must have been Susannah, who
else could it have been?

I slipped out of my jacket to find that even the
blouse beneath was grimy. Lifting the ewer from its
shelf, I poured a generous amount of water into a
washbasin. It was cool and soothed my skin. I
lathered and scrubbed with a cake of scented soap,
though nothing less than a long, hot bath would
remove the smell of burnt wood that clung to my
skin.

While I brushed my hair, I wondered how to
confront Susannah. I had been convinced that she
was much improved. Lately, in fact, she had begun to
cling to me almost as if she were my own child. How
then could she do such a thing? I had to make her see
that this was no mere prank. I could have been killed.

There was an urgent knock at the door.

"Come in," I called, still pulling the brush through
my hair.

I was surprised to see Matthew standing in the
doorway. Flustered, I dropped the brush on the
vanity and rose to meet him.

"Shall I send for Dr. Fletcher?" he asked, concern
plain on his face.

"Not unless he can recommend a laundress," I replied.

This brought a smile to his lips. "I've asked Mrs. Garen to have some water heated for a bath. Are you sure you're unharmed?"

"I'm fine, truly, though I will admit to being scared witless, and I must smell as if I've taken a roll on the hearth."

"I've spoken with Donnelly," he told me, his demeanor serious once again. "He will warn the men to be on their guard against thieves. All the same, I would be more at ease if neither you nor Susannah left the house unescorted. One of the grooms will accompany you if you wish to ride."

"As you wish, Mr. Wyndham."

There was a wounded look in his eye as if my formality distressed him. "You've been in my home too long now, Adrienne, for us not to be friends."

I was not sure what he expected me to say. "I do not wish to presume upon your kindness. Quite truthfully, my position here—"

"You've been listening to my stepmother's absurd discourse even though I've told you to pay her no mind."

"Circumstances being what they are, I must admit that Mrs. Wyndham was justified in her observations."

"Nonsense! I wish for us to be friends. You do me a great favor by your handling of Susannah. I've no stomach for the child's antics, and yet I must say that our relationship has improved with you as a buffer between us."

I was hesitant to accept his praise. My own perception of Susannah's well-being was on shaky ground after this afternoon's incident. I could say nothing to him, however, until I had an explanation from the child.

"Are we friends then?" he asked, extending a hand to me.

I took hold of it and managed a weak smile, nodding.

"Good," he said. "Now, I do not wish to presume upon our newfound friendship, but I am in need of a favor."

"A favor?" I echoed.

"Yes." He nodded to punctuate the statement. "My stepmother has made it clear that she intends to shut herself up in her room and sulk for the next few days. Ordinarily this would mean a pleasant respite for us all; however, I have planned a small dinner party for Saturday evening and find myself without a hostess."

I was incredulous. "Do you mean that you wish for me to—"

"It is a lot to ask, I know, but this is a business matter. I have invited a banker from Portland, Mr. Horace Putnam. We're seeking to obtain a loan from him for our Bristol steam line, and anything I can do to make a favorable impression upon him will certainly be done."

I could hear the pounding of my heart and wondered if Matthew could as well. "Could you not persuade Mrs. Wyndham?"

He laughed a curt laugh. "A lovely young lady at his elbow at dinner would be much more likely to impress our banker, by my thinking. Come, Adrienne, you were raised for this. You mustn't shy away when an opportunity presents itself, and you would be doing your friend a great kindness."

It seemed as though Matthew were goading me into a test of some kind. I had not permitted the still-vivid memories of Jason into my thoughts for some time, but now I was full of them. What was it he had said to me on that night when he stole out of my life? . . .

"You may not realize it yet, but Matt did not bring you here as a governess. He needs a wife, and you fit

the bill. . . . In a few months, you'll forget me, and
Matt will ask for you. . . .''

Could there be truth in those words?

At last I agreed to Matthew's request, and he left
me. I locked the door after him and collapsed onto the
bed, my body racked with uncontrollable sobs. Jason
was wrong; I had not forgotten him. I would never
forget.

Some time later, after I'd composed myself, I sought
out Susannah. Much as I might wish to deny it, she
could very well have been responsible for my
''accident'' in the tool shed. If she'd followed me to
the stables instead of going up to the house— If she'd
pushed me from behind— Too much speculation, I
told myself. But then I remembered the strange smile
she'd worn after she'd shut me in the mausoleum and
the malevolent glare she'd sent after Felicia just
before she destroyed the rosebed. Could one small
child be possessed of so much hatred?

I found her at the table in the schoolroom, bent over
her sketch pad.

''What's that you're working on?'' I asked.

'' 'Tis a picture of my horse, miss.''

She turned the pad around so I could see. ''A fair
likeness, don't you think?''

It was indeed, and I told her so. There was an
awkward silence as she went back to her sketching
while I paced a small section of the polished floor.
Finally I settled onto the small chair beside her.

''Susannah?''

The child turned a guileless face up to me. ''Yes,
miss?''

''Did you . . . after I sent you to the house this
afternoon, did you go back down to the stables?''

''Why no, miss. I came up straightaway to change
out of my riding things.''

I studied her expression for any hint of duplicity

and was surprised to see only an innocent smile.

"I wouldn't be cross," I assured her, "but you must tell me the truth."

"I don't understand," the child replied, a crease marring her brow.

"Susannah, did you try to shut me up in the tool shed this afternoon . . . the same way you locked me in the mausoleum when I first came to Wyndcliffe?"

She shook her head vehemently. "That was an awful thing to have done, miss. I knew the lock was rusty and would stick. I am sorry about it, truly I am. I'd never do anything like that now. We're friends, aren't we?"

I folded my arms around her slim form, still not convinced. Something was troubling this child; I could sense it. I'd heard that people who were not in their right minds could do terrible things and later not remember any of it, and Susannah had once denied to me that she walked in her sleep when I knew very well that she had. What was I going to do?

I sighed and kissed the top of her head. "Yes, we're friends," I told her.

Half a dozen women were assembled in the drawing room, listening to Mr. Putnam's eldest daughter demonstrate her expertise on the piano. We smiled at one another and made polite conversation while the gentlemen discussed their business in the drawing room over port and cigars. No one would have guessed that the elegantly dressed young woman perched on the settee was the governess in this house. Miss Adrienne Dalton, late of Beacon Hill, Boston, was certainly resplendent in a gown of robin's egg blue grosgrain with a point lace overskirt, and yet I did not feel so.

Miss Putnam completed the sonata and paused as the ladies gave her genteel applause. She riffled through the sheets of music before her and then touched her fingers to the keys again. The melody stilled all conversation. It was wrought with emotion in a style that could only belong to one man. I was very still until the echo of the last note died away. There was the awful ache of unshed tears at the back of my throat, and I was grateful for the ladies' enthusiastic response, for their attention was drawn away from me.

"What an unusual piece," commented one matron.

"Yes," agreed Mrs. Putnam, "but I don't believe I've heard you play it before, my dear," she told her daughter.

"It appears to be an original composition, Mama. The notes have been penned by hand."

"It is, I believe, one of Mr. Wyndham's brother's works," I heard myself say as I came to the piano. My voice was tenuous, and I cleared my throat to remedy that. "Though I can't imagine how it came to be here. He always worked upstairs."

I took the pages out of the girl's hand, running my fingers reverently over the notes that Jason had put on the page. I placed the sheets on a console table near the double doors just as the gentlemen came to join us. The evening passed uneventfully, with more innocuous conversation and a game of charades that managed to bring a smile to me despite my earlier upset.

It was very late when the last guest retired and Matthew and I were left alone in the drawing room.

"You see," he told me, "you were a success, just as I predicted you would be. I wonder if Mr. Landis knows what a superb hostess he lost when he let you get away?"

He studied my reaction to his words as he came to sit beside me on the settee. Matthew seemed pleased to find that I was unaffected by the mention of Phillip's name.

"Putnam seemed amenable enough to my proposals

this evening. Perhaps it was the extra attention you paid him at dinner.''

''Sometimes all that's needed is a warm smile and the exchange of a few pleasantries to soften the most irascible personality.''

''Not so very easy as you make it sound. You do have a talent, Adrienne. And I must tell you that you are an excellent charades player. Aaron told me as much and he's our expert.''

''That's Papa's doing. He loved games and riddles. When I was very young, before Mama died and he began to worry so much about the mill, he used to play games with us every evening.''

''He always told me that you were special. I thought he was only a proud father, but now that I have you here with me, I must say that you are all that he said and more.''

He took my hands from where they lay in my lap and drew them into his own. I listened to the vessel thump-thumping in my breast. It was not my heart, I knew, for that had been torn asunder on the night that Jason left me. My mind guided me now, telling me that here was an honorable man with whom I might find security and perhaps peace of mind. It would have pleased my father, of that I was certain, and even Jason himself had told me that such an alliance would be for the best. I met his eyes, noticing for the first time the gold flecks in them, like sparks from a fire. He drew me into an embrace that was all that I had expected. He was firm and possessive, and I could feel safe in his arms.

''How long I've waited, my dear,'' he whispered against my ear.

The foyer clock chimed the hour, breaking the spell that had come over him. He was ever the gentleman, and with a last, chaste kiss he released me.

''It's late now, and you must have your rest. We

shall see each other in the morning at breakfast, and then we will be riding with our guests.''

I could not find my voice. I had not anticipated that I would be included in the entire weekend's plans, but I gave him a smile as I headed for the open doors.

My eyes were drawn to the console table where Jason's music lay. I reached out for it, but before my hand could touch the pages, it recoiled as if on its own and dropped limp at my side.

It had been an exhausting evening, and yet even after I had pulled on my nightgown and settled beneath the bedclothes, I was wakeful. I got up and stoked the fire in the grate, put on a wrapper, and went down to the library for a book to occupy my mind.

It was not much later when I returned to discover that the lamp had blown out. The fire blazed in the hearth, casting an eerie red glow over the shadowed room. It cracked and popped, and as I relit the lamp, I was aware of an unusual odor. I went to see whether a spark had escaped the firescreen and alit on the carpet, but saw no spark there. On the grate, though, I saw the gown I had worn this evening, rolled into a ball, flames licking at the delicate and luxurious material. I cried out and set aside the firescreen to rescue the garment with a poker, but it was no use. I could salvage only a few singed scraps.

In disbelief, I sat down on the edge of the bed, cupping the scraps in my hands. Who would have done such a thing? My gaze drifted across the room as I wondered if the culprit might still be about, and then I saw the vanity table. Someone had made use of a cake of soap to write, in a childish scrawl, a message on the mirror: ''Go away!''

I opened the connecting door to Susannah's room. She appeared to be fast asleep, but I had to believe

that she was responsible for the destruction of my
gown and the message on the mirror. This was so like
her as she had been before, like that little girl who
had destroyed the rosebed and shut me up in the
mausoleum. She must have set fire to the tool shed as
well, though she had so convincingly denied it. I
could only wonder now what I had done to invoke her
wrath. The last time Susannah had displayed such a
passionate hatred was when she feared Rachel
Chandler would steal her father's affection. Could she
have such fears about me now?

Dreadful thoughts had begun to take form in my
mind. Matthew had intended to marry Rachel.
Susannah had wished her dead because of it, and only
days later Rachel's body was found on the rocks. I
remembered the time that we were on the Widow's
Walk and Susannah's touch had nearly caused me to
lose my balance. Had the child gone out walking with
Rachel on the night of the party? Dear God, what a
thought! And yet now when Matthew had begun to
show an interest in me, someone wanted to drive me
away . . . or kill me.

13

"Are they coming?
I can't see them on the road behind us. Where are they?"

"They'll be along shortly," Matthew assured his daughter. "They'd be here by now if you hadn't decided on the largest spruce in the grove for your Christmas tree."

"It's the perfect tree. Don't you think it's the perfect tree, miss?"

"Yes," I had to agree, "but you'll need a very tall ladder to reach the top."

"We've made paper chains to go round it, Father, and painted angels."

Matthew directed the pair of chestnuts pulling the sleigh around the curve of the drive. Last night's snowfall had so altered the landscape that I took it in as if for the first time. Puffs of white smoke floated out of the chimney pots and across the azure sky, and icicles hanging from window ledges cut the sunlight into brilliant rainbows that splayed across the granite walls of Wyndcliffe.

Susannah was beside herself with excitement, squirming beneath the fur robe that covered our legs.

Why she was not half-frozen by now, I could not imagine. The tip of my own nose had begun to tingle and my gloved fingers were stiff. We had drawn up under the porte cochere when she squealed, "Look, now they're coming up the road!"

We waited until the pair of Matthew's men drew up behind our sleigh in their wagon bed on runners. The top of the tree hung out of the back. Without hestitation, Susannah stepped over me and out of the sleigh to lead the men into the house, directing them to the spot in the drawing room that she had chosen for her tree. Matthew took my arm to assist me up the ice-glazed steps.

"She seems to be enjoying this," he observed.

"She does seem enthusiastic," I admitted.

I had watched over the child closely of late for a sign, any sign, of abnormality, but Susannah seemed as happy and normal as any nine-year-old child. What was there for me to do, then, but set aside my suspicions and get on with my life?

Matthew and I shed our wraps in the foyer and followed the rest into the drawing room where Susannah was imperiously directing the pair of men as they struggled to maneuver her tree into place. Matthew was greatly amused by her manner.

"What say you, boys? Shall I bring her down to the docks with me? She'll get a day's work out of our stevedores, I'll wager."

There was general agreement among those assembled and then the sound of a man's laughter of such a unique timbre that it drew my attention across the room.

He had been gone for more than a year and yet had not changed. He was so tall, his features so sharp. Those blue eyes sought me out, and I was so lost in their depths that a long moment passed before I noticed the woman on the settee and the fact that Jason's hand rested on her shoulder. She was pale and pretty but plainly dressed in serviceable brown merino.

"Jason," Matthew said with some caution, "I'd heard you'd settled in St. Louis."

I looked at Matthew, surprised to learn that he had known of his brother's whereabouts this past year, but then I could hardly have expected him to discuss that with me.

"Are you not pleased to see your brother come home for the holidays?"

I could feel the tension that laced the air between them though my attention was still focused on the dark-haired woman.

"We traveled the whole of yesterday just so we could spend Christmas Eve with you," Jason went on. "Oh, but you must forgive me. I've quite forgotten to make the introductions. Emily, this is my brother, Matthew, his daughter, Susannah, and . . . Miss Dalton. Emily is my wife."

My face drained bloodless, and the room began to spin. Matthew must have somehow anticipated my reaction for he caught my elbow to support me.

"Congratulations to you and your bride," he said.

She was quiet and mild-tempered. I wanted to dislike her but could find no fault in her demeanor. She seemed so intimidated by the family and the surroundings that I found myself sympathizing with her discomfiture. All the while, though, I was reminded that she possessed that which I wanted above all else in the world, and that which now I could never have.

I endured but a few moments more of polite conversation before I excused myself and sought the solitude of my room. Not long after, I sent word downstairs by Brenna that I was not feeling well and thereby escaped the torture of facing Jason and his bride across the dinner table.

I lay fully dressed on the bed with a damp cloth

over my eyes, and though I might have appeared to be resting, my mind was racing, fast and furious. I lifted a corner of the cloth to see that the twilight had ebbed away and left me to the comfort of the night.

The wound in my heart that had been healing had been wrested open that afternoon and the new pain was by far the worst. Why had he come back, after he'd left me with his talk of noble gestures and sparing me pain? Was I meant to stand by and watch while he settled into the household with his new wife and raised a family? I should have gone away then, left Wyndcliffe, but I had not the strength.

There was a knock at my door, and I lifted the cloth from my eyes as Brenna brought in my dinner tray.

"You don't look at all well, miss," she commented as she set the tray on the table beside my bed and lit the lamp.

I raised myself upright and smoothed my hair with my hand. "It's only a megrim. It will pass, I think, after I've rested. I only hope Susannah understands. She was so looking forward to my helping her with her Christmas tree."

"Don't worry yourself about Miss Susannah. When she heard you was ill, Missus Felicia offered to help the child trim the tree," she said as she went out.

I should not have been surprised, I supposed. When at last Felicia had emerged from the self-imposed exile in her room that had followed Matthew's censures and threats, she was a changed woman. Contemplation, it seemed, had made her realize how insecure was her own position in this household. She had learned to adapt to what must have been, to her, a most unpleasant situation, and so, too, would I adapt.

Thus resolved, I finished my meal and changed into an evening gown of rich burgundy faille with an overskirt and fichu of black lace. The visage which met me in the glass as I pulled my hair back into a caul of knotted black silk was considerably older than it had been this morning. The expression written upon it was one of reserve . . . and resignation.

The family would by now be assembled in the drawing room and I made my way through the darkened hall in that direction, but on the stairs I was diverted by Mrs. Garen.

"Evening, miss. I was just coming up to your room. The mister says if you're feeling up to it, he'd like to see you in his study."

"I am better, thank you, Mrs. Garen," I told her. "A little rest and Mrs. Black's excellent meal have been just the restorative."

"Well I'm glad to hear it," she said and headed back to the kitchen, where preparations for tomorrow's Christmas meal were already under way.

As I passed the drawing room doors, my attention was captured by the sound of Jason's laughter. My brow creased with the mental effort of staving off old memories. With each step I took, though, I managed to cast off another of them like the wilted flowers they were, until finally my thoughts were empty.

I rapped lightly and slid open the doors to Matthew's study. He stood before the fireplace, watching the blaze.

"Come in," he told me. "Are you feeling better then?"

"Yes, thank you," I replied in a voice that sounded hollow.

"Please sit down," he said, leading me to a pair of chairs before the hearth. I settled into one and he took the other for himself, leaning nearly out of it to address me.

"Where shall I begin?" he asked seriously, and only then did I begin to speculate as to the purpose of this interview.

"I shall be seven and forty years on my next birthday," he went on. "My head is not full of romantic notions as a rule. When you came into this house, though—"

He took a long breath, as if pausing to choose the right words. "What I am trying so inadequately to say is that I have grown fond of you, Adrienne."

He reached into the pocket of his dinner jacket and drew out a small, square box. And when I saw it, I knew what he intended.

"I thought you might prefer the privacy we have here now while you contemplate this Christmas gift."

He put the box into my hands, which had begun to tremble. I inhaled sharply as I lifted the hinged lid. Against a bed of black velvet lay a large diamond ring, flanked by blue sapphires.

"I don't know what to say."

"Say that you'll be my wife, Adrienne."

So many thoughts crowded into my confused brain all at once. I could have a husband who truly cared for me. Had he not proven his devotion in so many instances since I had come into his home? I could be the mistress of this household. Was it not what I had been reared for?

I had been within its walls for less than two years, and yet, I told myself, I loved Wyndcliffe as much as any Wyndham did. I could not think of leaving this house, of never again standing on the Widow's Walk, nor riding through its pine forests nor over its granite fences.

"I have ships and farms, buildings and land," Matthew said, "but I need someone to share my life with. Together you and I shall have sons who will carry the Wyndham name and fortunes into the next century."

I balked at the thought of producing a nursery full of sons for Matthew to turn into business magnates, but if they were my sons as well, could I not set a proper balance? Teach them to ride and dance and take time to enjoy their lives? Oh yes, I would adapt to my new circumstances, and as I told Matthew that

I would indeed marry him, I said to myself that his proposal was a godsend. At last I would find comfort and peace of mind.

He rose and, taking the ring from its box, slipped it on my finger.

"I shall make you happy," he promised.

Content, I thought sadly; content but never again happy.

It struck me then that I would, by my marriage to Matthew, become a mother to Susannah. Would she be pleased, I wondered? A shudder went through me as I remembered the warning that had been scrawled on my mirror. I knew that I must shortly deal with this problem of Susannah's resentment once and for all. She had to be convinced that I would not be stealing her father's love from her.

"I shall advertise for a governess for Susannah after the holidays," Matthew said, our thoughts having taken a similar tack.

"No, please," I replied quickly. "I think it would be easier for us all if I continued giving her her lessons . . . at least until after we are married."

"If you wish, my dear, but the matter must be seen to eventually. You shall have enough to occupy your time managing the household."

I could not rightfully tell Matthew of my suspicions about Susannah's instability without proof. She had been behaving so well lately. I could only proceed with utmost caution, for if the child was concerned about being displaced in her father's affections, this time I would most certainly be her target.

"I would like to announce our engagement to the family this evening, if you don't mind," Matthew said, and then almost under his breath, he chuckled, "My brother won't be the only one with something to celebrate."

It seemed perverse somehow that Matthew wanted to use our engagement to strike at his brother, but then it was too early yet for me to recognize that by accepting his proposal I was trying to accomplish much the same thing. What I could see, perhaps better than either of the brothers, was that if we were all to live together in this house, there must be some sort of peace between us.

"Could you not bind this rift between Jason and yourself?" I asked.

He regarded me, plainly surprised. "I should think that after the way you suffered at his hand— You may have forgiven him, my dear, but I have not."

I ignored this. "He is full of bitterness because of your father's treatment of him and envious of your success. Surely you can see that."

Matthew's chest puffed up with pride. "I have never borne him malice. It's only that, well, he does push one to the limit. His whole life he's been hell-bent for trouble."

"He needs to prove himself," I observed. "I think that if you made available some sort of position with the company as a peace offering, he might settle in."

Matthew pondered this. "Perhaps I could consider it, if you think it might bring peace to the house."

I smiled at him. "I'm sure of it."

I entered the drawing room on Matthew's arm, Mrs. Garen bringing up the rear as she carried in the punch bowl on its chased silver tray. The great tree dominated the room, the candles set in its boughs illuminating the decorations that Susannah and I had fashioned by hand. There were strings of cranberries like round, red beads, and hung on ribbons were sweet oranges brought in by Matthew's ships.

The whole family was gathered here with the few guests who had shared the Christmas Eve meal. Felicia was installed on the settee before the hearth, conversing with Dr. and Mrs. Fletcher. Jason and his bride were entertaining Mr. Donnelly, the estate manager, and his wife, and Susannah sat on the carpet with her knees drawn up, mesmerized by the flickering lights of the tree. Aaron Chandler was on hand as well, and when he saw us come in, he came forward.

"Ah, there you are, Matthew. You've gone to fetch Miss Dalton, I see. We were just preparing to toast Jason's marriage."

He seemed to be particularly enjoying this festive occasion. This was the boldest behavior I had seen him exhibit thus far. Mrs. Garen set her tray on a corner table, ladling the hot rum punch into silver cups, and Jason and Aaron came forward to carry them around.

I left Matthew's side and took a chair near where Susannah sat on the carpet.

"It's a beautiful tree, miss," she told me.

"Yes, it is," I said and laid a hand gently on her shoulder.

"I'm glad you're better now, so that we can see it together."

"Are you?" I wondered.

But she was staring into the depths of those evergreen branches again and did not reply.

Matthew cleared his throat and raised his cup.

"Ladies and gentlemen, let us drink a toast to my brother and his bride. May they enjoy many years of happiness."

"You must smile, Adrienne, and wish me well," I heard Jason say in a low voice as he came up behind my chair and pressed a cup into my hand. "Things are as they must be."

I pretended not to hear. Across the room, Matthew raised his cup once more. "And now, dear friends, we must have another toast. I am a happy man indeed, for this evening Miss Dalton has consented to be my wife."

There was a long moment of silence as all

assembled took in this unexpected news and then a
loud clatter as Aaron dropped a cup onto the tray.
"Clumsy of me," he said. "May I be the first to offer
you both my best wishes."

There followed a flurry of congratulations. Dr.
Fletcher offered his own toast to "the next generation
of Wyndham sons" and it was well received by all. I
sensed that Jason had not moved from behind my
chair, and I turned to him, expressionless, but cursed
the one tear that slipped out and trailed down my
cheek.

"Smile, Jason, and wish me well," I said, "for
things are as you have made them."

Susannah leapt up suddenly and put her arms
around my neck. "Oh, miss! Are you going to be my
new mama, truly?"

"Yes," I told her. "Will you like that, do you
think?"

She looked me over with a solemn expression and
then beamed. "Yes, I think so. Now we can be
together always, and you won't ever leave me, not
ever."

I pulled her close, and the tears came in earnest.

It was, I hoped, our engagement that put Matthew
into such a beneficent state of mind. Having offered
his brother a position in the company, he suggested
that Jason decide which facet of the corporation he
might best serve. I was amused to learn that they had
amicably agreed that Jason would oversee the
regulation of the tenant farms, which had been to
Matthew mostly a burden but was Jason's primary
interest. The situation could not have been more perfectly arranged. Jason was given a small office next to
Matthew's and in a scant two months was installed as
farm manager.

The entire household was surprised by the vigor
with which he approached his work. It was the con-

sidered opinion of the staff, who were by and large a
superstitious lot, that the Devil had met his match in
Emily. They all seemed to look askance at the dark
woman who moved about the house so noiselessly.
They were suspicious of her silence, though it was
clear that she was painfully shy and unaccustomed to
a large household. There was further fuel for the
gossips when one of the maids, after changing the
linens in the new Mrs. Wyndham's room, reported
that the woman kept a table with bottles and jars that
contained vile-looking concoctions of herbs and such.
It did not take long for them to conclude that Emily
was a practitioner of witchcraft and that she must
have cast a spell over her husband to make him so
unlike his former self. I was astonished that all of
them believed so heartily in their own fabrication. As
for myself, I was polite but cool toward Emily. I
found myself avoiding her if I could, though my own
reason was not superstition.

Again came the dream that for a fortnight had
threatened to shatter my fragile peace of mind.

I stood, all dressed in wedding-white, on the very
point of the Widow's Walk. The wind shrieked at me,
the cold rain stung my face, but through it all I was
unmoved. When at last all was still again, a fog crept
in on the chill night air and enveloped me. I was
utterly alone. I could not see Wyndcliffe behind me in
the distance nor the rocks far below my feet. A step
ahead meant certain disaster, yet I knew somehow
that I could not go back. I cried out in desperation
and, as if in response, lightning split the sky. In that
second my eyes were drawn downward and the
brilliant flash revealed a body on the rocks. It
was twisted and broken, and pale limbs lifeless,
Rachel's had been when I'd witnessed that horrible
sight, and yet this was very different. This time the
body I saw on the rocks was mine.

It was here that the dream ended, always in a silent scream that left me numb and filled with terror. This night was the exception, however. Tonight I could feel the cold of death creep over my limbs, stiffening them where they lay. There was, to my surprise, no pain in those last seconds of life, though I could feel very distinctly the soft sea spray as it settled on my face. . . .

I woke to the clatter of the french doors banging on their hinges. It was a relief to find that the chill I had felt was not the cold of death but only the winter wind that had blown open the balcony doors, and the spray I'd felt was only flakes of snow carried in on that wind. I rose from my bed and, crossing my arms over my chest, went to relatch the doors. I was shaking badly, from the fright more than the cold, so I took a poker to the ashes in the hearth but could not stir them back to life. Instead I pulled on my velvet dressing gown and sat down in the vanity chair, afraid to succumb to sleep. I lit the lamp, meeting my own vacant eyes in the glass, and admitted to myself that this was foolishness. It was, after all, only a dream that plagued me, persistent perhaps, but only a dream.

And then I noticed the box before me on the vanity. It was a marquetry box that Matthew had given me shortly after Christmas. Inside had been a length of the most exquisite Belgian lace, for my bridal veil, he'd said. I'd set the box up on the fireplace mantel, but two days later when I looked inside again, the lace had disappeared. I was distressed, but I could not believe that one of the maids was responsible. I questioned Susannah, and somewhat shamefully searched through her things when she was not about, but the lace was not to be found. I was loath to inform Matthew of the theft for fear of the interrogations that might result, and so I'd waited, leaving the box up on the mantel, and hoped that perhaps the thief would have a change of heart.

And now here was the box on my vanity table. Someone had been in my room this evening since I had fallen asleep. I did not breathe as I lifted the lid, and when it was open I could not. The length of lace was there, wrapped in tissue, just as it had been, but it was now dyed black. There was a note, scratched in pencil on the tissue, and as I read it, true fear crept over me.

"A bridal bed shall be her funeral bier."

It was another warning; someone wished me dead.

14

The marquetry box
was in its place on the mantel once more. Though I'd
not been able to sleep after I'd discovered what was
inside, I rose the following morning determined not to
let my fears overwhelm me. Someone meant to
frighten me, that was all. The best course of action
would be to ignore these incidents and go on with my
life. But in the quiet hours, I could not still the
speculations of my mind.

Did Susannah resent me still and wish to drive me
away? I did not believe it, and yet if not Susannah,
then who?

There was to be a formal reception in the banquet
room at the inn to welcome the new editor of the
Wyndham Harbor *Chronicle*, the small newspaper
that served the village. Matthew felt that he must put
in an appearance at the function and so informed me
that we would be attending.

I was delighted. It was the first such occasion since
our engagement, and I intended to enjoy myself.
Susannah was somewhat disappointed that she was to
be left behind, but she helped me choose the gown I
would wear. It was of lavender faille with a low

corsage and puffed sleeves. The skirt was gathered up at intervals, fastened by ribbons with bunches of pansies tied up in them, and revealed a white silk underskirt with a lace flounce round the bottom.

Susannah contented herself to watch as Brenna helped me dress that evening, and while Brenna arranged my hair with the same flowers that adorned the dress, the child expressed a wish that some day she might have a dress as pretty as mine. I assured her that she would and let her pin one bunch of flowers to her nightgown. Then we waltzed around my room together. When finally I put her into her bed, she drifted off almost at once, and I was relieved that she would not spend the evening lying awake in her bed, resentful at having been left alone.

I came downstairs full of anticipation of the night ahead. Tonight I would dance. I had not danced since before my father died. I paused on the landing and the lace on my dress caught on the carving of a baluster, but I did not notice unti I began to descend again and heard the rip as a section of lace was torn away.

"Oh, no!" I cried as I examined the damage.

Just then Emily came out of the drawing room, a basket on her arm.

"You've torn your gown, how awful," she said.

"I shall have to ask one of the girls to sew it for me. I hope there's time."

Emily bent down and took the lace gently in her hand.

"Let me mend it for you. I was just doing some patiencework and I have my needle with me."

"I couldn't impose—" I protested.

"Nonsense," she replied. "Come along. We'll go into the sitting room; we'll not be disturbed there. I'll have it repaired in no time at all."

"It's very kind of you."

I followed her into the sitting room and while I took

a seat on the divan, she knelt at my feet and threaded her needle. "Such a beautiful dress!" she said. "I've never seen anything to compare with it."

"It's a Parisian gown," I explained, "and I don't imagine I'll see its like again either."

Emily did not look up from her work. "Surely after you are married, your husband will allow you an extravagance now and again."

"Matthew is more than generous, but I shall never ask it of him. You see, I have a wardrobe full of Paris gowns upstairs, a trousseau for a wedding that was never to be. Such extravagances ruined my father. I won't see it happen to my husband as well."

I was as surprised as she by my revelation. I had not intended to make Emily my confidante, but she had been so kind to me, and there was no one else in the house to befriend her. What harm would it do?

"Were you born in St. Louis?" I asked, to break the silence.

"I was born on a farm in Kansas," she said in her mild voice. "My parents died when I was fifteen and I was sent to live with an uncle. All I've seen of St. Louis is his boarding house in Battle Row. It isn't a pretty place, Miss Dalton."

I was suddenly drawn to her, to her melancholy air and haunted expression.

"Please. If we are soon to be sisters, you must call me Adrienne."

She smiled up gratefully and then went back to her sewing.

"Jason was staying at your uncle's boarding house when you met him?" I surmised, prompting her to continue.

Emily drew up her needle slowly, then turned her dark eyes on me. She was hesitant and seemed to take care with her answer. "Yes, Jason was a boarder. My situation was not a pleasant one; my uncle is a cruel man. Jason was very kind to me when I needed kindness. When later he became sick, I nursed him. It was the Christian thing to do."

"Sick?" I echoed.

"He was in a bad way, from the drinking. When he was feverish, he suffered from awful nightmares and delusions. I sent for the doctor finally. He told me that the drinking would kill Jason if he didn't stop."

She paused a moment to reflect and knotted her thread. "At first I thought he wanted to die."

I gasped at this, before realizing that she might think me too concerned. And I was too concerned for anyone's good. Mild Emily, though, merely laid a hand over mine as if to reassure me. "It's better now," she said, "he's not had a drink at all since— since he decided to come home."

"I'm glad for you," was all I could say. Then I thanked her for mending my gown and left the room, more restless than I had been in weeks.

Emily had told me more than she could have imagined with her story and raised new questions that I was not sure I wanted to face.

I sat across from Matthew and pulled my pelisse closer around me as the carriage clattered over the cobblestoned main street of the village.

"You're thoughtful tonight," he said to me, "you've spoken nary a word since we left the house."

"I'm sorry if I've been poor company. I suppose it's that I'm apprehensive about this evening. I want to make the right impression."

"These people will be as pleased with you as I am," he assured me.

I smiled and went back to looking out of the window at the buildings we passed. The last of those in the row was the warehouse where Matthew kept his offices, and as I looked up, I was aware of lamplight in the window of the upstairs office.

"Someone must be working late," I commented.

"It's only Jason. You wouldn't believe how dedicated he's become. You were right, you know. There's been peace between us since I brought him into the business."

I did not tell him that the light was shining from his own corner office window and not Jason's. If, indeed, Jason was working late, he was doing so in his brother's office.

I should have been gratified, I suppose, that the village elite found me acceptable, but I began to suspect that the mixture of awe and fear that these people felt toward the man who all but controlled their lives would have made them appear pleased with any choice he made in a wife. I was, to them, no more than a shadowy presence on Matthew's arm, to be dealt with in polite but cautious fashion. I smiled a great deal and danced when I was asked, and yet even though my position in society had been effectively restored by this engagement to Matthew, I discovered that I was not happy. I feared I was never to be so again, and the evening that ensued seemed to corroborate my fears.

I was standing alone near the buffet table, Matthew having been caught up in conversation nearby, when a familiar voice startled me.

"Will you do me the honor of the next dance, Miss Dalton?"

Jason was the last person I'd expected to see here this evening. "If you will forgive me," I said firmly "I'm quite exhausted."

Dauntless, he took hold of my arm and whispered "I want to speak with you, Adrienne, and if I squire you to some quiet corner of the room, we're liable to set tongues wagging," he warned.

So I allowed him to lead me onto the floor, no

daring to acknowledge the quickening of my pulse when he took my hand.

"You're quite a success this evening," he said, and then pulled me closer so he could whisper against my ear, "You are the most beautiful woman in the room."

The compliment pierced my heart like a sharp needle, and I pretended not to hear.

"Where is Emily this evening?" I countered. "She'd enjoy this party surely."

His voice was suddenly cold. "She wouldn't like it."

"You would know better than I," I replied, and then more thoughtfully, I said, "She is a nice girl, Jason."

"I know that."

"Then what is this about?" I asked. "We've both made our choices."

"Or had them made for us, as you have pointed out."

"It doesn't matter," I said dolefully, and closing my eyes, allowed Jason to whirl me around the room.

My head was spinning.

"I didn't come back to Wyndcliffe to torment you," he insisted, "despite what you might think. I'd never have returned at all, but for— I've business to tend to."

"Business?" I echoed. "Is that what takes you into Matthew's office at night?"

"What do you know?" he asked and grabbed my wrist roughly.

He released me almost at once and dropped his head.

"I'm sorry," he said in a strangled voice.

Perhaps he had seen in my eyes some remnant of fear from that night on the garden terrace; certainly something had shocked him.

"Forgive me, Adrienne. I never meant— I promised not to frighten you ever again."

He looked so distraught, so tormented that it wrenched my heart.

"I only saw the lamplight in Matthew's office as we passed this evening," I explained, "that's all. Please, Jason, if this 'business' you're tending to will make you cross Matthew, I beg you to reconsider. He is comfortable with the peace between you. We all must live together in the same house, and I don't think I shall be able to tolerate it if there's warfare."

"Adrienne, I wish—" he said and then caught himself, "I wish I could explain to you now— Remember," he said finally, "no matter what may happen, your welfare has been foremost in my thoughts."

When the dance was over, he left me and I sought a quiet place to recover. There was hardly time, though, for Aaron Chandler approached and put a cup of punch in my hand. I thanked him and he shook his head.

"I don't envy you your position, Adrienne, with Matthew and Jason tearing at you like hungry dogs after a scrap of meat. It's always been that way, you know—what one has the other wants."

No doubt he had witnessed my encounter with Jason and reached his own conclusions.

"The question has been settled," I told him.

"Has it?"

He crooked a brow and searched my expression for any signs of doubt. I hoped he would find none. "Jason is married," I said, "and I am promised to Matthew."

My words did not allay his concern. "Listen to me, Adrienne. Those two destroy all that they touch. I am your friend and it pains me to watch them torment you, first one and then the other, the same way they did my poor sister."

Now I understood. Aaron was still grieving for Rachel, and my situation with the Wyndham brothers was a painful reminder of her.

I laid a hand on his arm. "You needn't fear for me, Aaron. I'm stronger than I look."

"Still, the best thing would be for you to leave here tonight, get away from that house and the both of them before the situation gets out of hand."

"I can't leave," I told him. "Wyndcliffe is in my blood, I'm afraid."

I was so sure of myself then, but there would come a time, very soon, when I would wish that I had taken Aaron's advice.

How easy things would have been if I had not begun to suspect that Jason now regretted the choices he had made. Surely he invented reasons to cross my path each day. At dinner I would turn to catch his eyes on me and I knew he was remembering. The hardest time of all was in the late evening when we all gathered in the drawing room and made attempts at conversation. Would it be this way, I wondered, year after year, until we had all grown old . . . and bitter?

The wind soughed gently, pushing an iridescent cloud of snow crystals against the long windows in the drawing room. The fire in the hearth snapped in response. I was seated at the piano, in the midst of a crude attempt at a Chopin waltz.

"Very nice, my dear," Matthew said when I had finished, though I sensed his thoughts were elsewhere.

I shook my head. "I'm afraid I've botched it again. It's that last progression."

"You've misplaced your hands. Let me show you," Jason offered.

He came up behind me and laid his hands over mine to show me the positioning. At his touch, my hands fluttered beneath his like two small birds. His cheek brushed against my hair as he bent over me.

"There, you see?" he said and cleared the hoarseness from his throat.

And then his hands closed over mine so tightly that I was sure he would crush my very bones. For a long while I did not breathe. Before the others in the room were aware of the silence, his senses returned, and he released me and stepped away. He went directly to the whiskey decanter and reached for a glass, but before he could fill it, Emily was there and caught his arm.

"No!" she said firmly.

He stood transfixed, looking through her as if she were not there, beads of perspiration standing out on his temples. He moved toward the decanter again, but she hung on to him. "No! Remember why you are here."

"We should never have come," he told her as he quit the room.

I sat, clad in my flannel nightgown, in the armchair beside my bed, feet tucked beneath me, and watched as the last embers in the grate twinkled and went out. The icy wind beat against the long windows, shrieking at me there alone in the dark, but my attention was caught by the argument raging nearby, seemingly for my benefit alone. The rest of the household was surely long asleep. The adjoining rooms belonging to Emily and Jason were just down the hall, close enough for me to hear clearly.

"She is the one," Emily said. "I saw it when you touched her."

"I warn you, Emily, do not meddle in my affairs."

Emily's implacable calm was a contrast to Jason's voice, fraught with emotion.

"You cannot have what belongs to another," she told him plainly.

"Damn it, don't tell me what I know well enough!"

"You want a drink, don't you?"

"Yes, yes, I wish I were blind drunk, then I'd have peace."

"The whiskey will kill you."

"Would that I were dead. I wouldn't be plagued by your censures . . . or my conscience."

"I will go if you wish it."

"It's too late," he said, his words full of dispair, "too late for us all."

I buried my head in the chair that was my cocoon. Theirs was a strange marriage. I wondered how Emily had come to be caught up in all of this. Had Jason loved her when he married her, or had he married her to forget?

When I learned, the next morning, that Emily had taken ill, I knew that the trouble in her marriage was taking its toll on her placid constitution and realized that I must make a conscious effort to discourage Jason.

With her illness, Emily became reclusive. She kept to her room, mixing her own herbal medicines and taking her meals on a tray. She had a peculiarly harsh cough that could be heard across the hall, and I began to fear for her health. My attempts to draw her out of her solitude proved futile, but I consoled myself with the confidence that soon Jason would admit that his place was with his wife. Then all would be well again.

Winter was by far the longest season in Maine and the cruelest as well. It kept one caged indoors, brought people too close for too long a time. But I refused to be shut up indefinitely, and whenever the day was sufficiently warm, I would trudge through the snow out to the Widow's Walk to take the air. Rather than turn seaward, lately I had begun to look back at the house, studying each stone and shrub and wondering if I would find it any less magnificent when I was its mistress. No matter the season, the

house stood there firm on its foundation. There was
comfort in that. I would sit on the stone bench and try
to imagine children that were mine and Matthew's
playing on the lawns, but try as I might, I could
picture no such future in my mind. More
superstitious persons in the household would have
told me that perhaps I could not imagine a future here
for myself because there was none.

Plans for a new Bristol steam line had taken up
much of Matthew's time lately, and so it was no
surprise when he announced plans for a trip to
London to complete the arrangements on that end.
Three months, he said he would be gone, but when he
returned, he promised me, we would begin in earnest
the planning of our wedding.

It snowed all morning on the day he was to leave,
blanketing the landscape anew. It was arranged that
he would catch the evening train to Portland, meet
with his banker, and sail the following morning. In
the afternoon, he took Jason into his study to discuss
how things were to be run while he was away. More
and more as Jason had shown his ability, Matthew
had come to rely upon him. After dinner he was
closeted with Aaron, giving him his final instructions.
When I came to tell him that it was time to leave, I
heard them talking.

"Where are the papers, then?" Aaron asked.

"They never left this house, I can assure you,"
Matthew replied. "I had everything that went out
carefully inspected. He couldn't have gotten them
out."

"She has them, I tell you!"

"Calm yourself," Matthew ordered. "Soon it won't
matter one way or the other."

"Not to you. You've ice in your veins. Well, I warn
you, Matthew, no one else had best be hurt by your
scheme."

I couldn't imagine what all of this meant and so I

rapped on the door and went in. "The sleigh is in the drive," I said.

"Rushing me off, are you?" Matthew said and smiled.

"You know that isn't so."

"We've about finished here at my rate," he said, rising from his chair.

He came to link his arm through mine and together we went into the foyer. "It is bitterly cold out there," I told him. "If you take ill, how shall I know of it when you aren't to return for three months?"

"Well, my dear, if I do, either I shall write to you about my recovery or you will read my obituary in the papers."

"Matthew, what a morbid thought to leave me with," I chided. "Have you said goodbye to Susannah?"

"Just after dinner, if you remember. Give her a kiss from me and tell her that I shall bring her something delightfully expensive from London."

He kissed me goodbye and went out the doors, only a few seconds before Jason came down the hall from the library.

"He's gone then?" he asked.

I nodded as Aaron came out of the study, agitated.

"He's forgotten his portfolio," he said waving it at me.

I took it out of his hand and grabbed my cloak from the rack. "I'll take it out."

"Are you sure?" Jason said. "I can run it out to him."

"No need," I told him, "it will give us a few moments more together."

"If you could spare some time when you come in," he asked hesitantly, "I'd like to speak with you in the study."

"As you wish," I said coldly.

I did not look to see what response there was to my barely civil manner, but went out of the door, waving my arm at the sleigh which was just then rounding the drive.

"Matthew, wait!"

When the portfolio was safely in his hand and the sleigh once again on its way, I turned back to the house. Yellow lamplight spilled out of the windows and onto the snow giving an aura of warmth, but the air outside was frigid and still. Stars hung suspended in the cloudless blue-black sky, and moonlight lent the landscape an eerie blue cast.

I breathed in deeply and felt the air burn my lungs. I did not want to go in, not just yet. I was afraid of what Jason might have to say to me, afraid of what he might suggest, but most of all I was afraid of how I would respond. I had vowed to myself that I would not stand between Jason and his wife. Emily was such a mild creature; she did not deserve more pain than she had already suffered.

The cold was invigorating, the stillness intriguing. I walked along the length of the house, listening as the crusty snow gave way beneath my feet, the crunch echoing in the quiet night. I considered going out to the Walk, but thought better of it. The joints of my fingers were already stiff with cold. So I came around through the topiary maze to the back of the house and paused only a moment, stepping up into the gazebo to look out on the luminous water and the round moon above. Gnarled brown vines of ivy reached up at the posts beside me like grasping fingers, and the lattice-work cast shadowy patterns on the snow.

Perhaps it was the incessant murmur of the waters below the cliffs that kept me from hearing the footsteps behind me until it was too late. One moment I was engrossed in the view and the next I clutched at a thick hemp rope that cut into the soft flesh of my throat. Lights flashed in the darkness before my eyes like stars exploding as I writhed to free myself, but a knee thrust into the center of my back made further movement impossible. My screams were but impotent gurgles, and I knew that I was to die here without knowing the reason why.

As the soft blanket of unconsciousness enveloped me, I must have become delirious, for I could hear Jason's voice calling out for me as if I were a lost child.

"Adrienne? Adrienne?"

15

"You can't die!
I won't let you, do you hear me? I love you, Adrienne."

The voice rose up and then dissolved into weeping. In that twilight which separates the conscious from the unconscious, the words echoed back again and again, dissipating the vapor of insensibility as the sun burns away the morning fog. It seemed that my whole body was leaden. Breathing was a difficult and painful task. Raising one eyelid took a major effort. The sunlight was brilliant and blinding, and the room spun around like a child's top. My first clear vision was of Jason beside my bed, and my still-torpid brain did not find this unusual. He was in his shirtsleeves, his shirt badly wrinkled, waistcoat hanging open. His face was haggard and stubbled with a day's growth of beard. I could feel his warmth as he squeezed my fingers bloodless, and with my free hand I reached over to touch the forelock of his bent head, running the back of my hand lightly along his jaw. Was this a dream?

At my touch he looked up, eyes rheumy, and grasped the other hand, kissing it fervently.

"Adrienne!" he said in disbelief.

It felt as if my throat had swollen twice its size, and when I forced out words, my voice was thin and reedy.

"I'm cold."

He reached up to touch my forehead. "It's the ice," he explained. "Dr. Fletcher said we had to bring down the fever."

He lifted me out of the bed of ice and into his arms, taking me to a chaise that had been placed for me before the fire. He laid me there and wrapped me in a quilt.

Slowly as I regained my mental faculties, I began to ask myself what had happened, why I was here in such a state and with Jason nursing me. I sifted through the memories until I could feel again the rope tightening around my throat, cutting off air. It was so vivid a memory that my chest heaved for breath and set off a spasm of coughing. Jason sat down beside me and put his arms around me until the coughing ceased. I lay weakened against his chest, and he stroked my damp hair.

"Who did this to you, Adrienne?"

I shook my head. "I couldn't see."

"I'll find whoever is responsible," he promised. "You won't be hurt again."

I looked at him, gray eyes dismal. "Someone wants me dead, Jason. I've known that for some time. They've tried before and they will try again."

He took hold of my shoulders and put me at a distance so he could read my expression.

"What do you mean?"

"While you were away, someone locked me in the tool shed and set it afire. If I hadn't broken down the door—" A frown creased my brow. "They decided it was thieves, after the livestock, but I knew better."

I paused to take a breath and when I continued, my voice was somewhat stronger. "One night I found my gown burning on the grate and a note scrawled on my mirror telling me to go away. And then there was the wedding lace.''

I pointed to the box on the mantel. After Jason examined it and the note penciled on the tissue, he returned.

''You told no one else of this?''

I shook my head. ''I thought it was Susannah, trying to frighten me away as she had tried to do when she shut me in the mausoleum. She hated Rachel Chandler, you know. She told me that she wished Rachel were dead, and soon after that—''

''You can't believe that the child would do such a thing?''

I looked up at him tearfully. ''I don't know what to believe.''

''It could not have been Susannah who attacked you in the gazebo,'' Jason said with conviction. ''A child would not have the strength for this.''

He cautiously touched the weal on my throat.

''No,'' I agreed, ''I suppose you're right.''

''It will do you no good to worry yourself about this. Leave that for me.''

You shouldn't be here,'' I told him, as if only just now realizing our position. ''Lord knows what the servants would make of this if someone came in.''

''You've been ill more than a week, Adrienne. The attack weakened you so much that you developed pneumonia. Dr. Fletcher did what he could, but still we feared— How could I leave you?''

A week I'd lain here? So gripped had I been by this illness that I had not even marked the passage of time.

''I belong with you,'' Jason insisted.

My eyes misted over. At first I'd wished I could be sure of his love, and then, when he went away, I'd wished to have him near me once more. Now when I had both, it was too late. How had things gotten so twisted?

"We cannot, Jason. It will hurt everyone around us. Learn to accept things as they are and go back to Emily," I said. "It's too late for us."

I turned my head away.

"I will not be without you," he said and touched my arm.

I would not respond. Finally I heard his footsteps as he walked to the door. There was a pause, and I imagined that he stopped to look back once more before the door swung closed.

All along I suppose I had believed Susannah responsible for the bizarre and frightening occurrences that had disrupted my life. My affection for the child, though, had tempered my fears. I was certain that she would come to accept me as a mother as she had accepted me as a friend. Now, with this latest attempt on my life, I was made to see that it could not be Susannah who threatened me, not a child whose aim had only been to play on my fears. There was someone in this house who wanted to be rid of me, one way or another, someone who had tried twice to end my life, and I could not imagine who it was.

The consolation in this new knowledge was, of course, Susannah's innocence. I could now believe in her gentle nature without looking behind each smile for something sinister. It was a joy to realize that I had won her heart after all, and before very long I had gained her trust as well.

It was a particularly gray spring morning. The fog clung to the landscape in wispy patches and the air was thick with mist, restricting me in my usual wanderings, so I prowled the house restlessly. As I crossed the upstairs hall, I was certain that I heard muffled sobs. I listened again for the sound, and it was repeated, this time ending in a mournful sigh. Deciding to investigate, I headed in the direction from

which the sound had come and found myself at the
room that had belonged to Matthew's dead wife,
Nora. I stood before the closed door, enveloped by the
shadows of the long hall, and my heart began to
hammer in my breast while the possible existence of a
Wyndham ghost crossed my mind once more. It was
the memory of Nora's portrait at Longfield that
settled my fears. She had been a gentle soul, who in
all her life had harmed no one, save herself. If indeed
it were Nora's specter within the room, then surely
she could mean me no harm.

I grasped the knob to try the lock and pushed open
the door. The sight of a slight figure sitting on the
windowseat gave me a start, but this was no
apparition, only Susannah, staring out of the tall
windows, tears trailing paths down her pale cheeks.
Could she be mourning her mother still?

The room was oppressive, the furniture shrouded in
dust cloths, the stale air full of the sickening sweet
scent of roses. Nora's belongings were just as she had
left them. It was not a healthy atmosphere for the
child.

"What is it, Susannah? What's wrong?" I asked as I
went to sit beside her.

To my surprise, she fairly threw herself into my
arms. "I've tried to forget, but I can't help it, miss.
Whenever I look out there I can see her, standing on
the Widow's Walk . . . just as she did that day."

"Who do you see? Diana Wyndham?" I guessed,
remembering how affected the child had been by the
legend.

She shook her head vigorously.

"Rachel?" I suddenly thought. "Did you see Rachel
Chandler on the night she died?"

Perhaps the child had witnessed the woman's
death. Susannah pulled away from me. Her brown
eyes were fixed and opaque. "She went straight to the
edge and looked down on the water and then . . . she

reached out her arms— Oh, miss, Mama wouldn't have left me if she loved me!''

She collapsed, sobbing in my lap, and I stroked her dark curls as her words sunk in. It had not been Rachel Chandler she'd watched out on the Walk but her own mother. Had the child truly witnessed Nora's suicide? It would explain so much about her behavior if it were so.

"Susannah," I said gently, "you must tell me what happened on the day your mother died."

She nodded, a blank expression overtaking her as she stared once more across the grounds. "I woke up early and came in to tell Mama good morning, but she was gone. When I looked out of her window, though, I could see her . . . out there on the Widow's Walk. I waved and called out to her, but she couldn't see me."

Her voice dropped until it was only a whisper. "Why did she want to die, miss?"

I felt helpless, for I did not know how to comfort her. "Poor child," I said at last, taking her small hands in mine, "how can I answer such a question?"

"I wasn't always good. Sometimes I made her angry, when I ran through the halls, and she had one of her headaches. Perhaps if I'd been quieter or worked harder at my lessons, she mightn't have—"

"No!" I captured her doll-like face in my hands to gain her full attention. Inside I was blaming myself for not trying to get to the heart of Susannah's problem long ago. As it was, she'd had to suffer alone with this terrible secret, drawing her own misguided conclusions.

"No matter what it was that drove your mother to take her life," I told her, "you can be sure that she loved you very much."

I folded my arms around her. "It is hard for those who are left behind to comprehend, but sometimes when a person must endure great pain, be it mental or physical, his only wish is for an end to his suffering. I think that must be what happened to your mother. But you were in no way to blame for what happened, do you understand?''

"I think so, miss.''

"Have you never told anyone what you saw?'' I wondered.

"It made everyone sad to talk about Mama,'' the child explained, "and at first I didn't want to remember. I think I should have tried harder not to be afraid, miss. I do feel better now that I've told you.''

I smiled at her. "I do love you, you know, and I'm glad that you've confided in me. It means that you're growing up . . . when you can face the truth and not be afraid.''

This seemed to please her.

"I think, though,'' I said to her then, "that we ought to talk to your father and explain about all of this. He needs to know the truth as well.''

She thought about it for a while, looking very grown up indeed. "Yes, miss. I will talk to Father when he comes home.''

It was gratifying to see how much Susannah's disposition had improved, how she was growing up, and to think that I might have had a hand in it. I did not imagine that it would be difficult to teach her self-reliance now that she had made such strides.

Susannah's mare kicked up clods of earth as she started back toward the house. I watched until she reached the road and then took Gypsy lightly over the low wall of trap rock and granite separating the fields. I rode inland past rows of apple trees, which in a few weeks would be fragrant and heavy with blossom and made my way beside the gentle curve of the river, its silver water still as glass. Along the bank on either side, the birches arched upward, their boughs meeting over the water like graceful arms entwined.

I did not wish to hurry back to Wyndcliffe, luncheon or no. I was sick to death of prowling the house like some caged animal. The crisp air was invigorating and I breathed deeply of it, savoring the sweet smell of grass and damp earth. I took whichever direction suited my fancy and, reveling in the freedom, admired the countryside. I led Gypsy at a canter along the road that split the Wyndham farms. Ahead I saw Mrs. Newell, bloated with pregnancy, hammering away at a break in the long fencerow.

"Good day," I said as I drew up beside her.

"And to you, miss," she replied.

Mrs. Newell did not look up, but lifted one end of a loose plank and hammered it back into place. I thought the woman's color was not at all healthy, and she heaved for each breath she took.

"Excuse me, ma'am, but surely there is another in your family to repair this fence. You shouldn't exert yourself this way. I fear for your health and the child's."

"You are kind to say so, miss, but Mr. Newell's laid up in bed. Broke his leg while tryin' to patch our roof. My boys is off with the fleet and, well, this fence won't mend itself. The cow's gone astray twice this morning."

"I see," I muttered, concentrating on her dilemma. "Surely Mr. Pagett can be of assistance."

"My Seth don't like to run afoul of Mr. Pagett. If you'll pardon my saying, miss, he's a hard man."

"I'm certain that if Mr. Wyndham were here, he'd see that something was done. I shall speak with Mr. Pagett myself," I decided, and as if she understood, Gypsy stamped the ground, ready to be on our way.

I pulled back on the reins and patted her.

"Go inside and tend your husband," I told Mrs. Newell. "I'll ask Mr. Pagett if it isn't possible to get some of the men from Wyndcliffe to repair this fence, and the roof as well."

"I don't want to be a bother, miss. Just 'cause we've had a hard chance—"

"Nonsense. You go on now. Something will be done about this, I promise you."

She looked somewhat relieved but still skeptical as I left her. "Thank you, miss."

I was feeling sure of myself as I rode into Pagett's yard. He was just coming in himself, stepping up onto the veranda as I called to him.

"Mr. Pagett? I'd like to speak to you, if I might."

He scratched his stubbled chin, and I thought from the way his clothes hung on him that he resembled a scarecrow. "Well, Miss Dalton, is it? This is a surprise."

I dismounted and slipped Gypsy's reins through the ring on the hitching post. He waited for me, and the bold stare he met me with stopped me on the steps.

"It's about the Newell farm. Are you aware that their roof needs repair?"

His eyes slid back and forth beneath their heavy lids, and his attitude seemed to change all at once.

"Can't see as how that's my business, nor yours either."

I ignored him, crossing my arms over my chest.

"I was riding just now and came upon Mrs. Newell mending fences. She tells me that her husband broke his leg while trying to repair the roof. She is forced to take over his chores. Now it seems to me—"

"It seems to me, missy, but what this ain't none of your concern. You ain't the missus here yet, and when you are, you'll be a lot less trouble for us all if you keep to plannin' tea parties instead of meddlin' where you don't belong."

I could hear the blood rushing in my ears as my anger peaked, but I only stood white-faced as he turned on me again. "Mr. Wyndham gives me a free hand to run these farms because I turn a profit for him. If Newell can't handle it, then he ought to give the land over to a tenant who can. There's plenty hereabouts would like to be in his place."

Without allowing me to reply, he stomped into the house and slammed the door. I was white-hot with anger and determined to have him hear me out. I opened the door with at least as much vigor as he had shown and stepped boldly inside.

"May I assure you, Mr. Pagett, my influence with Mr. Wyndham is not as slight as you might think. You will have the courtesy to hear me out, sir!"

There was no reply, and I hesitated as my eyes scanned the room. Pagett stood nearby, as confused as I. He was staring at his desk in the corner of the parlor, where sat Jason, a crooked smile twisting his lips.

"I don't recall inviting you in," Pagett told him boldly.

Jason folded his arms across his chest and, leaning back in the chair, stretched out his long legs, resting them on the desktop. "Surely you can't have forgotten, Pagett. We Wyndhams are your landlords."

"I work for Mr. Matthew Wyndham."

"Yes, so I heard you tell Miss Dalton, and by the way, that's no way to address a lady."

"That's none of your business, as I see it, so long as I do my job."

Jason pulled himself upright, and as I watched him, I thought that he had the look of a cat toying with a mouse.

"Precisely why I am here," Jason told him. "Perhaps you are not aware that I now run the farms for my brother."

The man looked at the toe of his boot as he scuffed it on the oak floorboards. "Just some fancy title and an office to keep you busy," he mumbled.

"Most assuredly not," Jason said, his voice gone cold. "An interesting ledger you keep here, Pagett, but pure fiction, of course.''

He drummed on the leather-bound ledger with his fingertips. ''None of these figures jibe with the information that I've gathered from our tenants. You've been able to squeeze enough out of the farms to keep Matt pacified and still have a tidy sum left for yourself, isn't that right?''

''You can't prove anything.''

''I won't have to. You'll be gone in any case.''

He rose slowly, each move deliberate. He was obviously enjoying this. He moved to stand before Pagett, and the man glared up at him, balling his fists, tensed as if he might strike. I did not breathe as they faced off, expecting violence to erupt with the next word. I was surprised by Jason's contemptuous smile and how easily it distracted Pagett.

''Pack your gear and be off the estate by morning,'' he told the man, and taking my elbow, he led me out.

He went first to where Cerberus was tethered behind the house, and then rejoined me so we might ride back to Wyndcliffe together.

We rode for some time in silence, Jason's attention full on me as I pretended to study the scenery.

''You shouldn't be riding by yourself,'' he told me. ''If someone means to harm you, it would be that much simpler to find you alone.''

It had been more than a month since I had been attacked and I had never left off speculating, but I would not give up my freedom.

''I won't stay locked up in the house, if that's what you're suggesting,'' I replied.

''Have a care at least,'' he said, ''for your own safety and my peace of mind.''

I nodded and thought I must have looked like a child who had been scolded.

''I'll talk to Donnelly about the Newells' roof,'' he told me, ''and we'll send someone out to see about the fences.''

"Thank you," I replied.

"You were truly concerned about Mrs. Newell, weren't you?" Jason asked, as if this surprised him.

"She should not be expected, in her delicate condition, to be mending fences."

Jason laughed at my wide-eyed reply. "Women such as she work with as much vigor every day of their lives. She's borne three healthy sons thus far and most likely stopped her chores only long enough to see them into the world."

I was wounded by his laughter and grew defensive. "I daresay that after we are married, Matthew will want me to show compassion for these people."

Whether intentional or not, I had chosen the right arrow to aim. At the mention of his brother, Jason pulled on Cerberus's reins and the black Arab stallion reared up, tossing his head impatiently. Jason pressed his mouth into a taut line. When I pulled up beside him, he reached out for my gloved hand, resting on the pommel of my saddle.

"There is a way for you and me, Adrienne, believe me. Do not rush into this marriage with Matt."

"I am promised," I retorted. "There can be no honorable way."

With that, I gave Gypsy my heel and we crossed the dirt road, jumped the stone fence, and galloped across the fields.

When Matthew returned at last, it was to find the estate well in order. It seemed to me, though, that he was unsettled by the capability Jason had shown in his absence. His concern at the attempt made on my life was to be expected, and I was by his order once again restricted in my wandering of the grounds. I felt that everyone in the household kept a watchful eye on me now, though it may well have been my imagination. In any event, I felt stifled by the restrictions placed upon me.

I had seen little of Jason since that day at Pagett's house. Perhaps this was due to a concerted effort on my part. I tried as much as possible to be where I knew he was not. I could not avoid him forever, though.

I had finished breakfast and was staring out over my second cup of tea when Jason came into the dining room. He poured himself coffee and drank it black. As he had ignored me thus far, I did the same, hoping someone else would come in so I might make my escape unnoticed. When I rose, though, he was beside my chair.

"I want to talk to you," he said.

"We've said all there is to say."

"Like it or not, Adrienne, you will hear me out this time."

His blue eyes dared me to refuse him, but he knew I could not.

"This very moment?" I protested. "Someone will come in surely."

"I've waited too long as it is," he told me, and opening the french windows, drew me out onto the terrace.

He turned from me, looking out over the lawns.

"I was wrong to have pushed you into my brother's arms," he began. "I thought it would be for the best. As his wife you would have the respect you deserve. This house would be yours, and money and fine clothes, a social position—"

I was fairly shaking with anger. "How dare you presume to know what is best for me? Do you think so little of me that you believe all I want of life is comfort and fine clothes? I am not a child!"

Tears collected on the tips of my lashes, distorting my vision, and I brushed them away impatiently. When he turned back to me, he seemed pleased at my agitation.

""There is a spark left in you, at least," he said, yet

there was a sad note in his voice. "I'm glad."

I did not understand.

"Matt is smothering you, bit by bit," he explained.
"You're no longer the firebrand who slapped my face
on the deck of the *Nora Jean*. You've grown positively
somber, and it's all Matt's doing. He's crushed the life
out of you."

"Perhaps I've only just now grown up," I
suggested.

"No," he said and shook his head vigorously.

"I'm betrothed to your brother," I told him. "All
that I do reflects on him."

"If you truly cared for Matt, you could never be so
cruel as to marry him, knowing that you do not love
him."

I turned away, looking out over the lawns as he had.
"Why would you say that I do not love him?" I asked
apprehensively. "I've never said otherwise."

"Oh, you can't fool me," he said and turned me
around to face him.

With his thumb and forefinger, he tipped my chin
up until my eyes were full unto his. As he took my
hand and put my palm to his, I felt sparks of
electricity, and a dangerous warmth spread over my
body from that place where his flesh touched mine.
My breath caught at the back of my throat.

"Do you feel this way when he touches you?" Jason
wanted to know.

He kneaded my shoulders and, on their own, my
arms wound around his neck. I let him kiss me and
when his lips settled on mine, I knew I was lost.

"You can belong to no other man," he whispered,
"don't you see that?"

It was true, God help me. I could never be
Matthew's wife, nor any other man's, so long as there
was Jason. This realization brought me no comfort.
My head dropped and I stepped back from him.
"There's no hope in this, Jason."

"You mustn't believe that," he told me and, reaching into his waistcoat pocket, drew something out and pressed it in my palm, closing my fingers around it.

I could tell by its shape that it was a key.

"Take it. It's for the cottage. Meet me there tonight, when you can get away. I'll explain everything to you then. There is a way, Adrienne. Trust me."

I did not watch him go when he left me but instead stared at the key he had put in my hand. When I came back into the dining room, it was to find Aaron Chandler there. The blood drained out of my face when I met his eyes.

"Have you been here—?"

"Not all along, but long enough," he said, "and so I shall be frank, Adrienne. You cannot be considering going to Jason as his mistress?"

My brow crooked upward. "Is that what he was suggesting?"

"Now you're being purposely obtuse. What else could he mean?"

"Yes, what else?" I said and let out a short laugh.

"Do you still plan to go through with this marriage to Matthew then?" he asked.

"I cannot . . . now," I admitted. "Once you said you'd help me if I needed to get away. Will you help me now, Aaron?"

"If it's what you want. I've told you what my feelings are. You know that I'll see you safely away from them both."

And so it was decided. Aaron would book passage for me on the packet to Boston, and I would leave on the morrow. Perhaps if I had been a braver sort, I'd have chosen another destination, but Boston had been my home for so many years and there was comfort, at least, in that. I had saved enough money to take a small room while I sought another position, and Aaron promised to provide me with a reference.

When we'd made our plans, Aaron went back to Matthew's study where he'd been working, and I went up to visit Emily, hoping this would help me reaffirm my decision.

I found her in bed, eyes half closed, her dark hair splayed across her pillow. "If you're resting, I can come back later," I said.

"No," she said and raised up on her elbows, "please come and sit by me. I was going to brew some tea, and I'd welcome the company."

"Let me do it for you," I offered.

She propped herself up with pillows while I put the kettle on the spirit lamp. "You'll find the tea in the tin on the table," she said, pointing it out to me. "You may have a cup yourself if you like, though you might find it bitter. It's an herbal blend I've concocted. It seems to ease my cough."

"Thank you, no," I told her. "I've only just had mine at breakfast."

While I waited for the water to boil, I went to the windows and drew apart the draperies, hoping the sunlight would brighten the dreary room. From behind I heard the rasp of Emily's breathing, followed by a spate of coughing that brought me to her bedside. She had covered her mouth with a handkerchief, and when she drew it back I saw blood on the cloth. Only then did I realize how seriously ill she was.

"Emily?" I said in a bewildered way after the coughing had subsided.

"I'll . . . be fine," she assured me. I sensed that she would rather I had not witnessed the attack.

I tended the teapot without a word. When I brought her her cup, she smiled at me but did not speak. I sat in the chair beside her bed and studied her for a long while as she sipped her tea. What kind of life was this for her, imprisoned in this room, in this bed, without the comfort of her husband's love?

"Are you happy, Emily?" I asked, not thinking what an odd question it must have seemed.

"It's peaceful here," she said, "and I'm grateful for that."

"You will want more when you are well."

"No." Her breathing was uneasy still, but her expression serene. "How can I make you understand? Until I came into this house, I never dreamed such luxuries existed. It must have been much harder for you . . . to have had such things and then to have had them suddenly taken away."

My gaze drifted off. "Such things are not so important as they once were."

I left my chair and paced the room, pausing to examine the jars of herbs lined up on the table. "I'm going away," I told her.

"You mustn't."

I turned back. "I can't stay here, surely you—"

"I know that you cannot run from one who loves you . . . one whom you love."

How could I tell her that I did not love Matthew? That what might happen if I stayed could destroy too many others, herself included?

"Promise me you will wait, Adrienne," she said, suddenly very serious. "Talk to him tonight, before you do anything rash. All this will work out. You must believe that."

"Talk to him tonight." Had I misunderstood? Surely she had meant Matthew, for how could she know what Jason had planned for tonight?

16

When Emily came to the table dressed for dinner that night, all conversation stopped. The maids hastily set another place, and she settled quietly into it, looking pale but more rested than she had been that afternoon. No one was so surprised as Jason, who continued to stare across the table at her in a perplexed way, long after Matthew and Aaron had resumed their business discussion.

"Are you feeling stronger then?" Felicia asked her at last.

"Yes, thank you," she replied. "Dr. Fletcher said some activity would do me good."

"Maybe you can come riding with us in the morning, Aunt Emily," Susannah suggested.

"I don't think she's ready just yet for riding," I cut in.

"Not yet," Emily agreed, "but I can watch you from my window. I see many things from my window."

Susannah squirmed in her chair. "Can you see the Widow's Walk?"

I put my hand over her small one, which rested on the edge of the table.

"No, child," Felicia put in, "Emily's room looks out
onto the back of the house."

Emily sipped at her soup and then laid down the
spoon. "Yes. I have a lovely view of the gardens . . .
and the gazebo and the stables below that."

"I shall wave to you when I go out tomorrow,"
Susannah said.

"I will watch for you," Emily promised.

Jason had followed the conversation without
contributing and now appeared to be more than a
little perturbed with his wife. "Don't tax yourself, my
dear," he warned.

"It really is quite a view," she went on, unheeding.
By now she had garnered everyone's attention. When
she paused for breath, I sensed that she was not so
well-recovered as she would have us believe. "If I
cannot sleep at night, I put my chair by the window
and admire the scenery. When the moon is full, it's
bright as day."

She was nervous, I saw as much, and her strength
was waning. What was the purpose of this exercise
and her senseless chatter? To remind Jason that he
had a wife, frail though she may be? Or to remind me?

Tension laced the air. Everyone felt it, it seemed.
The meal was interminable, with only the barest
snatches of conversation to relieve the pall that had
settled over us. Jason escorted Emily back up to her
room before dessert, and I thought she leaned too
heavily on his arm, despite her insouciant smile.

After dessert, Matthew returned to his study, and I
managed a word with Aaron, apart from the others.

"The arrangements have been made," he informed
me. "The packet leaves in the morning at seven."

I sighed in relief. "Thank you."

"Come to Chandler House late this evening, when
you can get away, and in the morning I shall drive you
into the village and see you safely on board myself."

"I have to explain to Matthew—"

"Do what you must, only don't let him know that you're leaving. He can be very persuasive if he has to be."

I promised to do as he asked and thanked him once more before I went up to put Susannah to bed. After she had fallen asleep, I kissed her good night for the last time and went to my room to pack those things that I could carry with me. The next half hour was spent in an attempt to compose a letter to Susannah that would explain in terms she could comprehend why I could no longer remain at Wyndcliffe. This completed, I steeled myself and went down to face Matthew.

There was no answer when I knocked at the study door and no one about when I peeked inside. The lamp on the desk was lit, and there was paperwork scattered on the desktop, but the room was empty. I came and sat in Matthew's chair, wondering as I settled back if he had only stepped out for a moment. And I thought while I waited of what I would say to him beyond "I cannot marry you."

When the mantel clock struck half past ten, the door slid open, and I looked up to see Mrs. Garen there with a tray.

"Oh, miss," she said, as startled to see me as I was to see her. "I've brought Mr. Wyndham's coffee."

"I've been waiting here for him, Mrs. Garen. Do you know where he is?"

"He told me after dinner he'd be in here working. He's not been to bed. I was only just upstairs myself."

She left me then, and I waited a quarter of an hour more, becoming more unsettled as each second passed. My resolve was waning, and had Matthew walked in then, I believe I'd have let him convince me to stay, but he did not appear.

I had to get to Chandler House soon, so I twisted the ring he had given me off my finger and left it on his desk. I did not commit my feelings to paper as I had done for Susannah. I sensed he would be more disappointed in me if I tried to make feeble excuses.

I met no one as I went up for my bag nor as I came down the back stairs and stole out of the house.

The full moon shone down bright as day on the footpath, and the night air was redolent of pine. I alternately walked and ran, slowing only to catch my breath and looking back only once to bid Wyndcliffe farewell.

I did not remember until I saw it before me that this path would take me past Jason's cottage. There was no thought involved as I mounted the steps and wrapped my hand round the knob, but a rush of thoughts followed. I had put the key on a ribbon round my neck this morning and kept it beneath my bodice all day long. Even when I had decided to leave, I'd not left it behind. I would only meet him to say goodbye, I told myself, to have an end to it. I would not let him touch me.

No lamp was lit, and the cottage was full of eerie shadows. I dropped my bag and maneuvered through the entryway and into the parlor with the aid of the moonlight streaming in through the unshuttered windows. I lit the lamp and gasped to see Jason, still in his evening clothes, sitting in the corner chair. His face was edged in shadow, and I could not read his expression. "I'd convinced myself that you weren't coming," he said.

"I've come only to say goodbye."

He rose from the chair then, and I stepped back in response. "You can't leave. I won't let you."

"I cannot be what you want," I told him. "No matter what I feel for you, I'll not be any man's mistress."

His brow creased into a frown, but I saw that one corner of his mouth had turned up in that familiar twisted smile that told me he was amused. "What? Is that what you think?"

He was laughing at me but I did not understand why. "What else is there for me?" I demanded to know.

He expelled a long breath. "Sit down," he said and gestured toward the sofa.

I did as he asked, wondering what explanation there could be for his behavior.

"There have been too many misunderstandings between us, but no longer—"

He sat close beside me, and I reluctantly allowed him to take my hands in his. "Listen to me, Adrienne. I want what I have always wanted. I want you to be my wife."

I stared at him in disbelief. Surely he had lost his reason. "You have a wife, or have you forgotten?"

He clasped my hands tightly in his, holding my gaze with his own as if I must look deep into his eyes to understand. "This marriage between Emily and me is a sham, contrived purely to scotch any feelings you might have had for me . . . and to make sure that I would never have the chance to harm you again."

I sat very still, trying to comprehend what he had imparted. "Emily is not your wife?"

He shook his dark head, his eyes still not leaving mine. "When I left here, after I'd hurt you so badly, I went to St. Louis. One night across a poker table, quite by chance, I met a ship's captain who was bragging of how he had run the Union blockades during the war, supplying arms to the Confederacy. After a few more drinks, he told me the name of the man who'd employed him. That man was my brother."

My jaw dropped. "Matthew, a traitor? I don't believe it. Why would he take such risks?"

"Money," Jason replied. "The blockades had cut off his shipping routes and were strangling the business. The blockade-runners were realizing a three-hundred-percent profit on each successful run.''

Jason made it all sound quite plausible.

"He may well have put the gun into the hand of the rebel who nearly killed you," I observed.

"And did kill thousands of others, the mercenary bastard! Do you see now why I had to come back?" he asked, barely able to restrain his anger. "You said once that I didn't care about the family business because there was no profit in it for me, but I do care, Adrienne, and one day I might produce the son who will inherit it all. So I had to be sure that Matt's lack of judgment wasn't eroding the foundation from under a business that took my family a hundred years to build.''

"I understand all of that," I told him, "but . . . Emily.''

He settled back against the tufted cushion of the sofa, and I studied his face carefully, needing to hear the truth, no matter what it might be.

"Emily's uncle ran the boarding house in St. Louis where I had a room," he explained. "She cared for me when—I was ill. And when I'd decided to go back, I knew I couldn't leave her in that place. She had consumption. She was dying, and if I'd left her behind, her uncle would have tossed her out in the street when she wasn't able to do a day's work for him.

"And I'd made a vow," he continued, "never to return to Wyndcliffe if there was a risk of hurting you. So I hired Emily to pose as my wife. It was beneficial to us both. She could spend the remainder of her life in comfort, under a doctor's care, and I could keep an eye on Matt, without standing in the way of your happiness.''

Tears had filled my eyes, blurring my vision, and were brimming over. "But, Jason—''

He pressed his fingers over my lips. "I am asking you to forgive me for complicating things. If I tell you now that I love you, that nothing is so important to me as your happiness, will you believe me?''

"How can I doubt it after all you've told me?''

"I swear to you, Adrienne, I'm a different man than I was a year ago. I have a place at Wyndcliffe now, and I'm making something of my life.''

"I never doubted that you would,'' I told him.

"Emily will agree to a comfortable sanatorium, if it's what you want. I'll see that she has the finest care. And of course, the family will have to be told of the deception.''

"Can we not wait,'' I asked, "and let Emily have her peace? We've waited this long, after all—''

Concern was plain on Jason's face. "But you will marry me when the time comes?''

It was what I'd wanted more than anything, to spend my life with Jason, to be his wife. I reached out to trace the sharp square of his jaw with the back of my hand. "Yes, Jason,'' I replied, amused that he might believe I'd have said otherwise. "Yes, I'll marry you.''

He pulled me into his arms all at once. "Take care, my dear,'' he whispered against my ear, "for I'll not give you the chance to change your mind!''

He scattered fevered kisses across my brow, and as his lips trailed the sensitive flesh of my throat, I felt the warmth of desire rise in me. "We'll not leave this house tonight, you and I, until I've made you mine,'' he vowed, "until all of the doubts and questions are swept aside.''

I met his eyes unreservedly. "No more doubts.''

With that, he lifted me easily into his arms and swept me up the stairs. When he set me down once more, we were in a cozy little room that he must have used for himself on occasion, for I noticed items of his clothing hanging in the wardrobe. He left me to stir the fire in the grate, and I stood there in the darkness, unfastening the buttons of my pale blue basque one at a time.

It struck me that I was not the slightest bit afraid of him or of what was to come, despite my ignorance on that score. That Jason and I belonged together I knew wholeheartedly, and this knowledge struck dumb the little voice inside me which might on another occasion have cried for reason. I would wait no longer for happiness.

The basque slid to the floor. I pulled the pins from my coiled hair, one by one, and shook it free until it drifted over my shoulders and down about my waist like a mantle. By the time Jason had finished his task, I'd shed my corset, and it lay, along with my skirt and petticoats, in a pool at my ankles.

Jason returned the poker to its place and left the hearth, and when he turned his attention to me once more, I reached out for him. It seemed an eternity before he'd crossed the room and caught me up in his arms. Recklessly, I pressed closer to him until I could feel his long, muscled legs against mine. Finding the ribbons of my chemise, he untied them, and I shrugged it off, watching for his reaction, hoping he was pleased. His eyes had darkened to the color of the midnight sky, and his bold gaze lingered. I waited, breathless, until at last he cupped my head, losing his hands in the tangle of my hair, and his mouth sought mine.

I was drunk on the taste of him, and I wanted more. The room spun crazily as I was drawn down into the maelstrom. Firelight whirled about in a kaleidoscope of amber light, and a pleasant warmth enveloped me as Jason's hands traveled lower, down to the hollow of my back. I unfastened the buttons of his waistcoat and linen shirt, my fanned fingers slipping beneath the fabric, seeking out the muscular definition of his chest. On their own, my hands moved upward to his shoulders and drew off waistcoat and shirt in one deft move, pinning his arms momentarily until he shook them free. I pressed my palm to his scarred shoulder and carefully massaged the twisted flesh. A harsh rasp in his breathing told me that his patience was very nearly exhausted. He lifted me onto the bed then, and as I settled back against the cool sheets, he shed his trousers. He came to me and fitted himself along the curve of my body, and I found myself boldly exploring his hard-thewn frame, marveling at the way our two disparate forms fit together so perfectly and surprised by the delightful sensations his insistent hands wrought in me. Jason was such a skillful lover that I could only hope that my lack of experience would not be a disappointment to him. But it was not so, for he was a thoughtful lover as well, who guided me until I was sure of myself and my own sensuality was awakened. After a first tender joining, inhibitions fled and we both reveled in the passion we had waited so long for.

Later, as we clung to one another, watching the patterns cast by the fire in the grate, I tried not to think about the inevitable set of circumstances we had set into motion this night. I did not wish to spoil my happiness. I must yet face Matthew with an explanation, I realized, and Aaron as well, whose aid I no longer required.

A heavy hammering on the door downstairs rumbled through the stillness, and Jason's body tensed in response. He was on his feet and had slipped on his trousers in an instant. He stood for a moment by the closed door, listening to the harsh shouts of men who had assembled on the porch outside. His hands clenched and unclenched at his sides, and as he reached for the doorknob, he turned back to me. I had raised myself on one elbow and was clutching the bedclothes to my breast.

"Stay here," he warned, "and open this door to no one but me."

"Jason, what is it? What do they want?"

"I don't know; just do as I say."

No sooner had the door closed behind him than I felt the very bed beneath me shudder as the door downstairs was forced open. "He's here!" someone who was now inside called to the others.

Alarmed, I sprang to my feet and went to where my clothes lay in a heap on the floor, but, thinking better of it, I pulled Jason's dressing gown from the wardrobe and wrapped myself in it. What could these men want of Jason to break in on him in the middle of the night? I put a hand cautiously against the closed door and listened.

"Looks to me as if he's been asleep, boys," I heard someone say. The voice sounded like Mr. Donnelly's.

"Sure and that's what he'd have you believe."

There was a mumbled assent from the group.

"What's the meaning of this, Donnelly?" Jason demanded.

"I'm sorry to have to be the one to tell you, sir, but it's your wife. She's been—that is to say, well, she's dead."

"Emily?" Jason asked. "What happened?"

"Well, sir, one of the girls found her in her bed, strangled, she was, with a length of rope."

"Are ye daft, Donnelly, tellin' him like he don't already know it?"

"He done it," called yet another voice, "just like he killed that poor Miss Chandler."

"If you'd just come with us, Mr. Wyndham," Donnelly asked, trying to placate them all, "we'll all go down and talk with the constable."

I could almost feel the hatred that infused the mob downstairs.

"No more talk," someone shouted, "we need a sturdy tree and our own length of rope."

Without heed to Jason's warning, I opened the door and walked purposefully down the long staircase until I was in full view of the group assembled there.

My eyes swept the room, hoping to capture the attention of every man there. They were Wyndcliffe men mostly, many blearly-eyed with drink and every face full of a hatred of Jason Wyndham. They were a dangerous lot. They hated and feared him, this man who was everything to me. He could never have harmed Emily nor Rachel. Why could they not see that? At last my eyes came to rest on Jason. From his place a few steps below me, he looked up, a pained expression on his brow. "Adrienne, no."

I merely smiled in reply and rested a hand on his shoulder. Barefoot and with his Chinese silk dressing gown pulled close around me, my hair hanging loose to my waist, still I had lost none of my dignity.

"I'm afraid, gentlemen, that you shall have to look elsewhere for your suspect. Mr. Wyndham has been here with me all evening."

All eyes were cast downward and a collective silence came over the men.

"You can't mean that, miss," Donnelly dared to say. "He must have enticed you here. We all know Mister Jason has his ways."

"Nevertheless, I came here this evening of my own volition, and I am Mr. Wyndham's alibi should he require one."

I was amazed at my own calm. For a fleeting moment I thought I had convinced them. Why hadn't I realized that my words would keep them from their purpose for only a short time? Even now as they ruminated on my words, there was a grumbling amongst them.

"His poor wife lies dead, and we find him here in the arms of another woman," someone called out. "How are we to know but what she ain't in it with him, plottin' to kill his missus?"

I did not move, did not breathe. There were murmurs of assent, and someone spat out, "Whore!"

Jason balled his fists and took a threatening step

toward the group. A slick sheen of perspiration shone
on his skin, and the murderous glare in his eyes was
menacing by the light of the men's lanterns. They
closed ranks and seemed to move a step backward in
response. I greatly feared that if Jason could identify
the man who had hurled the epithet, he'd have struck
him down regardless of the consequence. Though
their fear of him gave Jason a certain power over
them, he was still hopelessly outnumbered. I went to
him, carefully controlling my movements so that
none would see my trembling, and I took Jason's arm
to hold him back. He responded by placing himself
before me as if to shield me from them.

"Damn your soul, Donnelly," he said, sounding
very tired. "She's done nothing . . . nothing."

"I only came to see there was no trouble, sir,"
Donnelly explained. "Perhaps you'd best come with
me to see the constable. I can't guarantee what might
happen if you don't."

A long silence ensued, and I knew that Jason had no
choice but to go with them.

"You drunken fools! Out of my way!"

The group turned around so they might identify the
newcomer who was making such a commotion as he
cut through them. "You're a brainless mob, the lot of
you, out for blood! If you'd have waited to hear from
me instead of some feeble-witted serving girl, you'd
know that Mrs. Wyndham was murdered by the same
person who attacked Miss Dalton. Yes, there is a
murderer in our midst, but as for these two, I saw
them leave the house together hours ago. I can assure
you that neither of them has been back since. Does
any man here dare dispute me?"

The crowd parted, and the speaker stepped into the
lantern light. It was Matthew.

The men were silent. If they were afraid of Jason,
then they were doubly so of Matthew. He held their
jobs, their lives and those of their families in his

hands. This was enough to disperse the crowd, with men shaking their heads in sympathy for Matthew Wyndham, who had been betrayed by his brother and his intended bride.

When the room was empty but for us three, I found that I could not meet Matthew's eyes, then meeting them could not look away.

Never had I felt so ashamed. I had betrayed this man who had taken me in and offered to share with me all that was his. Yet still he had forgiven me and had lied in my defense.

Jason went into the parlor where the lamp was lit, but I could not move. Matthew's dark eyes held me there and only left me as he followed his brother. As he passed, I noticed my engagement ring on his little finger.

"How did it happen?" Jason wanted to know.

"Just as I said."

"In the same way as Adrienne was attacked? Damn it, Matt, what do you know about this?"

"Certainly less than you," Matthew replied, enmity plain in his voice.

"If you truly believe that, then why did you mislead the men just now?"

"I will not have a lynch mob roaming the estate, even a half-hearted one. Fortunately for you, brother, most of those here tonight found their courage at the bottom of a whiskey bottle and were easily enough dissuaded."

Without another word, Matthew turned on his heel and went out. I wanted to call out to stop him and offer some words in explanation, but what could I say that would not hurt him more?

I went upstairs to dress and when I returned, it was to find Jason seated at the piano in the parlor. His head rested in one hand, and with the other he picked out discordant notes, one at a time.

"Who is doing this?" he wondered aloud. "Emily

never harmed anyone. It's my fault for bringing her here. Someone killed her to strike at me. That must be it.''

"You can't know that,'' I argued.

He expelled a long breath and shook his head. I handed him his shirt and waistcoat, realizing that I could not keep him from feeling responsible.

"I'm going to leave in the morning,'' I said, as he dressed, "and go home to Boston.''

"There's no home for you there. I won't let you leave,'' he said and grasped my hand. It was cold as death.

"What else can I do? I've shamed Matthew more than any man deserves, and after all his kindness—''

"He's not the innocent lamb you make him out to be, Adrienne, or have you forgotten? He may well be—''

I let my fingers slip from his. "Please, Jason, no recriminations tonight. I've returned his ring, but I must go to him now to apologize . . . as if words can erase this night.''

Jason rose and grasped my shoulders roughly.

"And would you take away what we've shared this night? I thought, when you stood there before those men and threw away everything for my sake, it meant that you loved me. It was more than I had any right to expect.''

I looked up at him, my eyes aflood with tears. "Did you doubt that I would give up everything for you? I do love you, Jason, and I shall love you as much when I am in Boston. If you decide that you want me, I shall be waiting for you there, only do not ask me to stay here where I shall be a constant painful reminder to your brother of how he was betrayed.''

He pulled me close and pressed his lips to my forehead. Coward that I was, I buried my face in the warmth of his chest, loath to leave him and face Matthew. He pulled back all at once and lifted the chain that hung at my throat. "And will you return this to my brother?" he asked.

"You've never let me explain," I began. "The brass ring was a gift from my father, his last gift before he died. I've always thought there was some message attached. You see the Wyndham roses engraved on it?"

"Then it wasn't a present from Matt?"

I shook my head vigorously.

"Brass ring, you say?"

He sat again at the piano, and his right hand picked out a light, chiming melody. My heart began to beat double-time and thoughts whirled around in my head at such a rate as to be jumbled nonsense. "What is that?" I managed to say.

The melody released a flood of memories . . . of a little girl, only five years old, and the gift her papa had brought her one winter day. He had been gone for months on business and had promised me a present when he returned. As he stood there in the entry hall, his greatcoat and tall beaver hat dusted with snow, I came running down the stairs with Nanny at my heels to claim my prize.

"How's my little one? Have you taken good care of Mama?"

I nodded. "Oh, Papa, she'll be so pleased. You've been gone forever almost."

I had waited ever so patiently as he removed his coat and hat, eyeing the parcel on the steps behind him, and when at last he set the box before me and lifted the lid, my mouth made a round O. It was a carousel music box, and when he turned the key, the painted horses went around and a bright melody filled the air. I clapped my hands together. "Oh, Papa, this is the best present ever!"

"Do you like it? You may take it up and show Mama if she's not resting. But first, my sweet, I want you to imagine that you're riding on that gray stallion

right there," he said pointing to one of the tiny
wooden horses. "You see him, the one tossing his
head? Now, if you were riding on that carousel, what
would you do?"

"Reach for the ring, Papa, the brass ring."

"Reach for the brass ring!" I said aloud and Jason
looked at me as if I'd lost my senses.

"It was a message," I told him. "My father meant
the ring to be figurative, like one of his games."

I turned from Jason and hurried to the door. He
followed close on my heels. "What are you talking
about?"

"It was a message, and I've only just now realized."

I'd have gone out then if he hadn't caught my arm
and held me fast. "I don't half understand what this is
about, Adrienne, but we need to talk about your
leaving. Wait and I'll walk back to the house with
you."

I shook my head. "Go upstairs and finish dressing.
I'll come back when I've found out what all this
means."

I left him then, slipping out into the night before he
had an opportunity to argue.

17

There were still lights in the windows
of the house despite the hour. But when I went
through the halls, I did not encounter a soul until I
opened my door and found Brenna within.

"Oh thank heavens, miss, thank heavens! When I
saw you'd packed your things, I thought you'd go off
and me never gettin' the chance to tell you how sorry
I am—"

"Brenna," I said, "it's after midnight, what are you
doing here?"

She looked so distressed that I led her by the hand
to the bed. She sat down and I beside her, but when
she began again, she was no less incoherent.

"Constable Hewitt was here, about Mister Jason's
wife, and I heard him talkin' to Dr Fletcher. He said
that whoever done them things to scare you tried to
kill you as well, and 'tis the same person that
murdered Missus Emily. But 'tis not that way at all,
Miss, I swear to you."

I was far too tired to attempt another riddle tonight.
"Brenna, what are you going on about?"

" 'Twas me who put your dress in the fire and
ruined the lace and wrote them notes. I was scared for

271

ye, miss, and couldn't see no other way."

She was wringing her hands as she watched my expression.

"Why?" I asked her. "Why did you want to drive me away?"

"On account of him. He's the cause of all the troubles in this house, yours and mine as well. 'Tis his sinful pride sent me Tim to his grave. I were good enough to bed but not to wed, and so my boy had no proper father."

"Jason," I said aloud. She was talking about Jason, and her words were especially hard to take after what had passed between us this night.

"No, Miss. Few know, as I, where the true danger lies in the Wyndham family. 'Tis Matthew fathered my son, and 'tis Matthew I watched follow Miss Rachel Chandler out to the Widow's Walk on the night she died."

"Matthew? But why didn't you speak out at the inquest?"

She looked up at me, eyes wide. "I daren't, miss, lest my pa and me be sent packin'. I'd not have been believed anyhow. Who would there be in this house, or in the whole village, to gainsay Matthew Wyndham?"

It was all true. Matthew's power over these people protected him absolutely.

"I never tried to kill you, miss, nor Missus Emily neither. I swear to it. I only wanted to scare you off so he couldn't do to you what he done to Miss Chandler. You was always nice to me, and I didn't want to see you hurt. You will tell the constable, won't you, miss, that I had no hand in murder?"

Her head dropped into my lap, and she was sobbing. The weight of this secret had taken its toll on her. I stroked her hair to soothe her.

"Dry your eyes, Brenna. I shall stand by you. I want you to go home now and go to bed. Speak to no one else about this, do you understand? I will explain everything to Jason, he will know what to do. He cannot be hurt by his brother's wrath."

When she was calm enough, I sent her home, but before I could carry her news to Jason, I had to find the carousel and learn Papa's secret. I went quietly into Susannah's room and found the music box on her bureau. Without hesitation, I reached into it for the tiny brass ring that would release the latch. It had been easier to manage when I was five years old. My hands had grown since then, and my fingers strained now to reach the ring. At last I got hold of it and pulled. The catch sprang open and the hidden tray slid out, but instead of the hank of hair ribbons that Papa had put there for me when I was a child, I found a packet of papers.

I took them into my room and examined them by the lamplight. There were various bills of lading, sales receipts, and contracts whose legal jargon I found impossible to decipher. Again and again, I went over them. This was Papa's secret, a collection of old papers? I could make neither head nor tail of the mess and decided that it would be best to see them safely into Jason's hands. Knowing the shipping business, perhaps he could ascertain their value.

This time I took Gypsy from the stables and saddled her myself. I reached the cottage in half the time, only to find that Jason had gone. I couldn't imagine where he might be at this late hour. I tried to wait for him but patience eluded me. I needed to know what message my father meant to send to me by these papers, and also, while sitting alone in the quiet cottage, I began to realize that what Brenna had told me tonight meant that, for whatever reason, it must have been Matthew who had tried twice to kill me. Surely after the ugly scene we had put him through this evening, he would be even more intent on ending my life. I decided at length to go to Aaron with the papers. He was my

friend and had made no secret of the fact that he
despised Matthew. Later I could explain everything to
Jason.

And so it was that I found myself on the steps of
Chandler House at such an unseemly hour. Before I
knocked on the door, though, I noticed a light at the
side of the house, shining out of Aaron's study
windows. He had not yet gone to bed, perhaps he was
still awaiting my arrival. I went to the french
windows and peered in. When I saw him at his desk, I
sighed in relief and rapped lightly on the pane. When
I rapped a second time, he came to let me in.

"Aaron," I said, stepping over the threshold, "I've
so much to tell you. I found these papers just now
hidden inside my music box. My father left them
there for me, but I don't understand what—"

Only when I had come full into the room did I see
Matthew, seated by the fire. He rose when he saw
me. I stopped mid-sentence and took a step
backward.

"You see, she's had them all along," Aaron said as
he latched the doors.

With the feeling that the ground had fallen out from
under my feet, I realized that Aaron and Matthew
were allies.

"You're a fool," Matthew told him, "she doesn't
even know what she has."

"Then someone tell me, please," I said, clutching
the packet tighter in my hand.

I stood between them, shifting my gaze from one to
the other, and Aaron obliged.

"Those precious papers, my dear, detail the unholy
alliance formed by Matt here and your father to run
the Union blockades during the war."

His words hit me like a blow, knocking the wind
from me. "No," I told him. "No, I don't believe you.
My father would never be party to anything of the
sort. He was no traitor."

"I'm afraid he was," Aaron said, "whether you like the sound of it or not. When the war broke out, he couldn't get cotton enough for the mill. Matt's trade routes were cut off by the Union ships. They both needed money, and running the blockades was a lucrative venture, though in the end, of course, only one of them made a profit."

Aaron returned to sit behind his desk. Matthew, by comparison, seemed to be paralyzed, standing there beside his chair. "She doesn't understand any of this," he said, "she can't possibly—"

I turned on him. "Don't I, though? I understand that you're a murderer, that you murdered my father, just like you murdered Rachel!"

"What?" Aaron exclaimed, on his feet now.

"You killed him, didn't you? Didn't you?" I shouted at Matthew, my voice rising to end on a hysterical note.

"Your father had a heart condition," Matthew replied, remaining calm, "you knew that."

"You pushed him too far," I argued, "the strain was more than he could bear."

Suddenly, Aaron was before me. "What do you know of my sister's death?" he demanded.

Grabbing me by the shoulders, he shook me, his fingers like claws in my flesh. The mild expression he usually wore was gone, replaced now by a frightening, wild-eyed glare, his lips pressed into a thin line as he waited impatiently for my reply.

"Aaron, you're hurting me," I told him and stepped out of his grasp.

The man who had been my friend seemed to return all at once. "I'm sorry," he said. "Please, I must know."

"One of the Wyndcliffe maids saw Matthew follow Rachel out onto the Walk on the night she died," I explained.

"She waited in my room that night," Matthew tried

to explain, "until I'd come back from the village. She threatened to throw herself into the ocean if I didn't agree to marry her. I didn't believe her. I told her I was tired of her theatrics and then she ran out of the house. When I saw her heading for the Walk, I followed her. I'm not sure, even now, if she meant to kill herself, but she was awfully close to the edge. I went after her. We struggled, and she fell."

"Damn you, Wyndham! Damn you to hell!" Aaron shouted. "She loved you, and you killed her!"

Matthew took a step closer. "No, Aaron. It was an accident. I swear to you."

Aaron began to pace a small section of the carpet, and his limp seemed more pronounced. "You're an ungrateful bastard!" he said. "Why do you think I've always done the work for you when you wouldn't soil your hands? It wasn't for myself, it wasn't for the money. It was for my sister. 'Get the papers from Dalton,' you said, but when I asked him for them, he told me that they were his insurance. He didn't trust you, Matthew. Imagine that! He didn't trust the word of the great lord of the manor. He threatened to expose you. If he didn't get his share he had nothing more to lose, he said. I believed him. I couldn't let him drag you down. Where would that have left my sweet Rachel? She was going to be your wife, mistress of Wyndcliffe. It was all she'd ever wanted, since we were children."

Aaron paused in his discourse. He was struggling with his lame leg now and edged back toward the desk chair to rest himself. Removing his spectacles, he tossed them onto the desktop and ran a hand through his lank hair. His complexion was a pasty white, and I guessed that the leg was giving him pain. From a bottom drawer, he drew out a bottle of whiskey and one tall glass. Without a word, he poured and downed a generous swallow. It was the first time I'd seen him touch spirits. There were many things about Aaron Chandler I had yet to learn, I was beginning to realize, and I was honestly afraid as I waited for him to continue with his explanation of my father's fate. With this strength restored, he leaned back in his chair, seeming to enjoy the power of the moment as he held our full attention.

"I had to stop Dalton any way I could," he said matter-of-factly, "and so I put my hands around his throat. It was easier than I thought it would be, really. He struggled at first and then grabbed at his chest. In the end it was his heart that failed him. So, you see, my conscience was clear."

I could not speak as my rheumy eyes met those of the man who had murdered my father. There was in them no remorse, no feeling at all. What sort of man was Aaron Chandler that he could end another's life without a second thought? He must be mad, I decided, and this was the most frightening realization of all.

"I never told you to kill him, Aaron," Matthew insisted. "We could have come to some sort of agreement. Adrienne, you must believe me. I didn't know about any of this."

Still I could not speak.

"You're a fool, Matt," Aaron put in. "Dalton would have announced to the world that Matthew Wyndham was a traitor to his country, and your empire would have crumbled. Where, pray tell, would that have left the Chandlers? What would become of Rachel's dreams? 'Without the Wyndham fortunes,' she used to tell me, 'we Chandlers are less than nothing.' And so I save your contemptible hide, and this is how you repay me? By sending for Dalton's brat and causing Rachel's death?"

I turned to Matthew then. "Why *did* you send for me? If you thought my father such a threat—if you thought he'd gotten these papers to me—?"

"I felt that I owed you something for all you'd lost,"

he explained. "I thought that by marrying you I could do some justice on your behalf."

"You could have told me the truth from the first," I replied, feeling more weary now than sad.

"There wasn't only myself to consider," Matthew told me. "I'd used your father's share of the money to rebuild. If Wyndham Shipping went bankrupt, it would have affected the lives of many people, people who needed their jobs to provide for their families. How was I to know that you weren't just a spoiled child who'd have demanded the cash and to hell with my company? The business was not stable enough, I could not take such a chance."

I considered what he'd said. If I had known of the existence of these papers two years ago, before I'd come to know this place and its people, what would I have done? I was afraid to search within myself for an answer. Matthew had certainly made the right decision by bringing me here to Wyndcliffe. I knew that the well-being of the Wyndham business interests was of vital importance to many people's lives, and I could not take that away.

I went to kneel before the fireplace and stretched out my hand to let the tip of the packet of papers touch the flames in the grate. They licked the paper greedily and the edge promptly browned and curled. Soon the packet had a flame all its own.

"What are you doing?" Matthew asked, astonished.

I tossed the papers into the grate and watched as they crumbled into ash. "This won't haunt you any longer," I said.

"I shall repay you all of the money that was owed your father," he promised, "as it can be managed."

I shook my head. "Keep your money. I don't want it. I'm partly to blame for Papa's getting himself into such a tangle. He thought he had to buy my love with all of his expensive presents. I should have told him that he had it all along."

Matthew drew nearer. "You've had your revenge on me," he said. "Tonight when I saw you with my brother, I realized that the money, the power, all that I believed to be important, would never be enough again."

"A touching moment, but you don't imagine that this is the end of it, do you?"

Aaron's caustic comment brought me to my feet. I heard the wood scrape as again he pulled open his desk drawer. There was a flash of metal this time, and he drew out a pistol, aiming it at my heart.

"I'm sorry, Adrienne, but someone must pay for Rachel's death. I did warn you to leave, and now it's too late. Be still; I've had poor luck with you thus far."

"Then it was you who tried to kill her?" Matt said. "But she's done nothing. If you must lay blame for Rachel's death, blame me."

Aaron got to his feet somewhat unsteadily, his eyes darting rapidly beneath their lids from Matthew to me and then back again. "Killing you would be too easy. You have to suffer the way I've suffered. After I watched you make a fool of yourself over Adrienne, on that day you gave Felicia a dressing down, it was then that I realized that she had to be the one to die."

Matthew's brow furrowed as Aaron's words sunk in. "And so you locked her in the tool shed and set it afire?"

Aaron nodded. "Not a well-planned attempt, I'll admit. I'd have succeeded the next time, though, if Jason hadn't come looking for her."

My heart fell. There was no escape for me this time if Aaron meant to kill me.

Matthew took a step toward the desk. "Stay where you are!" Aaron ordered, his voice unsteady.

"Emily?" I said, drawing his attention. "What about Emily?"

"You heard her at dinner this evening," he replied.

"She was telling us plainly that she'd seen someone in the gazebo with you. How was I to know that she hadn't recognized me? I couldn't be found out, not before I'd made *him* pay!"

"You're mad!" Matthew told him. "Venting your hatred of me on innocents. Leave Adrienne out of this, do you hear me?"

"You're responsible for her fate," Aaron countered. "You should have married Rachel, but you tossed her aside without a thought when you fell in love with Adrienne. Now you must watch her die."

Sweat beaded his brow, and the wild look had come over him once more. I stood, paralyzed, awaiting the pistol's report. Aaron's extended arm trembled, and he steadied one hand with the other.

Just then, there was a heavy pounding as someone tried to force the locked study door.

"I've found the ledgers, Matt. I've proof of what you've done."

It was Jason!

I screamed his name, and again he tried to force the door. "If you've harmed her, Matt, I swear I'll kill you, brother or no!"

As Aaron's attention turned to the shuddering door, Matthew rushed at him.

"I won't let you do this!" he said.

Aaron fired twice and, to shield me, Matthew put himself between us. There was a crash of splintering wood as Jason finally broke through the door, and I watched in horror as Matthew slumped to the floor, two small holes in his waistcoat flooding crimson.

Across the room, Aaron did not move as if amazed by what he'd done, and when Jason had discerned what had transpired, he grabbed for the pistol, wresting it from Aaron's hand. For a time Aaron only stood there in stunned silence, but when we turned our attention to Matthew, he cried out all at once and smashed through the french windows, making off into the night.

I knelt beside Matthew and put my hand on his heart to see if it still was beating. He was alive but barely drawing breath, and Jason looked at me to see if I needed his assistance. I could hear the servants stirring now, and Kathleen's head peeped in between the splintered sections of the door.

"Go after him," I told Jason. "We'll manage here."

18

I forced open my eyes
to discover that I was at Wyndcliffe once more and
had fallen asleep on the drawing room settee. I pulled
myself upright and felt the ache of cramped muscles.
Nearby on the hearthrug, Jason sat feeding pages of a
ledger book to the flames.

"So you're awake at last," he said when he heard
me stir.

"I was waiting for Dr. Fletcher to come down. I
must've fallen asleep. What time is it?"

"Nearly noon, I think. I saw to it you weren't
disturbed."

"And Matthew?" I asked, breathless.

"Hanging on. The doctor seems to think he'll pull
through."

I sighed. "Thank God for that."

"One of the bullets has lodged near the spinal cord,
though. Dr. Fletcher can't be certain of the extent of
the damage, but he says that Matthew might not walk
again.'

I closed my eyes a moment and said a silent prayer.
"Did you find Aaron?"

He tossed a last handful of pages into the grate and

came to sit beside me. "He decided to join his sister. We found his body this morning on the rocks below the Widow's Walk."

"It's finished, then?"

"Yes," he said, "it's finished."

I rested against his shoulder. "Why did you let me go on believing that Brenna's Tim was your son?" I asked him.

"The truth would have served no purpose but to damage Matt's spotless reputation. Mine was far beyond redemption as it was. And I think that somehow you wanted to believe me a rogue."

"I've my own black secrets now," I admitted.

I feared his reaction when I told him my father's secret. He had despised his brother on the same account

He took my hands. "I shan't abandon you, if that's what you're thinking."

I was not so sure.

"Matthew had a partner in his blockade-running venture," I began, "someone who helped him to procure arms and sell them to the Confederates."

My chin dropped to my chest. "That man was my father."

Jason's brow furrowed. "A partner?"

"Yes," I told him. "When Matthew tried to cheat him, my father threatened to expose him, and Aaron killed him to keep him silent."

Jason groaned. "What a mess they made for themselves!"

"My father had hidden some papers for me in my music box. I only found them last night, and when I couldn't find you, I went to ask Aaron's help. It wasn't a wise move, I see now."

"So Aaron was Matt's pawn," he concluded.

"Not exactly. Aaron only helped Matthew for Rachel's sake, and when she died, his hatred for Matthew boiled over. He struck out at me to hurt

Matthew, and he killed Emily because he thought
she'd seen him in the gardens on the night he attacked
me."

Jason was quiet for a while, and when he found his
voice, it was strained. "She never saw anyone that
night. She thought it would be a clever plan to draw
out the murderer."

"And it cost her her life," I said.

"She wanted it that way, I think. She feared the
slow, painful deterioration the consumption would
have made her suffer, and she knew that whether our
marriage was real or not, she stood between you and
me."

He drew me close and put his arms around me.

"The papers from my father," I said to him, "I've
burned them, Jason."

He only smiled.

"You're not angry that I've thrown away a chance
. . . our chance for a part of your family's business?
Isn't that what you've wanted, what was rightfully
yours, what your father robbed you of?"

I felt the laughter vibrate through his chest. "My
darling, before you came into my life, I couldn't have
cared a whit for the family business. It was only when
I realized that I had nothing to offer you— Matt has
signed over the farms to me, that's enough, and I
suspect that I shall be managing more than that until
he recovers.

"I have ideas, plans, but precious little experience
in the business world," he admitted. "I know that my
temper will prove a disadvantage, and I will need
help, someone to smooth the ruffled feathers I will
surely cause along the way."

He drew back and took both my hands in his. "I
need you with me always, Adrienne. Matt once said
you'd be a valuable asset to him. Well, you'll be more
so to me."

His blue eyes sought out mine, and I met them

without reservation. Rising, he drew me by the hand
from the drawing room through the foyer and out of
the doors onto the drive. The sun was high in the
cloudless sky, a gentle salt breeze carrying with it the
murmuring of the tide rushing over the rocks below.
The lawns were lush and green and the woodland that
bordered them was alive with the singing of birds.

We turned back toward the house, ever formidable,
a bastion high upon the granite cliffs. Surveying it all,
I felt comforted. This house would stand forever.
Jason must have felt this, too, for he spoke solemnly.
"In time I may amass some degree of wealth, some
manner of respectability, but for now all that I have to
offer you is my love and a home here in this house."

He pulled me to him and our lips met. It was all that
I wanted.

Epilogue

Could it be that ten years have passed since that day when old Mr. McKeon set me out under the porte cochere and I began my life at Wyndcliffe? As I watch my children playing on the lawns, I know that it must be so, but those intervening years have been kind to our family, slipping by almost without notice.

It is the year of our nation's centennial, and today's Independence Day celebrations were especially grand. The children and I were pleased and proud as Jason, in his blue cavalry officer's uniform, led the contingent of war veterans who paraded through the village, and from our place in the reviewing stand, young Thomas, baby Sarah, and I cheered heartily. Ben, our firstborn, ran beside his father through the streets until finally Jason pulled him up into the saddle to ride with him.

The cheering of the villagers meant a great deal to my husband, I think, to show how far he had come in these ten years. There had been skepticism, to say the least, when Jason first took over in Matthew's stead, but in time he proved equal to the task, restoring the Wyndham fortunes through wise investments and sound judgment. Now even those who'd whispered behind their hands about his reputation had to admit they'd misjudged him.

Matthew and Susannah are with us once more, having only just returned from a visit to the Centennial Exposition in Philadelphia where, Susannah tells me, fifty countries have sent exhibits. None would argue but that these years have wrought the most change in Matthew. While he did recover from the injuries inflicted when he'd saved my life, he never regained the use of his legs. This was difficult for one who had been so vital, to find himself suddenly dependent upon others. Ironically, it was the daughter he had so neglected who become his constant companion, and through her tender ministrations, his soul was healed, even if his body never would be. He was content to allow Jason the freedom to control the Wyndham assets; he'd lost his taste for business. His interest now lay elsewhere.

It began, I believe, at dinner one evening. Matthew had been railing against the blatant corruption in President Grant's administration, and Susannah quietly suggested that rather than complain, he ought to do something about it. Though his physical limitations might prevent him from achieving personal glory, we soon realized that Matthew had much to offer as an advisor and organizer, and he was soon dividing his time between Wyndcliffe and the state capital in Augusta.

And Susannah? Susannah had grown from precocious child to graceful young woman before we realized it. Matthew plans to take her on the Grand Tour of Europe in the spring, for her eighteenth birthday, and when she speaks of the trip, I can see all of her dreams in those bright eyes. She is more thoughtful than many young girls her age, visiting her grandfather often and taking an interest in the farm that will one day be hers. She spends hours with the

children, telling me that she hopes to be able to give
back some of the love I gave to her when she so
needed it.

Felicia Wyndham died quietly in her sleep last fall,
and though I cannot say that we'd grown closer with
the passage of time, there had been peace in the house
at least. We buried her in the family graveyard, close
to Jason's father, and when spring came, Susannah
planted a rosebush beside her headstone.

Chandler House stood vacant for several years after
Aaron's death, but when Jason finally succeeded in
locating a Chandler cousin who'd been living in
Charleston, South Carolina, the man was grateful for
the opportunity to remove his family from the
unsettling climes of a South reeling under the abuses
of Reconstruction, and brought life to Chandler
House once more.

Evening is upon us now, and all of the inhabitants
of our estate have gathered on the lawn, anticipating
the fireworks display that Mr. Donnelly and his men
have arranged. Wyndcliffe stands before us,
unchanged, as it was a hundred years ago and
doubtless will be a hundred years hence. I am never
less than awed when I gaze upon these granite walls,
and in the circle of Jason's arm with tiny Sarah's fair
head resting against my shoulder as she sleeps, I
watch the rockets soar and burst into a million
colored stars overhead and form my thoughts into a
silent prayer of thanks for my good fortune.